THE
WITCH'S WARNING

Also available by Joseph Delaney

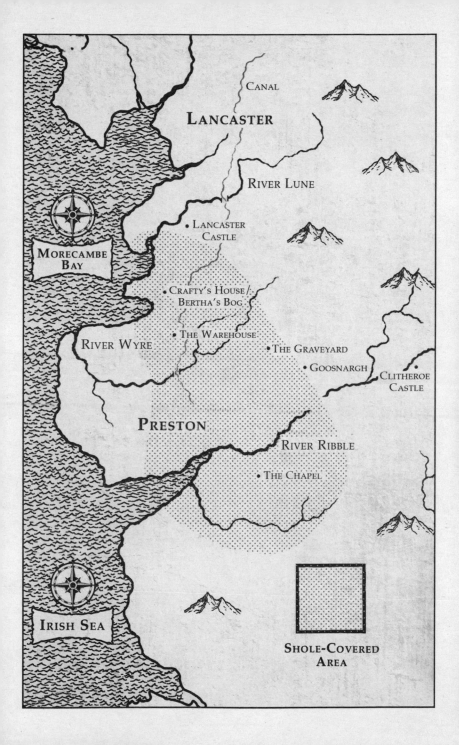

ABERRATIONS

THE
WITCH'S WARNING

JOSEPH DELANEY

PUFFIN

PUFFIN BOOKS

UK | USA | Canada | Ireland | Australia
India | New Zealand | South Africa

Puffin Books is part of the Penguin Random House group of companies
whose addresses can be found at global.penguinrandomhouse.com.

www.penguin.co.uk
www.puffin.co.uk
www.ladybird.co.uk

Penguin
Random House
UK

First published 2019

001

Set in 10/15.5 pt Palatino LT Std
Typeset by Jouve (UK), Milton Keynes
Printed and bound in Great Britain by Clays Ltd, Elcograf S.p.A.

A CIP catalogue record for this book is available from the British Library

ISBN: 978-0-241-34995-3

All correspondence to:
Puffin Books
Penguin Random House Children's
80 Strand, London WC2R ORL

MIX
Paper from
responsible sources
FSC
www.fsc.org   FSC® C018179

Penguin Random House is committed to a
sustainable future for our business, our readers
and our planet. This book is made from Forest
Stewardship Council® certified paper.

For Marie

OLD NELL

Crafty halted, his heart lurching with fear, his mouth dry. There were footprints in the white snow, each one smeared with red as if the owner of the clawed feet had stepped in a puddle of blood.

Trying to control his terror, he walked on until he reached the grave – a black tombstone shrouded by leafless trees. There was no wind, but the branches were moving slightly, the twigs twitching with a life of their own.

The black soil of the grave had recently been disturbed. There was no doubt: this was where the dead witch dwelt. This was where she slept, bloated with blood. This was her secret refuge.

Her name was carved on the tombstone:

OLD NELL

Crafty took a deep breath and prepared to leave. He had found the aberration. His work was done. He need not face her alone. Armed couriers would deal with her.

But when he turned round, there was no comforting blue circle showing his escape route back to the castle. The gate had winked out. He was trapped in the Shole.

All at once there was a noise from the grave. A slithering, sucking, squelching sound. The soil was moving. Something was slowly emerging – the clawed hand of the witch, twitching with hunger. Grey and warty, it reached out through the soil as far as the elbow. The hand writhed, opening and closing as if searching for something. A second hand joined it, quickly followed by the head and shoulders of Old Nell.

Her long grey hair was matted with black grave slime, and a sudden stench of loam and rotting flesh filled the air. Her face was wrinkled, the deepest line a vertical furrow between her tightly closed eyes. Then she opened her mouth wide. Both jaws had three rows of pointed teeth: this aberration was a predator that fed upon raw flesh and drank warm blood.

Crafty's own blood froze in his veins. He watched as, finally, Old Nell opened her eyes and stared straight at him. He wanted to run, but he was held frozen to the spot by her pitiless gaze.

As she reached for him, she spoke, her voice halfway between a growl and a croak:

'*This is what you deserve!*'

And then she lunged for him.

*

Crafty woke with a gasp, his heart racing even faster than it had in the nightmare. He sat up in bed, but the terrifying dream still hadn't left him entirely. It felt as though the witch's words had been spoken straight into his left ear. It was as if she had been in the room, leaning over him while he slept.

It might have been only a dream, but the witch herself had been all too real. Crafty remembered her saying something similar to him when she was alive. He and his fellow gate grubs, Donna and Lucky, had walked down the dark steps of the dungeon where the witch was imprisoned. It had smelled terrible, and was empty but for a bundle of what looked like dirty rags in the middle of the floor.

Then, seeing a leg protruding, Crafty had realized that it was the witch, Old Nell. She'd been fastened by a chain to a ring set in the floor. The bundle of rags had then sat up slowly to reveal a wrinkled face, eyes like tiny brown buttons and a shock of white hair streaked with dirt.

The friends had been curious about her, but their visit hadn't gone well; she'd cursed the three of them:

'May you get what you deserve!'

Well, what *did* he deserve? Crafty wondered. To be grabbed and eaten by the dead witch, as she'd promised in his nightmare? What did Lucky deserve? Would he too die in the Shole as so many gate grubs did? As for poor Donna, she was already dead. Had she deserved to die so young?

Shuddering, Crafty climbed out of bed and went over to the window. It was barely light, but as he looked down the hill across the cobbled streets of Lancaster, he could see the edge of the Shole, a black curtain stretching from the ground high into the sky.

Old Nell had been hanged, but it was rumoured that other witches had taken her body into the Shole, where people were killed or changed – though some of the dead were brought back to life there. Is that what had happened to Old Nell?

Had his dream been more than a nightmare?

Had it been a warning?

That morning Crafty and Lucky received their usual early training session. Theirs was a dangerous job, and the more you knew about the dreaded Shole, the greater your chances of staying alive there.

The Shole was a kind of mist that had been expanding for about seventy years. Most forms of life caught inside died very quickly. A few survived and changed into deadly monstrous predators that were called *aberrations*. The northern edge of the Shole had now reached Lancaster: it had crossed the canal to threaten the heart of the city and the castle itself.

And Lancaster Castle was where the main resistance was based. Here a team of people, the Castle Corpus, studied the Shole, attempting to learn as much as possible about it. There were boffins, mancers, couriers and many other specialists; right at the bottom were the lowliest of them all, the gate grubs like Crafty and Lucky, who formed the front line and faced the greatest danger in the struggle against the Shole. They assisted the gate mancers, and went out into the Shole to collect specimens or retrieve other useful information. Crafty was thirteen and Lucky a year older. Their chances of reaching another birthday were very slim.

Their training today was only a question-and-answer session, but that was better than nothing, and their eager questions were being answered by Leticia Crompton-Smythe. Despite her young age, she was the brightest and best of the castle boffins, but she was currently working as a gate mancer in order to study the Shole more closely.

Leticia was slightly older than Crafty and Lucky. Her hair was cut very short, and although her expression was usually serious and challenging, when she gave a rare smile her face softened into something much more attractive and welcoming. Although far superior to them in rank, she was now their friend and allowed them to call her by her nickname – Lick.

All three of them had nicknames. Pete Proudfoot's was Lucky, although Crafty didn't know how he'd come by it. Crafty was also a nickname; his real name was Colin. His parents had given it to him when he was a baby. Rather than crawling, he'd found a clever way of rolling over and over to reach something he wanted.

Now, he suddenly realized that he wanted to put a question to Lick: he'd remembered something from his dream.

'Lots of aberrations have three rows of fangs in both top and bottom jaws. Is that also true of those who are reanimated – the ones who come back from the dead?' he asked.

'All the evidence so far is that those returned to life by the Shole do not have fangs like other dangerous predators,' Lick answered, 'but they may still need raw flesh and fresh blood for sustenance.'

So why did Old Nell look like that in my dream? Crafty wondered – though he knew that dreams didn't always follow the logic of the waking world.

He had just opened his mouth to ask another question when there was an interruption.

The far door of the Waiting Room opened and the Chief Mancer appeared. He wore a black gown and an even darker frown. Crafty could tell that something bad had happened.

'Sorry to cut your morning briefing short,' he announced grimly. 'Let's all go down to my room – and quickly. You'll be going into the Shole.'

'Is it an emergency?' Lick asked.

'It certainly is, Miss Crompton-Smythe. An *excursion* is taking place!'

Lick gave a little gasp. Crafty wondered what an excursion was but, before he could ask, the Chief Mancer had turned on his heel and left the room.

All three of them immediately got to their feet and pulled on their greatcoats. It was extremely cold in the Shole. That alone could be enough to kill you.

Crafty followed Lick and Lucky down the steps to the Chief Mancer's office. Here the mancer beckoned Lick inside. 'Benson and Proudfoot, you wait outside for a moment while

I brief Miss Crompton-Smythe!' he commanded Crafty and Lucky. Then he closed the door in their faces.

'What's an excursion?' Crafty asked Lucky.

'It's when something nasty leaves the Shole and enters the Daylight World,' he replied.

Crafty was just wondering what kind of aberration it could be when the silver knocker on the Chief Mancer's door caught his eye. It was shaped like the narrow skull of a dog, but with two horns.

'Ever come up against one of those?' he wondered.

Lucky shook his head and grinned. 'Don't want to either!' Then, with a frown, he went on, 'I wonder what Ginger Bob's got to say that's not fit for our ears? We're always the last to know anything!'

Ginger Bob was their nickname for the Chief Mancer, but it had nothing to do with his hair colour. It came from his habit of sharing ginger biscuits with the gate grub who'd assisted him.

Crafty smiled at his friend. Lucky had been on the job for three months longer than him – not much, but any experience was valuable in their line of work. Lucky had two fingertips missing from his left hand – the result of frostbite suffered in the Shole. His nose was also broken, squashed sideways against his face. Crafty had never asked him how he had received that injury.

Neither of them spoke again. Crafty waited nervously, his mouth dry and his heart beating rapidly in anticipation. No doubt Lucky felt the same, he thought.

This was what they did, he told himself, attempting to stay calm. Despite the increasing danger, their work must continue. At the moment their priority was to hunt down and destroy a dangerous killer – a new aberration that had used a gate to enter the Daylight World, even when it was not being used by a mancer. It was killing gate mancers in their rooms. They must find out what it was, how it was getting through the gates – and stop it.

Before long Lick opened the door and beckoned them inside. Ginger Bob was seated behind his desk. Papers were littered across its surface, and on top of them was a scattering of biscuit crumbs. They sat down on the three chairs facing him.

'Miss Crompton-Smythe is aware of what we are now about to face – but what about you, Proudfoot? You are the senior gate grub here. Do you know what an *excursion* is?'

'Yes, sir,' Lucky replied. 'It's when an aberration comes out of the Shole and into the Daylight World.'

'Indeed. Have you heard of the White Lady?'

'No, sir.' Lucky shook his head, looking worried.

When the Chief Mancer raised his eyebrows and turned to Crafty, he shook his head too. Aberrations were usually called something horrible – the White Lady sounded like someone aristocratic.

'Well, I suppose that's good,' said the Chief Mancer, 'because we try to keep such aberrations secret so as not to alarm people. The Shole is terrifying enough as it is.

'The full title of this particular aberration is the White Lady of Whittingham,' he continued. 'Whittingham is a hamlet north-east of Preston; thirty years ago, when the Shole was about half a mile away, many of its inhabitants fled north or east but a few of the poorest families remained there. One day an aberration in female human form came out of the Shole and spoke to some children who were playing by a riverbank. She said she had a message for their parents: if they brought their sick and lame to the edge of the Shole the following morning, she would heal them.'

'Why would anybody be stupid enough to believe that? How could they trust anything from the Shole that made crazy promises like that?' Lucky asked.

The Chief Mancer frowned at him. He didn't like being interrupted, and Lucky's tone was disrespectful. Lucky hadn't been the same since Donna was killed a few weeks previously, Crafty thought. He often failed to think before he spoke.

'All accounts of these meetings claim that she wasn't at all threatening,' the Chief Mancer replied. He was clearly trying to control his anger and make allowances for Lucky. 'She had a very pale, beautiful face and wore a long white dress, white shoes and white gloves – hence her name. Her hair was also silver-white; it was so long it reached the ground and trailed behind her as she walked. In short, she didn't look anything like a normal aberration.

'But there was another very good reason why the parents believed their children. One little boy she'd approached had been born with a withered leg – he limped badly. When the children gave the White Lady's message to their parents, they saw that his leg had been healed.'

'Did anybody from the castle get involved?' Crafty asked.

Ginger Bob shook his head ruefully. 'Not until it was too late. The White Lady healed many people, and word of her powers spread. People came from miles around. She seemed particularly fond of children. Every afternoon she talked to them – parents were asked to keep away. And they trusted her. After all the terrible things that had happened to them, people wanted to believe in something good.' He paused and sighed. 'Then one afternoon the children didn't return. Neither they nor the White Lady were ever seen again. It's believed that she led them into the Shole.'

I knew this story couldn't have a happy ending, thought Crafty.

'That happened very many years ago and, as far as we know, the White Lady hasn't left the Shole again. Not until this week . . .' There was an ominous pause.

'She's back?' asked Lucky, his eyes wide.

'Very much so,' said the Chief Mancer. 'This time near a village called Goosnargh, not far from Whittingham. For days she's been healing people and then talking to the children – though not everybody was happy about this. As you pointed out, Proudfoot, she comes out of the Shole, and that in itself is enough to alarm some people. A farmer arrived at the castle just before dawn today. He'd walked all through the night, skirting the Shole as closely as he dared in order to hurry here and warn us about her . . .'

He steepled his fingers and closed his eyes for a moment. 'Unless we intervene quickly, history will almost certainly repeat itself. Unfortunately, no couriers are available at the moment. All those fit for duty are already out patrolling the Shole. We usually retain two couriers in reserve, but they have already been dispatched to deal with another supposed excursion. There was a report that a dead witch known as Old Nell had visited the village where she used to live . . .'

Crafty's heart lurched. The mention of Old Nell reminded him of his nightmare. Could it really just be a coincidence that this report of her had surfaced on the same morning?

'Were you going to say something, Benson?' asked the Chief Mancer, staring at him.

Crafty realized that he must have gasped out loud, but he shook his head. He knew that his nightmare would be dismissed as irrelevant. No – he had to believe it was just a coincidence.

'All right. Well, as I'm sure you've realized, in the absence of couriers trained to deal with this, we are the only ones who are able to help. It will be very dangerous, but we need to go to Goosnargh, deal with the White Lady and avert the threat to those children.'

Crafty's mouth was dry. Lick, Lucky and Crafty were Fey, which meant they had certain abilities and, most importantly, they could enter the Shole without dying or being changed. The Chief Mancer wasn't Fey, and wouldn't be able to go into the Shole. So that left just the three of them to deal with the threat.

His mind went briefly to his father. He was a courier – he had been one of the best – but he had only recently been rescued from a mission that had gone horribly wrong, and was still in the Infirmary recovering from his injuries. Crafty hoped he would be better soon. Things were getting desperate: their resources in the fight against the Shole were stretched to breaking point.

He pondered about the White Lady. She could heal people, but no doubt she also had dangerous powers. From an early age, everyone was taught to fear the Shole, and yet those poor children from Whittingham had followed her to their deaths or worse. However kind she had been to them, it seemed unlikely that they would have done so willingly. Maybe she could control people's minds . . .

Suddenly it occurred to Crafty that *she* might be the dangerous new aberration that had been entering the castle and killing gate mancers? Three of them had been murdered already, the most recent just two days earlier, and the Castle Corpus were on high alert.

It looked like they had a new threat to deal with – but maybe they were one and the same . . .

2

THE WHITE LADY

As usual, Lucky was to be the Chief Mancer's grub while Crafty would work with Lick.

Once he had followed her to her room, Lick pulled back the curtain to reveal an alcove in the wall. Within it, four ornate iron legs supported a silver frame, which was about five feet in diameter. At first glance it could have been mistaken for a mirror, but it showed only a swirling darkness, a vortex of dark clouds.

Crafty took a long look at it. The gates were used to see directly into the Shole and if, like all gate grubs, you were one of the Fey, you could actually climb through it. But, although you had *some* immunity against the Shole, you were still vulnerable to its fierce aberrations. Many gate grubs had been slain or had disappeared, never to be seen again.

Crafty knew the dangers of their job only too well. Brock and Ben, his two brothers, had been gate grubs. They had died in the Shole. A wave of sadness washed over him, but he quickly pushed it to the back of his mind. He had to concentrate – because there were other ways in which a gate grub could die . . .

On either side of the gate – between Crafty's chair and the silver circle – stood two shiny metal poles. Between them, high up, was a sharp horizontal blade that seemed ever-ready to descend. It was a guillotine. To the left of the gate was a foot pedal, which could be pressed to bring the deadly blade swishing down on to whatever was below it. In theory it was a defensive weapon: when grubs went into the Shole they were often pursued by aberrations, returning with a bloodthirsty killer hot on their heels; any aberration could then leap through the open gate and into the Daylight World. If that happened, the mancer could depress the pedal, causing the guillotine to descend and kill the intruder.

However, sometimes the guillotine killed both the grub and the aberration. That was how Donna had died – although this had been no accident. She'd been murdered by Viper, a nasty, vindictive character who was working as a gate mancer at the time. He'd been a member of an organization called the Grey Hoods, a cult that worshipped the Shole and sought to obstruct the work of the Castle Corpus. When Crafty had tackled the traitor, he had managed to push him through his own gate and out into the Shole. Viper wasn't Fey, so the Shole should have killed him. But it hadn't. Instead he'd been changed. Now he was even more dangerous, an aberration that was full of hatred for Crafty. Crafty knew he was lurking somewhere in the Shole, plotting revenge. He had wondered if Viper could be the killer entering the Daylight World. It was possible. The White Lady sounded equally powerful, but Viper definitely had a motive.

No time to think about that now, Crafty told himself. *Just focus on the job at hand.*

He sat down in the chair and waited for instructions from Lick. He glanced nervously up at the guillotine blade, taking a slow, deep breath to calm himself.

'Here, Crafty,' Lick said, handing him a small metal cylinder.

It was called a locator and he'd used one before. What he now held was part of an object that had previously been cut in half; the other half was usually buried close to the edge of the Shole. When the Shole advanced and engulfed that area, a gate grub could take the locator and, using his Fey abilities, move the gate to where its other half was buried. It was a quick and easy way of moving within the Shole – though grubs could sometimes use items such as pieces of clothing to locate things.

'This one will take us to the part of the Shole nearest to Goosnargh. Cheer up – it might not be too bad,' Lick said with a smile.

Crafty shook his head. 'For me, maybe, but I'm the only one with a weapon,' he said, patting the right-hand pocket of his greatcoat where he kept his dagger. The gate mancers hadn't bothered to arm gate grubs, but Crafty's dagger had been a gift from a friend, and he had then been authorized to carry it by the Duke himself.

'True,' Lick admitted, 'but all that's about to change. I'm getting new weapons – hopefully within a few days. I'm refining something that might one day become standard issue for anyone venturing into the Shole – though unfortunately not in time to help us now. Still, things may not be as bad as they seem . . .'

'You've already said that!' said Crafty. 'Do you really believe it, or are you just trying to convince yourself?'

Lick laughed, and patted him on the shoulder to reassure him. 'Look, the Chief Mancer always exaggerates the danger just to keep you on your toes. What he *didn't* tell you is that two or three couriers are due to report back to the castle today. As soon as they arrive they'll come through the gates and join forces with us.'

That reassured Crafty. Couriers, who routinely patrolled the Shole, were all recruited from the Fey and were usually heavily armed.

'In the meantime,' Lick continued, 'we'll monitor the danger, which shouldn't become critical until late afternoon anyway. The White Lady heals people in the morning and talks to the children in the afternoon. Even if today is the day she chooses to lead her victims into the Shole – and we don't know that it is – it won't be for several hours, and the couriers should be back by then. So let's make a start. Take us into the Shole, Crafty.'

Crafty gripped the locator and concentrated, staring at the swirling vortex of dark clouds within the frame. It cleared instantly, and through the gate they could see a meadow bordered by half a dozen leafless trees standing starkly against the grey sky. The light was dim and everything looked grey. There was also a dusting of hoar frost on the ground; Crafty knew that it would be cold.

'You head towards the edge of the Shole,' Lick told him, picking up the lock of his hair that she kept nearby. 'I'll follow you as far as I can.'

Gate mancers were not usually Fey, which meant they couldn't go through a gate into the Shole. Nor could they find people or objects inside – or move the gate. So the mancer stayed behind while the grub ventured out, sometimes no better than bait on the end of a fishing line. The gate stayed where it was, and the further from the gate the grub went, the more dangerous it became for them.

But because Lick was also Fey, she and Crafty had an advantage: she could use that hank of Crafty's hair to track him closely and make the gate follow him so that, if danger threatened, it would never be too far away. But even this trick had its limits. Silver gates couldn't move about in the Daylight World – so once Crafty was out of the Shole, he was on his own.

He clambered through the gate and took six paces forward, his boots crunching on the frozen ground, his breath steaming. It was bitterly cold. Another dozen paces, and then he looked back at the gate. From this side it looked

like a blue circle floating in the air. Lick gave him a wave –
and suddenly the blue winked out. Crafty wasn't worried:
this simply meant that she was jumping forward to stay
close to him. He carried on walking, and when he glanced
back over his shoulder the blue circle was much nearer.

As he walked, Crafty listened carefully. Most aberrations
slept during the day, but a few were still active. Often the
first warnings were their shrieks and howls as they
approached, eager to kill and eat you. And with each step
Crafty realized that it was getting darker. That meant he
was nearing the edge of the Shole. It was always gloomy
there, and the sun could only penetrate weakly; it was now
becoming darker and denser – and more terrifying.

Then he suddenly stepped out into the Daylight World.
What a change! The sun was shining and the air was
much warmer. He could hear birdsong and the trees were
still in leaf, the grass green underfoot. He turned round
and looked back at the Shole. It was like a black curtain.
Everything inside it was now invisible, and he could no
longer see the gate.

Then he realized that the singing of the birds was not the
only thing he could hear. There were voices – the distant
murmur of people. They were out of sight somewhere
beyond a coppice of trees.

Crafty stepped back into the gloom of the Shole, then
approached the gate so that he could talk to Lick. 'There's a
wood, and beyond it I can hear people. Sounds like a crowd.
I'll go and take a look.'

'Take care, Crafty – don't let anyone see you,' she said. 'Good luck!'

He stepped back and glanced around. He was looking for the blue circle of the second gate. Heading back to the gate again, he said, 'Lucky should be out here somewhere. I'm surprised I can't see him already.' He gave Lick what he hoped was a brave smile.

She suddenly looked shifty. 'Ah, sorry, Crafty, I should have mentioned it. The Chief Mancer says that we can't risk both of you, so Lucky is being held in reserve.'

That wiped the smile from Crafty's face. Without any backup he was in even more danger. But he understood Ginger Bob's thinking. A lot of gate grubs had died recently – at the moment Crafty and Lucky were the only two left – and they were very hard to recruit, so the castle had to use them sparingly. Still, he didn't like the implication he was expendable.

However, he nodded to Lick and set off through the Shole, once again carefully listening for danger. Soon he was back in the sunlight. He couldn't help smiling with relief as he entered the wood. It was early autumn, and although a few leaves had fallen there was still a riot of colour overhead – gaudy reds and yellows. Crafty walked forward cautiously and kept glancing at the ground. If he stepped on a twig, it might alert others to his presence.

As he advanced, the murmur of voices grew steadily louder. How many people were there? he wondered. He reached the edge of the wood and hid behind one of the last trees, peering round the trunk to see what was ahead of him. A grassy slope led down to a small river which was spanned by a wooden bridge.

The water sparkled in the sunlight – but not half as brightly as the White Lady. The sun reflected off her so strongly that it almost hurt Crafty's eyes. She was all in white, and her gleaming white hair formed a coil on the ground beside her. Her face was partially obscured by all that dazzling hair, but he remembered Ginger Bob saying that she was very beautiful.

She was sitting on a big rock on his side of the riverbank, close to the bridge; along the far bank and across the bridge, people were queuing. It was a long queue, and at the front was a man bent over a walking stick who was bowing before the White Lady. Suddenly he gave a cry of joy, straightened his back and threw his stick into the river. As it floated downstream, the man knelt down before her and the waiting crowd began to cheer.

Crafty couldn't see any children and the queue was moving very slowly; it seemed certain to occupy the White Lady for some time. She certainly took her time over the healing. She seemed to engage each person in conversation and, although he was too far away to hear what was being said, Crafty could see the smiles on their faces. *She's more like some kind of fairy-tale princess than an aberration*, he thought.

On returning to the gate, Crafty told Lick about the long queue. They both relaxed, and Lick ordered a plate of sandwiches from the kitchen – it was as well to grab a bite while they could. Crafty consoled himself with the thought that, as time went on, it was all the more likely that the couriers would return.

Soon afterwards he set off for the riverbank once more. By now the queue was much shorter and it was growing late. Soon the adults would have gone and the White Lady would be talking to the children. Maybe she *wouldn't* turn nasty today? Crafty fervently hoped not – though he wished the couriers would return soon in any case.

What if she led the children towards the Shole and he was the only one who could stop her?

YOUR FRIEND; MY ENEMY

When he returned to his lookout point, the sun had been obscured by dark grey clouds and rain looked imminent. The White Lady was still perched on the rock, surrounded now by a couple of dozen children. They were sitting on the grass looking up at her, their faces shining with happiness. She was certainly holding their attention.

Crafty looked up at the sky again; he was concerned by the change in the weather. Would a downpour mean an end to her talk with the children? She might decide to lead them into the Shole as soon as it started to rain. Even as the thought entered his head, the first heavy drops of rain began to patter on the canopy of leaves above his head.

The White Lady glanced upwards at the sky and gave a slight shake of her head, as if annoyed by the rain. Was she about to climb to her feet and lead the children away?

Crafty felt a moment of panic. His worst fears were being realized. What hope had he of stopping a powerful aberration like the White Lady by himself? He needed help – and quickly. He moved back through the wood and began to run, oblivious to the twigs cracking under his boots. When he passed through the dark wall of the Shole, the temperature dropped sharply and the rain immediately turned to snow.

By the time he reached the gate he was breathless and struggled to get his words out.

'Calm down, Crafty,' Lick told him. 'Take a deep breath and tell me what's happened.'

At last he managed to explain his fears. 'Are the couriers back?' he asked finally, hopefully.

Lick shook her head, her expression grave, and Crafty's heart sank. Then she yanked the cord that hung over her desk and he heard a bell ring in another room. She had summoned some of the castle guards.

He didn't know how much help they would be: they weren't Fey, so they couldn't come out into the Shole to help him deal with the White Lady. And the gate couldn't emerge elsewhere within the Daylight World. There was no way to get them close to the threat.

'Listen, Crafty,' Lick said. 'She might simply send the children home and return to the Shole. But we had better check. I'll have to come with you. We need to make sure that those children are all right.'

He was grateful that she was coming with him – though he was the only one with a weapon.

Half a dozen armed guards entered the room and Lick gave them their orders. They would be staying to guard the gate and stop aberrations getting into the castle; it was a dangerous job.

'If there's *any* trouble at all, call for the Chief Mancer. He'll know what to do,' Lick said, then stepped through the gate and set off. As Crafty turned to follow her, he saw that the snow was almost a blizzard now; back in the Daylight World the rain would be torrential.

As they emerged from the Shole, the rain drove into their faces, making it difficult to see. They ran through the wood, the ground sodden and squelchy underfoot. Then he heard something above the drumming of the rain. It was cries of terror; the sound of children trapped in a waking nightmare.

They came to a halt just inside the wood. Crafty gazed down the slope: his own worst fears had just been realized. The White Lady was heading directly towards them with the children in her wake. At first Crafty couldn't make sense of what he was seeing. And then it hit him with a jolt. No wonder the children were crying. She wasn't just controlling their minds, she was dragging them towards their doom, for they were entangled in her long hair; it was wrapped around their arms or waists or throats.

Then Crafty had a moment of inspiration. He knew what to do.

'Back the way we've come!' he hissed to Lick, then set off without waiting for her answer.

She followed him back to the edge of the Shole, where they stayed within the cover of the trees. When Crafty pulled the blade out of his greatcoat pocket, Lick's eyes widened and he put his finger against his lips to silence her. His heart was thumping and his mouth was dry. He was terrified at the thought of what he must do.

The crying grew louder; some of the children were screaming from both terror and pain. It must hurt to be dragged like that, bound up in the hair of an aberration.

The White Lady was coming through the wood, her white shoes and the hem of her dress splattered with mud. The black curtain of the Shole was directly ahead of her – less than a hundred yards away. She seemed to be singing, but it was a weird sound. There were no words, just a shrill eldritch keening that sounded more like musical pipes than a human voice.

But then she isn't human, is she? thought Crafty. *Her appearance makes you forget the truth – that the White Lady is a dangerous aberration.*

He took a deep breath to steady himself. It was now or never!

Just before the first of the children emerged from the trees, he raised his blade, took a deep breath and sprinted towards the White Lady. He seized her hair from behind and sliced down with his blade. It was very sharp and the hair was stretched taut, which made it easier to cut through.

It was very coarse, but Crafty hacked through the thick strands in a couple of seconds.

The White Lady screamed and staggered forward, tumbling on to her knees. Glancing back, Crafty saw that the children had fallen too, still tangled up in her hair. He turned to the aberration and saw something that chilled him to the bone. The severed ends of her hair were weeping blood; rivulets were trickling down her back, staining the white dress.

The White Lady clambered to her feet, turned and took a step towards him. The front of her white dress was covered in grass stains and her face was twisted in anger. Crafty realized that she was changing before his eyes, her face elongating, purple talons extending from fingers that were now webbed like the wings of a bat. She was taking on her true evil shape.

Within seconds the beautiful face had been replaced by that of a malevolent demon. Fangs curved down over her lower lip, short black horns protruded from her forehead and her skin had grown mottled and leathery.

She took a step forward and her right hand lunged towards Crafty's head. The blow was fast and forceful, but somehow Crafty anticipated it and stepped backwards. The sharp talons missed his eyes by the breadth of a cat's whisker. Now she struck again with her other hand, and again Crafty managed to evade those terrible talons; if he hadn't, she would have blinded him and shredded the skin from his face.

Then she spoke to him, her voice a hoarse rasp that vibrated through his body. It sounded like a huge predatory cat sharpening its claws on a tree trunk.

'Begone from here or die!' she threatened. *'The children are mine.'*

Crafty stared back at her, determined not to show fear. Glancing over his shoulder, he saw that Lick was helping the weeping children. She had already managed to free a few of them from the aberration's hair, and they were either staggering away or helping their friends. He only needed to buy them a little more time.

He lifted his blade again and pointed it at the White Lady.

She hissed and stared at it, her eyes widening. *'Where did you get that?'* she demanded.

'A friend gave it to me,' Crafty replied, measuring the distance between them. He had been given it by Bertha, the Bog Queen. She was an aberration, but she was also an ally; she was his friend.

'Your friend; my enemy!' the aberration rasped.

She lunged towards him again, but this time Crafty moved aside and sliced up at the taloned hand with his blade. It made contact, and she shrieked and stepped backwards, blood trickling from the cut. Crafty saw that the blood wasn't red, but black and viscous, dripping like beads of tar on to the sodden grass. Her eyes flared with hatred and she prepared to attack him again.

Suddenly, out of the corner of his eye, Crafty saw Lick moving towards him. What could she do? he wondered. She didn't have a weapon – though she was balancing something in the palm of her hand; something Crafty recognized. It was one of the orbs that she used to light their way and drive back aberrations, which loved darkness and feared light. It would float upwards and cast a sudden blinding white light.

This time Lick used it as a weapon. She hurled it towards their enemy. It broke against the aberration's forehead with a bright flare. The White Lady screamed and fell to her knees, hands fluttering up to her face.

All at once Crafty heard shouts. Men were running towards them through the black curtain of the Shole. The couriers! They'd arrived at last.

The aberration glanced back at them and dropped down on to all fours. Then she bounded away like a hare, following a long curve that took her round the advancing couriers and into the dark wall of the Shole.

The couriers didn't attempt to follow her but headed towards Crafty and Lick. The man in the lead was even bigger than Crafty's father. As he approached, Crafty noticed his stern expression and the insignia of a green crown on his left shoulder. This must be the commander of the couriers, Captain Clayton.

Crafty had never met him, but his father had often mentioned him. He was an excellent courier, but a strict disciplinarian with a fanatical hatred of aberrations.

'You're Brian Benson's son, aren't you?' he demanded.

Not even a 'hello', thought Crafty.

'Yes, sir,' he answered.

'Well done, boy. You showed real courage there. You too, Miss Crompton-Smythe. Now, let's take these children back to their parents . . .'

Some of them still needed to be freed from the thick tangled hair, some were too weak to walk, but within half an hour all were safely back on the riverbank, where the parents had gathered to collect their offspring.

None of the children had been permanently harmed – at least not physically. But Crafty knew that their experiences might lead to years of nightmares. They would never forget the White Lady's attempt to abduct them.

And it could have been much worse, he reflected. If they'd been taken into the Shole, those children would have died, been eaten or changed into aberrations, and then they would never have seen their parents again.

Had Crafty and Lick not confronted the White Lady, this is what would have happened; the couriers would have arrived too late to intervene. Together, they had made a real difference.

Crafty was cold, tired and soaked to the skin – but he felt very pleased.

BERTHA, THE BOG QUEEN

The following morning, instead of the usual question-and-answer session, they had what Lick called a 'debriefing'. They discussed what had happened and considered how their response to the threat might have been improved.

'Under the circumstances I think you did well,' Lucky said. 'But one thing would make it easier the next time an aberration comes out of the Shole. There should always be at least two couriers stationed in the castle.'

'But that *was* the case,' Lick said. 'Don't you remember what the Chief Mancer said? They had two in reserve, but they were called to deal with another excursion – the one supposedly by the dead witch. The threat from the Shole is growing and they are stretched to the very limit.'

'They can't possibly be any more stretched than us gate grubs!' Lucky protested. 'I should have been there to help, not kept out of harm's way in case something happened to Crafty. We really need to recruit more gate grubs, don't we?'

'We certainly do, Lucky,' answered Lick, 'but Fey are rare enough, and those who can use a silver gate are hard to find. But the Chief Mancer is searching for others to help us. I know he's doing his best.'

'Do you think the White Lady could be the killer we're looking for?' Crafty asked.

Lick pondered this. 'Not long ago you thought it might be Viper – he's still a real possibility. What makes you think it might be her?'

'She's very powerful and, unlike other aberrations, which are just wild and driven by hunger for raw flesh and blood, she seems capable of planning and behaving in an intelligent way. I can imagine her finding a way to enter the castle through one of our gates and kill the mancers.'

Lick nodded. 'Yes, but there are other questions. She last left the Shole thirty years ago. What has she been doing since, and where was she hiding? And why did she suddenly emerge again after all this time?'

'And what about the witch?' Crafty asked. 'Was she really there? Did the couriers who went to the Crook o' Lune manage to deal with her?'

'It seems that by the time the couriers arrived she'd retreated into the Shole. She hadn't done any harm – other than terrify those who saw her. However, a few brave souls spoke to her and insisted that she really *was* Old Nell back from the dead. She cured a few warts, a few colds and headaches, and said she'd be back. Of course, the White Lady also starts off by helping people . . .'

'Was there nothing different about Old Nell?' Crafty asked. 'What about her teeth?'

'Teeth?' asked Lick, looking puzzled.

'The triple rows of teeth that some aberrations have . . .'

'Her teeth weren't mentioned, so I don't suppose they'd changed. You asked me a question about that not long ago. As I said, not all human beings changed by the Shole have them. And those returned from the dead certainly don't. Bertha is a good example of that.'

Crafty nodded and decided to shut up. This was one more reason why he shouldn't worry about his nightmare. Even if Old Nell had returned (and it seemed she had), she didn't seem to have any interest in eating anyone – let alone him. It had just been a scary dream, but one that he was finding it difficult to forget.

The discussion ended when the Chief Mancer came to collect Lucky for another mission.

'Let's go and talk to your friend Bertha again,' Lick said to Crafty after they'd gone. 'I've a couple of questions I want to ask her . . .'

Thousands of years ago Bertha had been a tribal queen, sacrificed by her own people and buried in the bog outside Crafty's house. When the Shole engulfed the place, Crafty had spent many lonely months there, taking refuge in the cellar. But it had also brought Bertha back to life, and she had visited him and kept him company during those dark times. He owed her a lot.

Once in Lick's room, Crafty sat down facing the silver gate. They wouldn't be using a fixed location so there was no need for a locator: Crafty's emotional bond with Bertha would be enough to take the gate close to where she was.

He stared into the gate and concentrated. Almost immediately the clouds cleared to show a familiar view. In the distance, through the grey murk, Crafty could just about see three houses; his old home was the one in the middle. The sight of it made him feel terribly sad.

The last time he visited his former home he had made a shocking discovery. Crafty's mother was not Fey, and he'd always assumed that she had died when their house was engulfed by the Shole. But it turned out that she'd been changed by the Shole and had been hiding in their old house. She'd told him to go away and never to come near her again. It had been terrible to hear those words from his own mother. It had upset him deeply, and he hadn't yet told his father what had happened. He would wait until he became stronger. But one day soon he would have to break the news to him.

Between the gate and Crafty's house was Bertha's bog. At the moment it was bubbling gently, but Crafty had seen Bertha turn it into something much wilder. She would be somewhere beneath its surface. It was her home.

'I'll go out and see if I can find her,' Crafty said.

He went through the gate and Lick followed him. There was no frost on the ground and the air was milder than usual for the Shole. This was often the case close to the bog. As he walked slowly towards its edge, there was an immediate disturbance. Bertha's crowned head surged up, followed by the rest of her body, and she stepped out on to the bank to face him. She was a slim, brown-skinned girl with large green eyes.

The last time, Bertha had been wearing armour. Now, at first glance, she didn't seem to be wearing any clothes – though in fact the garments she'd worn at her sacrifice had become fused with her skin, making it look like stretched brown leather. It was strange, but the mud and slime didn't stick to her at all. Her hair was her glory. It flowed down on to her shoulders in shiny, leathery black coils; atop it was the slim golden crown of the Segantii Queen with a large lustrous green gem affixed to the front.

'Hello, Bertha,' said Crafty, greeting her with a smile. 'I'm so glad to see you again. I'm with Lick, the gate mancer you met before. Would you mind talking to her again? She has some questions she'd like to ask you.'

'Very well,' said Bertha, looking past Crafty. 'I like Lick. She is sensible and thinks very quickly. Ask her to come forward.'

Crafty beckoned to Lick, and she approached Bertha while Crafty took up a position halfway between Lick and the gate, ready to intervene and warn her if anything nasty tried to go through; he was still within earshot and heard Lick's first question clearly.

'Hello, Bertha. Thanks for agreeing to answer my questions. My first one is about the Shole: do you think it's alive?' Lick asked. 'Do you know – is it controlled by something invisible, an entity that we can't see?'

Crafty remembered Lick asking something similar the last time they met Bertha on the edge of the bog. But before she was able to answer, Crafty had deceived Lick and run off in a desperate bid to rescue his father. He was curious now – what would Bertha say?

'I do *not* know,' said Bertha curtly. She sounded annoyed.

Crafty was disappointed. He'd been hoping for some sort of revelation. There was a long silence while Lick and Bertha stared at each other, each suddenly a little hostile.

Lick then asked another question. 'Do you ever hear voices, Bertha? Do you ever hear voices inside your head that tell you what to do?'

Crafty was shocked and surprised by that. It was a really strange question. What had made her ask that?

Bertha's response was even stranger. She turned her back on Lick and, without another word, walked back into the bog and disappeared from sight.

Lick headed back towards Crafty, shaking her head. 'Well, that didn't go very well! I don't think Bertha likes me,' she said.

'That's not true. She told me that she thought you were sensible and quick-thinking. But I wonder why she didn't answer your question.'

Lick merely shrugged and they clambered back through the gate.

Crafty was starting to get annoyed. 'There's something you aren't telling me!' he snapped. 'Why did you ask her that question about the voices? Did you guess that it might upset her?'

Lick nodded. 'I did think it might make her angry, but it had to be asked. Still, I didn't expect her to leave like that. Look, Crafty, I'm sorry for being secretive but I'm trying to figure out some things about the Shole – I want to know why some aberrations kill humans and others, like Bertha, don't. Why some seem to have a mind of their own, and others don't. Also, why are some of them – like the White Lady – able to move freely in the Daylight World, while others aren't? When I have my thoughts clear and I've arrived at an answer, I'll tell you. Is that all right?'

Crafty wasn't happy but he had to accept Lick's explanation.

THE RELIC ROOM

The following day was Sunday, which meant a free day.

When he was looking forward to something, Crafty could usually will himself to wake up early. It certainly worked this time. He jumped out of bed and glanced through his narrow turret window.

It was just after dawn and the sky was grey, with fast-moving clouds coming in from Morecambe Bay. He looked down the hill towards the Shole, the dark, impenetrable curtain that had recently engulfed the southern reaches of the canal. It didn't seem to have advanced during the night so, reassured, Crafty dressed quickly. He was really looking forward to his day off.

Everyone in the castle got a lie-in on Sundays, so breakfast wouldn't arrive for a couple of hours. Crafty had got up early because he planned to do something.

After he had rescued his father, the commander of the castle, the Duke, had given him a silver key which he kept around his neck, hidden under his shirt. The Duke had told him that it would grant him access to anywhere in the castle.

The Duke had been impressed by Crafty's cunning, and wanted him to find out what was going on within the Castle Corpus. The guilds all kept secrets from each other – and maybe even from the Duke. Crafty was going to be his spy! It was something he had kept hidden from Lucky and Lick. Maybe even the Chief Mancer didn't know about it. He was very curious to find out about the different departments.

But there was another task the Duke had charged Crafty with, although it would be difficult and probably dangerous. The sinister Grey Hoods – of which Viper had been a member – had supposedly infiltrated some of the departments; they were working to hold back their progress and thus aid the Shole. The Duke hoped that Crafty might be able to identify these people.

Now he was going to use the Duke's key for the first time – and he was going to demand access to the Relic Room.

On Sundays neither Crafty nor Lucky wore uniform – after all, it was their one day off, and they liked to walk the streets of the city anonymously. However, today, as he was going to use the silver key on behalf of the Duke, Crafty thought it better to wear his uniform, with its short-sleeved shirt and the letters *GM* emblazoned on it. *GM* stood for gate mancer. It showed that gate grubs were the property of members of the Mancers' Guild.

The Relic Room was on the ground floor of the castle. Crafty followed the long corridor lined with closed doors, the name of each room printed above them. He passed the Dead Room, the Forensics Room and then the Optimists' Room.

Next came the Ducal Chambers, where the Duke now lived, surrounded by servants and guards. This used to belong to the Pessimists. Crafty didn't have a clue what they actually did, or where they were now. Next he passed the Grey Library, and came at last to the door of the Relic Room.

He paused and pulled the silver key out so that it rested on his chest. Then he took a deep breath and rapped twice on the door. He was nervous. In spite of the right of entry the key bestowed, he didn't expect a friendly reception. The guild wouldn't appreciate his trespassing on their territory. Whatever secrets they had, they would want to keep them.

Crafty wanted to see inside this room because it housed samples after the other departments, such as Forensics, had finished with them. It would contain some of the earliest and oldest materials brought out of the Shole.

There was the sound of a bolt being drawn back and a key turning in a lock before the door opened. A giant of a man was glaring down at Crafty. His arms were like tree trunks, each one twice the thickness of Crafty's legs. He wore black trousers, a thick brown leather belt and a leather jerkin with the letters *RR* in red across his chest. The man stared down at him, his expression filled with contempt.

Crafty lifted the silver key on its chain and showed it to him. 'This gives me the right to enter any room in the castle,' he said. 'I'd like to look around the Relic Room, please.'

Before the key could fall back against Crafty's chest, the man's huge hand closed around it. Then, to Crafty's astonishment and dismay, he snatched it away, breaking the chain. He studied it closely and then shouted out one word: 'Guards!'

Two burly men rushed towards Crafty; lifting him off his feet, they held him against the wall.

'Keep him here while I deal with this!' said the giant, still staring at the key.

But he didn't return. Instead, ten minutes later, the Chief Mancer came into the Relic Room. He dismissed the two guards with a curt nod, then scowled at Crafty and held the key under his nose.

'Where did you acquire this, Benson?' he asked.

There was no point in lying – Crafty knew he'd only make things worse for himself. 'The Duke gave it to me, sir. It gives me access to any department in the castle. He said that nobody could refuse me. All doors would open to me the moment I showed the key. That's what the Duke said.'

'Did he now?' Ginger Bob mused, stroking his chin. 'And why would he do that? I wonder. Well, we'll soon find out if you're telling the truth. I've sent someone to inform the Duke that you were caught in possession of his silver key.'

A castle guard soon entered the room, and Ginger Bob went over to the door so that they could speak out of Crafty's hearing. When the Chief Mancer returned, he gave Crafty the faintest of smiles, then held the silver key out to him. 'All is well, young man. The Duke has confirmed that he did indeed give you that key. But it might have been better if I had been informed that you had it and intended to use it. However, no harm is done. You wish to look around the Relic Room?' he said, gesturing with his arm around the gloomy anteroom. 'I will smooth your path by introducing you to the curator. Follow me!'

He led the way and Crafty followed, putting the key in his pocket; the guards and the big man who had confiscated it were nowhere in sight. As far as Crafty understood the castle hierarchy, Ginger Bob was second in rank only to the Duke. But although he was in charge of all the mancers – not just those who managed the gates – each department was self-governing and it seemed that the curator commanded the Relic Room.

Crafty realized that he knew nothing about mancers other than gate mancers. What did they do? he wondered. What magical skills did they possess? The castle held so many mysteries.

It wasn't long before the curator himself came looking for them. Crafty was astonished at his appearance. He had expected a large, imposing man; someone slightly pompous and strict like the Chief Mancer. But he was very small – he barely reached Crafty's shoulder – with an impish face and long silver hair that hung down over his shoulders. Although the hair suggested age, his face was youthful and his blue eyes twinkled with humour.

He and the Chief Mancer exchanged polite nods, and then Crafty was left alone with the curator.

'Well, young Benson,' he said, beaming, 'I believe you have a key and are here to use it. Had you asked for me by name, you would not have been so badly treated! I do apologize for that. However, if I may, I propose a guided tour first so that you know your way around. Would that be satisfactory?'

'Yes, sir,' Crafty agreed. A guided tour would only show him what they wanted him to see, but he had to start somewhere. He wasn't expecting to discover all the secrets of the Relic Room on his first visit. 'What *is* your name, sir, if you don't mind me asking?'

'I have only one name – the one everyone uses when addressing me, even my own wife and children, I may add. That name is *Curator*. I live and breathe this job. It is my life. Now come this way . . .'

Crafty felt sorry for the man's children. Fancy having to address your own father as *Curator* all the time. Talk about taking your work home!

He was led through a door and stepped into a very large room. It was filled with glass display cases, the largest one mounted on a dais.

'This is what we call the Old Museum – it contains the very first samples collected from the Shole.' The curator pointed towards the large case. 'What do you think of that?' he asked.

Crafty peered through the glass. The aberration inside seemed perfectly preserved; it stood on four muscular legs that seemed made for speed. It was sleek like a greyhound but, like many predators from the Shole, it had three rows of teeth in its narrow skull, and two horns which jutted forward aggressively.

Suddenly Crafty realized that he had seen something similar before . . . 'Curator? Is the silver knocker on the door of the Chief Mancer's room made in a likeness of this creature's head?'

'Indeed it is. Well spotted, young Benson! It is of tremendous importance because it was the first aberration to be snatched from the Shole. It lurked around Water Lane, back when the Shole was only a few hundred yards across, but then wandered into the Daylight World and terrorized Preston. We call it *One-Bite* because of its method of attack. It would run down its human prey, taking a single bite of flesh. It never went back for more. Of course, that one bite killed many of its victims outright, depending on where the wound was.'

Crafty didn't want to meet the creature any time soon. 'Was this the only one?'

The curator shook his head. 'Others have been sighted in the Shole – and there is even a live one in the Menagerie. The good news is, they don't hunt in packs like other similar aberrations. One-Bite always bites alone!'

The curator was walking quickly past the display cases, not giving Crafty a chance to look at them properly. He began to feel frustrated, and halted before a case that was over eight feet tall and at least twenty long. It was full of what looked like bats; bats of all shapes and sizes that hung from a beam.

The curator came back to stand beside him. 'They almost look alive, don't they?' he said, his eyes twinkling. 'Of course, they are quite dead by the time the Menagerie or Forensics hand them over – though we don't use a taxidermist; there's a special substance that preserves them. Do you like bats?'

Crafty looked up at a giant bat that was covered in fur. 'I've nothing against them,' he replied, 'but I don't like the look of that one! I wouldn't want to meet anything like that in the Shole.'

'No, you certainly wouldn't. None of these are true bats, of course. They are aberrations that have been changed by the Shole. And we have deduced that not all were originally bats – most were birds and a few were mice or rats – but we term them bats for convenience. In fact, that large specimen is what we call a *corpse bat*. It's similar in appearance to the huge fruit bats that are found in some tropical areas of the world.'

The curator paused and tapped on the glass of the case for emphasis. 'All these bat aberrations are dangerous. The smaller ones are commonly found in attics and lofts – those are places to be avoided in the Shole. You must know by now that buildings are usually more dangerous than the countryside. As for the corpse bat, it prefers to be in the open; it hangs from the branches of tall trees, hidden amongst the leaves. Of course, it doesn't eat fruit!' he said ominously before once more striding on.

Each room they came to contained the same glass cases. Some were filled with bones or skulls, others with twisted woody plants that had human characteristics – branches in the shapes of hands or feet.

'We are in effect moving from the past to the present,' said the curator. 'This final area we call New Arrivals – it contains our most recent acquisitions. This is work in progress. We are so busy at present that we've had to ask the staff to work on a Sunday morning.'

They had entered a room furnished with tables and benches at which the Relic Room staff were working. They were measuring objects, sketching them and making notes. Most of them were grey-haired men – though Crafty saw one who was younger, probably in his early twenties. The man caught Crafty's eye, then frowned and looked away. He probably didn't like having to work on a Sunday morning, and being stared at added insult to injury!

Crafty didn't blame him. Being the Duke's spy had its perks – he would be able to satisfy his curiosity about the castle's different departments – but it also made him feel slightly uncomfortable.

He would have liked to question some of the workers, but he knew it was better to wait until he returned, this time without the curator at his elbow. Besides, he was hungry and didn't want his breakfast to go cold! So he thanked the curator and took his leave.

Ten minutes later he was back in his room, just in time to take delivery of a plate of ham and eggs and warm, freshly baked bread.

Not a bad morning's work, he thought.

That afternoon Crafty and Lucky walked down into the city together. The sky was overcast and it looked like rain. The weather was still relatively mild, but it was autumn now and winter was coming.

Crafty turned to look at his friend: Lucky hadn't been very talkative and now Crafty saw that he seemed sad.

'What's wrong?' he asked.

'Just thinking about poor Donna,' Lucky replied. 'I still really miss her.'

Crafty nodded sympathetically, but he didn't know what he could say to make things any better. Donna had been killed by the gate mancer Viper, the guillotine chopping off her legs. It was a terrible way to die. Crafty knew that Lucky had been close to her: before Crafty arrived at the castle it had been just the two of them working together and sharing danger. He knew that Lucky still felt her loss keenly.

They walked through the streets in silence. Because of the increased threat from the Shole, lots of people had left Lancaster and gone to live further north – Kendal being one of the more popular choices. But today the city seemed unusually busy, as if all the remaining inhabitants had come out on to the streets.

At last they reached their unspoken destination – a shop which sold the tastiest pies in Lancaster. They both peered in through the window, and the smell of meat and potatoes wafted through the open door, making their mouths water. Soon they were sitting on the wall outside, each with a big steaming-hot pie, and at last Lucky looked slightly more cheerful.

All at once Crafty realized that the people walking past them were all moving in the same direction. They were heading up the hill towards the castle – and with a shock he saw that some of them were dressed in grey coats, with hoods to match. These were members of the Grey Hoods cult.

'Where are they going – to the castle?' Crafty asked. He noticed that most of the passers-by wore surly, angry expressions.

'Looks like it,' Lucky replied, 'though what they hope to achieve when they get there is anybody's guess. There are a lot of Grey Hoods out stirring things up. They say we're not doing enough to protect the city. The truth is, they just want to make things as difficult as possible for us. It's a good job we don't wear our uniforms on a Sunday. The least that might happen is we'd be spat on. The worst . . . Well, best not to think about that. Feelings are running high.'

After eating, they walked down towards the dark curtain of the Shole, approaching to within fifty yards of it. Anything might be lurking just inside, but it was still afternoon and most aberrations would be sleeping, so the risk was small. Most – except, of course, for the White Lady – stayed inside the Shole.

'I used to like coming down here. I miss being able to look at the canal,' Lucky said.

Crafty nodded. 'When I looked through my window every morning, that was the first thing that caught my eye. But at least the Shole isn't advancing much at the moment.'

'Just a couple of inches a week. Let's hope it stays that way.'

They both glanced back up towards the castle. A big surge might engulf it one day; it could happen at any time.

The pair began to trudge back up the hill, each lost in his own thoughts. Crafty was thinking about his mother and wondering sadly how she was coping alone in the Shole. He was also worried about his dead brothers, Brock and Ben: the Shole might bring them back to life. He would like to see them again, but part of him wondered whether it would be a good thing. Bertha survived by catching creatures and eating their raw flesh. If Brock and Ben had to do that, they'd be very different from the brothers he'd once known and loved.

Just then there were shouts from above them, near the castle. Crafty and Lucky began to walk faster, wondering what was happening. An angry crowd had gathered near the main gate, yelling abuse at the guards stationed there. A few people were even throwing stones.

Suddenly the crowd fell silent. A tall officer of the Castle Guard moved forward to stand directly below the raised portcullis. He held aloft a sheet of paper so that everyone could see it. Then he began to read from it. Crafty and Lucky were too far away to hear most of what he was saying, but as they drew closer they caught the final words.

'Disperse now or face the consequences! This is by order of the Duke.'

'He's just read them the Riot Act!' exclaimed Lucky. 'If they don't clear off now, force will be used against them.'

But the crowd didn't disperse. Instead everyone started to roar in anger and to push forward towards the gate. But then the Castle Guard surged out of the castle in force. Crafty saw that they were using clubs, not swords. Within moments people were running down the hill, desperate to escape. Some were bleeding from the blows they had received.

For a moment Crafty feared that he and Lucky were in danger of being caught up in the scrum, but the fleeing mob didn't even glance in their direction as they ran past. Then he saw a couple of Grey Hoods hurrying past too. The hood of the nearest one had fallen back, revealing his face – and a gash over his left eye.

With a shock, Crafty recognized him. It was the youth who'd been working overtime in the Relic Room that very morning.

IT HAS TO BE DONE

Crafty knew that this evidence of a Grey Hood working within the castle should be reported to the Duke immediately. As soon as he'd parted from Lucky, he went straight to the Ducal Chambers.

Two armed guards dressed in full ceremonial uniform stood outside the big door. As Crafty approached, they crossed their long spears to bar him from entering. They were big men and merely stared over his head as if he was unworthy of their attention.

'My name is Colin Benson and I'd like to see the Duke, please,' Crafty said politely.

They continued to ignore him, and Crafty realized that he was wasting his time. Maybe he should go and ask the Chief Mancer to get him an appointment.

But then, suddenly, the big doors were thrust open and another guard with a large black moustache and a sergeant's triple stripes on his shoulder stared down at Crafty and spoke in a loud, booming voice. 'Master Colin Benson! The Duke will see you now!'

How could the Duke have been aware that he was waiting outside? Crafty wondered. Then he understood. The Duke had once been trapped in the Shole, and rather than kill him it had changed him. Before he could be rescued, the lower half of his body had been transformed into a tangled mass of fibrous roots. These roots now extended from the huge container he'd been planted in, right down below the foundations of the castle. They were very sensitive, and the Duke had told Crafty that they were like ears, enabling him to listen to conversations some distance away. He must have heard Crafty's plea to be admitted and noted the silence of the guards.

Without a word, the two guards moved their spears aside, and Crafty followed the sergeant into a vast room. He walked along a red carpet and up a set of steps, glancing up at the Duke.

The ruler of Lancashire was dressed in a green tunic with gold buttons, and his neat blond beard covered more than half his face. The lower part of his body was planted in a huge cylindrical container, with three sets of steps leading up to it; one at the front, and one at each side. A rich purple cloth encircled his waist and flowed across the container and down to the floor.

When Crafty reached the end of the red carpet, he bowed. The Duke then beckoned to him and Crafty climbed the central set of steps. He looked up at the Duke. 'Sir, today, for the first time, I used the key you gave me to gain entry to the Relic Room. The curator showed me around. When we reached the New Arrivals room, I noted that the staff were mostly elderly men – though the one young man working there caught my eye. This afternoon I went down into the city, and on my return saw a mob being dispersed by the Castle Guard. One of the Grey Hoods fled past me down the hill. I think it was the young man I saw in the Relic Room.'

The Duke stared hard at Crafty. 'You *think* it was him? How sure are you, Crafty? You do realize that if that young man is found to be a member of the cult and is using his position in the Relic Room to work against us, then the consequences for him will be severe. He would at least face a very long term of imprisonment; even his life could be forfeit . . .'

Crafty had thought about this already; he realized that, if he reported his suspicions, the young man might be hanged. He didn't want to point the finger at an innocent person. He himself had also been wrongly accused and sentenced to be hanged. He remembered how terrified and wretched he'd felt, waiting in his cell. He wouldn't wish that on anybody.

'Sir, I am reasonably sure, but there is some room for doubt. However, there is one way to be more certain. As the youth came past, I noticed that he had a gash over his left eye – he'd probably been hit by one of the guards. So, if the young man shows up for work tomorrow with a cut over that eye, his guilt will be confirmed.'

The Duke nodded. 'Well done, Crafty. But tell nobody else what you have just reported to me. Even if the young man *is* a member of the Grey Hoods, we will allow him to continue working, though we will watch him closely. He may lead us to his fellow conspirators. If you are proved to be correct, you will have done very well indeed.'

'I think I was just fortunate that he came past. It was a bit of luck, that's all.'

'It was more than luck. You were observant and remembered his face. Well done!'

Every few days Crafty went to visit his father in the Infirmary, where he was staying while he recovered.

It was a while now since Crafty's father and two other couriers had gone missing in the Shole. They had disappeared for over a month, drawn by a strong magical summons that had led them into captivity. Breaking all the rules, Crafty had found the missing couriers and played a big part in their rescue. But one of the couriers had been slain by aberrations, and Crafty's father still hadn't fully recovered from his ordeal.

On this visit, Crafty had decided to do something he'd been putting off for a long time: break the news about his mother.

The first time he visited his father he had been sitting with a rug over his knees, staring into the embers of the fire and looking very low. Crafty couldn't imagine how he would ever recover his former health. But now he was well on the mend. He met Crafty at the door of his room, gave him a warm smile, patted him on the back and invited him in. They sat side by side facing the fire.

'You really do look a lot better, Father,' Crafty told him.

'My health is much improved and I'm getting stronger by the day. The doctor says that I can return to duty in another week or so. I'm getting tired of spending all my time in this room. I'll get fitter once I can start walking!'

By that Crafty knew he meant walking in the Shole, going back to his dangerous duties as a castle courier. He frowned at the thought.

His father looked closely at him. 'Is there something the matter, Crafty? You look worried.'

'I *am* worried, and I have to tell you something, Father. Something that will be a shock.' He drew a deep breath. 'Before I tried to rescue you, I needed something of yours so that I could find out where you were. So I went back to our house to get your pipe. But as soon as I reached the top of the cellar steps I knew that something was wrong. There was some sort of climbing plant rooted at the bottom; it had grown over every step, covering the silver alloy completely.'

The silver alloy had been a protective measure put in place by his father, a ward against aberrations. When Crafty was forced to take refuge in the cellar, no aberration could set foot on that metal. Nothing could go down to the cellar. But with the steps covered in foliage, this was no longer the case.

'It suggests the use of very powerful malign magic,' his father said, shaking his head. 'Something must have been hiding in the cellar. Did you still go down there?'

'Of course, I did, Father. I had to get your pipe. How else would I have found you?'

'You were very brave. An aberration could have been using the cellar as its lair.'

It was now or never, Crafty thought. He steeled himself. 'There *was* an aberration. It was hiding in the cupboard. At first I thought it was hiding there, and planning to leap out and attack me. But I was wrong. She just didn't want me to see her . . .'

'*She?*' his father asked.

'There's no easy way to tell you this, Father. The aberration . . . it was Mother. It was *Mother* who was hiding in the cupboard.'

Crafty watched his father as all the colour fled from his face. His hands began to shake and he clamped them tightly around his knees.

'I thought your mother was dead. Are you *sure*? Did you see her face?'

When their house was suddenly engulfed by the Shole, Crafty's mother had been out shopping at the local market. His father had searched and searched, but then, unable to find her, had assumed that she was dead.

Crafty shook his head. 'I didn't see her face because she wouldn't come out of the cupboard. But there was no doubt about it. Her voice was slightly changed – a bit husky – but it was definitely her. She said she didn't want me to see her like that; I should go away and never return. She said that I mustn't take you there either. She can't bear to be seen now that she's changed.'

His father became very still and sat there silently. When he finally spoke again, his words were chilling.

'I need to go and talk to her, Crafty, and as soon as possible. I can't wait until the doctor declares me fit.'

This made Crafty even more worried. 'Do you think that's a good idea, Father? You're still unwell, and Mother did say she didn't want to see either of us.'

'It has to be done. I want you to come too. I'm still weak – I might have to lean on you if I get tired. And it's better if we both speak to her. We'll go at noon – the safest time – on your next day off. At least I won't need to blindfold you this time! You're a gate grub now and have quite a bit of experience of the Shole . . .'

Crafty wasn't sure he wanted to be part of his father's plan. It was dangerous, and he was worried about what they might find. But how could he refuse? If he did, his father would almost certainly go anyway, and in his weakened condition it would be very dangerous.

Crafty worried about it all week, and for once Sunday came all too quickly. Crafty was forced to make an excuse to Lucky, saying that his father wanted to spend the day with him. Of course, he didn't say what they planned to do.

They set off at noon, both wearing their greatcoats. Together they approached the dark churning wall that marked the place where the Daylight World ended and the Shole began. Two patrolling guards watched them from a distance but did not interfere. Nobody hindered the work of a castle courier.

One moment the sun was shining and it was a mild autumn day; the next the temperature dropped alarmingly. Now the sky overhead was dark grey, their surroundings murky. They had entered the Shole.

Crafty's father led the way, but soon his pace dropped and he became breathless. After about fifteen minutes he had to rest.

'It's too soon for you to be doing this,' Crafty told him. 'Why don't we wait until next Sunday? You'll be stronger then.'

'I'll be all right,' wheezed his father. 'I'll get my breath back in a few minutes.'

Crafty glanced around. It was gloomy and there was a slight powdering of frost on the grass, but all was silent and nothing moved. There wasn't even a hint of danger. 'It's very quiet,' he said.

His father nodded. His breathing was slowly returning to normal. 'It looks harmless enough at the moment – and so it should be at this time of day. But you should never grow complacent. The Shole can change in an instant,' he said.

'What's the strangest thing you've ever seen in the Shole?' Crafty asked curiously.

His father was staring into space and it was a long time before he finally answered. 'That's hard to say. What would you say if I told you there were trees that could move?'

Crafty smiled. 'What? Trees with legs! That's got to be a joke.'

'It's not a joke – far from it,' his father replied with a shake of his head. 'They don't have legs, but their roots do a similar job. Their progress is slow – maybe just a few dozen yards a year: we've measured it. But there are also things that look like trees but aren't. They're *really* dangerous – they can move very fast and feed on flesh.'

'Is there any way to distinguish them from an ordinary tree?' Crafty asked, staring nervously at a tangle of tall trees about fifty yards away.

His father shook his head. 'Visually there are no clues at all. We call that category of aberration a *mimic* because it pretends to be something else while it waits for its prey. But when you're in the Shole, always listen carefully,' he said, pointing to his ears. 'A rustling when there's no wind – that could be the only warning you get. But, you know, there's something even stranger than trees that can move or mimics that can kill . . .'

Crafty's father paused, briefly lost in thought, then continued. 'There are lots of really strange phenomena that we simply can't make sense of. But, for me, one stands out. There's a black barge drawn by a horse-like creature. It goes along the canal, through the Shole to Preston and back. Leading that strange horse is a tall, skinny, hooded figure – it must be over seven feet tall. That barge always leaves Lancaster at midnight on a Tuesday and returns three nights later. We're keeping it under close observation. Each week a different courier is sent to watch it.'

'Have you seen it, Father?'

'Of course – that's one of my duties. I've followed it three times so far.'

'Have you any idea at all what its purpose is?'

'There are theories – mancers and boffins throw out theories like confetti at a wedding – but the most sensible one is often the most likely to be true. In this case, there's a suggestion that a bargeman and his horse were changed by the Shole and are just mindlessly continuing the work they once did.'

'Sounds likely,' said Crafty.

'Yes – though there is a problem with that explanation,' his father told him. 'The barge has a cargo of mysterious coffin-shaped boxes. It moves them from place to place. So far, it's been too dangerous to get close enough to find out what those boxes contain. But somehow I doubt whether it's coal, wood, salt or any of the things that were previously transported along the canal.'

'Is the bargeman dangerous?' Crafty asked.

'Almost certainly – and the horse even more so. It has very long legs and, instead of hooves, three long toes tipped with talons. Both horse and bargeman have three rows of needle-like teeth, which tells us that both eat raw meat. And they operate at night, which is always the most dangerous time in the Shole.'

Crafty's father shifted uncomfortably, as if he'd remembered where they were. 'Anyway, that's enough for now – let's be on our way. We've lingered too long . . .'

He set off north-east again, but at an even slower pace. Fortunately there was still no hint of danger. This time he managed almost half an hour before he had to rest again.

'Did we take this route when you blindfolded me and led me out of the cellar?' Crafty asked.

'Not exactly. I always vary it slightly – force of habit, I suppose,' his father said. 'Something might be hiding and notice you passing by. Next time it could be lying in wait for you.'

'I remember that we halted because something big and dangerous was close by. I could hear it eating. Did you see it?'

His father nodded grimly. 'It was hidden by trees, but I caught a few glimpses, Crafty. Luckily it didn't notice us. It reminded me of a giant caterpillar – it had a hairy, tubular body and was munching leaves and bark. Most likely we weren't on the menu, but it's always best to be wary. Never trust anything in the Shole.'

Crafty wondered if his father's advice also applied to Bertha, the Bog Queen. He knew now that she'd played a part in his rescue, but his father still didn't realize that she'd visited Crafty in the cellar: he didn't trust aberrations, no matter how friendly they might seem. Crafty wondered how he felt about a changed wife.

They walked on in silence until, at last, the bog came into view, with the three houses right on its edge. Crafty wondered if Bertha was somewhere nearby. Would she know that he and his father were visiting their old home?

'If the bog keeps on expanding, it will soon undermine our house,' observed his father. 'It's almost up to the back door.'

The bog had already swallowed the back gardens of the three houses, and they had to sidle along the rear walls. No doubt mud would eventually fill the cellar and then the house would collapse. Where would his mother take refuge then? Crafty wondered.

As they trudged towards their back door, their boots sank into the mud almost as far as their ankles. The gently bubbling bog and the squelching of their boots were the only sounds to be heard.

Crafty's father led the way into the gloomy kitchen, took a candle from his pocket, lit it with a match and handed it to Crafty. Then he lit one for himself.

But as they descended the first set of steps that led down to the cellar, Crafty suddenly felt uneasy. His father had pulled a long-bladed dagger out of the pocket of his greatcoat. In theory there was nothing unusual about that. After all, they were still in the Shole, and danger was everywhere.

However, when they reached the silver-alloy stairs, Crafty's father halted and turned to face him. 'I think it's probably best if you wait here. I'd like to talk to your mother alone.' Sometimes he could look very stern; more Courier Benson than the father Crafty loved. That unyielding expression was on his face now.

Crafty was about to protest, but then thought better of it. If his father wanted to speak to her – so be it. It was his right. And anyway, Crafty wanted to obey his mother's wishes – she had told him she didn't want him to see her again – even if it hurt him terribly.

'Whatever you think best, Father,' he replied.

His father turned and began to descend the steps, the candle casting his flickering shadow behind him. Those silver stairs were covered in plant foliage, no doubt summoned by his mother. Her gardening skills had been enhanced now that she was changed. It seemed that she could make plants do her will by magic.

Crafty watched his father complete his slow, cautious descent and cross the cellar past the graves of Ben and Brock, heading for the tall cupboard.

Its doors were closed. Was his mother hiding inside? he wondered.

Suddenly Crafty's whole body began to tremble and he felt sick to his stomach. *No!* Bile rose in his throat as he raced down the steps, though he knew he wouldn't be fast enough. He would never reach his father in time.

Courier Benson was raising the knife in his right hand. He'd placed the candle at his feet and his left hand was turning the handle of the cupboard door. The tautness of his body and the grimace on his face confirmed that Crafty's instincts had been correct.

He intended to kill Crafty's mother.

'Father! No! No!' Crafty shouted.

But he was too late.

His father opened the cupboard door and thrust the knife inside.

THE BEST SOLUTION

Instead of screams, there was the sound of metal striking wood, and when Crafty reached his father's side he saw that the cupboard was empty. Crafty was trembling, but was filled with an intense relief. He had feared the worst. He looked up at his father and saw that he was crying, tears rolling down his cheeks and dripping from the end of his chin.

'Why, Father? Why?' Crafty asked. 'Why would you want to hurt Mother?'

'She's no longer your mother!' his father shouted, brushing his tears away with the sleeve of his greatcoat and thrusting the knife back into his pocket. 'She's changed, Crafty, and could be a danger to us all. I was just going to put her out of her misery. Somebody has to do it, and it's best that I take care of it. That's the best solution. You do see that, don't you?'

Crafty watched his father slump to his knees and bury his face in his hands; his shoulders shuddered with deep sobs. He felt desperately sorry for him, but he couldn't let him kill his mother. He knew she might return at any time, so he had to get his father out of the house. Either that or somehow change his mind.

'I know that Mother's no longer fully human, but couldn't we just leave her to live out her life as best she can?' Crafty tried to keep calm, but his heart was thudding and he felt breathless.

His father shook his head sorrowfully. 'Use your imagination, Crafty. Put yourself in her shoes. How do you think she feels – an aberration cut off from everyone she loved? She'll be lonely and terrified. Think of the happy life she led before and everything she's lost. It'll be a kindness to put an end to such a miserable existence.'

'But while she's alive, there's still hope,' Crafty persisted.

'Hope! There's no hope at all. No going back to what she was before. Besides, she's a danger to others. It's my duty,' his father insisted.

Crafty thought briefly about using Bertha as an example of an aberration who was kind – someone you could talk to. But he remembered that even Bertha, who was his friend and had saved him from death in the orphanage, sometimes killed and ate humans to survive. Even Lick might have been on the menu if she hadn't been a friend of Crafty's.

Courier Benson began to pace backwards and forwards, clearly agitated; he kept staring at the steps. All Crafty could do was hope that his mother stayed away.

Then he had a sudden moment of inspiration. 'If you hate aberrations so much, why did you bury my brothers here in the cellar?' he challenged.

His father came to a halt, glanced at the graves and turned towards him. His eyes were filled with a mixture of alarm and surprise. He opened his mouth but no words came out.

'You did it because you hoped that one day the Shole would bring them back to life, didn't you?' Crafty went on.

His father continued to stare at him wordlessly, and Crafty kept talking. 'Don't you realize that, if it ever happens, they'll be changed? They'll be aberrations too, and will do whatever is necessary to survive. How is that different from Mother's situation? Would you want to put them out of their misery too, Father? If so, what's the point of hoping they'll be brought back to life?'

His father clenched his fists, and for a moment Crafty thought he might hit him. But then his shoulders slumped and he went over to pick up his candle. Finally, without another word, he headed for the steps.

Carrying his own candle, Crafty followed him up into the kitchen. Soon they were trudging through the mud and then heading north towards Lancaster. This time his father never halted once. Anger was giving him strength. Crafty walked at his heels, and they didn't exchange a single word until they were safely out of the Shole and back inside the castle walls.

At last his father turned and met his gaze. 'Today's been hard for both of us, Crafty. Maybe things will seem clearer in the morning. But nothing you've said has changed my mind. Take care, son. We'll talk again soon.'

Then he set off without a backward glance.

On Monday morning, as usual, Lucky was first in the Waiting Room.

'Did you have a good day with your father?' he asked Crafty.

'We stayed in his room most of the time – he's still a bit weak – but we took a short stroll around the city. It was good,' he replied.

He felt bad lying to his friend, but he couldn't bear to tell him what had happened the previous day. Something so terrible had to be kept in the family.

A few moments later Lick arrived and they had the usual fifteen-minute question-and-answer session. Crafty's heart wasn't in it; he didn't ask a single question. He saw Lick looking at him curiously because he was usually desperate to get as many answers as possible in the time allowed.

When the session was over, she stood up and smiled at Crafty. 'Come with me. We've got a job, but it's just routine – nothing to worry about.'

Nodding goodbye to Lucky, he followed her down to her room. She sat at her desk and gestured that he should take the seat opposite.

'There's something wrong, isn't there, Crafty?' she said, frowning. 'Care to tell me about it?'

For a moment he just stared at her without speaking. But what he'd kept from Lucky he now shared with Lick. Everything came out in a torrent of words like a dam breaking. Lick knew about his first descent into the cellar, but later he had omitted the fact that his mother had been hiding in the cupboard. He told her about it now. With tears brimming in his eyes, he added that his father wanted to put his mother out of her misery.

'He's getting stronger by the day. He won't wait for my next day off – he'll go to the house without me. He could even be on his way there now. I've got to warn her. We could use the gate . . .'

Lick buried her face in her hands – something she often did when there was a difficult decision to make. Then she pulled her hands away and stared straight into Crafty's eyes. 'Did you have a happy childhood?' she asked.

Crafty was surprised by the question. Lick never talked about her own background and had never asked him about his. 'I was happy being with my mother, father and brothers,' he replied. 'But the neighbours were far from friendly. They never spoke to us because we were Fey. And they thought even worse of my mother because she'd married a Fey man.'

'I see. I can sympathize. It's hard to be Fey,' she said. 'I should know. We have something in common, Crafty. We *both* come from mixed marriages. My mother was Fey but my father wasn't. They didn't get on well either. There were a lot of rows.'

Crafty could see the sadness in Lick's eyes, but he was surprised by what she had just revealed. Her mother was the famous Myra Crompton-Smythe who had invented the silver gate. He knew that she had died several years ago. He wondered where Lick's father was – whether he was still alive. But now was probably not the best time to ask.

'I'm sorry,' he said simply.

Lick nodded, and was about to say more, but then she closed her mouth firmly and sat staring down at her desk. Finally, she raised her head and looked him straight in the eye again. 'I want to help you, Crafty, but I can't let you return to the cellar – it's far too dangerous. However, there is another way. You told me that Bertha used to visit you there.'

Crafty nodded, wondering where this was leading.

'Then let's visit Bertha and ask *her* to warn your mother!'

'That's a great idea!' he said, suddenly filled with new hope. 'Let's do it!'

He got to his feet and headed towards the chair. Lick followed and pulled back the curtain to reveal the silver gate. Crafty stared at the swirling clouds and concentrated on finding Bertha. Moments later he was gazing at the gently bubbling bog. They were much closer to Crafty's house than usual. Bertha must be somewhere nearby.

'You go out and talk to her, Crafty,' Lick said. 'She didn't seem to like me very much last time. I'll stay and guard the gate.'

He buttoned up his greatcoat against the cold and clambered through. He hadn't gone far before Bertha's crowned head appeared, and seconds later the slim, brown-skinned girl stepped out of the mud to face him. Wasting no time, Crafty told her what the problem was.

'My father might even be on his way here now. I need to get a warning to my mother. Would you do that for me?'

'I will, but it may take me some time to find her. She doesn't always stay in the cellar. She has other hiding places that your father won't know about.' Bertha paused, and seemed to be thinking. 'We must make sure that neither she nor your father can ever go down to the cellar again. She could get trapped and he could take her unawares. Go back to the castle. I'll deal with this.'

Before Crafty could ask her what she proposed to do, Bertha slid back into the mud. He turned and walked back to the gate, clambered through and told Lick what Bertha had said.

'I wonder what she intends,' he said, thinking aloud.

Moments later the bog supplied the answer. It was no longer calm. Waves rolled across its surface as if driven by a gale-force wind, each one bigger than its predecessor. The tide was moving towards the three houses. As the waves struck, windows shattered and doors were smashed inwards.

Crafty gasped with shock. Bertha was destroying his home!

The final wave of mud swamped the three houses, striking them just below the roofs. Then, with a load roar, it swept forwards. Within moments the bog had moved on fifty yards, and Crafty's home was now part of it; only the roof and chimney showed above the surface.

He was stunned. The mud would have surged into the house, then down the steps into the cellar. By now it would be swamped. Bertha had certainly made sure that Crafty's father could never catch his mother in the cellar. He was grateful to her for that . . . but what about Brock and Ben? His brothers' graves were now buried under all that mud. He would never again hear them whispering to him.

He'd never told anyone that he could hear them – not even his father or Lick – and he didn't feel like telling her now. It was a mystery to him why this was; after all, they were dead. Did it mean that there was a place where the dead went? Would they wait there until the Shole brought them back to life?

After he'd closed the gate and he and Lick had sat down at the desk again, Crafty explained his concerns about what Bertha had done: 'She's prevented any immediate threat to my mother, but I'd hoped that one day the Shole might return my brothers to life. Now their graves are buried under all that mud.'

Lick gave a shrug, as she often did, but it was a sympathetic shrug. 'I think you'll have to try not to worry about it, Crafty. There's no guarantee that the Shole will ever return them to life; if it does, well, no doubt Bertha will help them. From what we've just seen, it's clear that she has a lot of power over the bog. Your brothers are in her territory now. I'm sure she'll keep them safe.'

Crafty nodded sadly but tried to be optimistic. What Lick said made sense. He trusted Bertha to take care of his dead brothers and to help them if they were returned to life.

'Yes,' Lick continued. 'In fact, we've just learned something *really* important. We suspected that Bertha could control the bog – remember you told me that it became agitated when Viper was hunting for her, and that mud had splattered his face and shirt while leaving you untouched?'

Crafty nodded. The mud had come straight through the gate as if directed at Viper.

'Well, Bertha has just confirmed that she does indeed control it. It's as if the bog is an extension of her body. She's like the mind of the bog, its controlling spirit. This is a real breakthrough – what if there are other entities out there that can do the same? What if there are aberrations that control aspects of the Shole?'

THE WITCH'S WARNING

That night Crafty dreamed about the witch again.

She was about to be hanged, and he watched as the guards lifted her on to the barrel and positioned the noose around her neck. The mob were excited, shouting at the executioner to get on with it. The hangman tightened the rope, and then, with a savage kick, knocked the barrel out from under Old Nell's feet.

It was only a dream, but it was more like a memory of the scene he and Lucky had actually witnessed when they hanged Old Nell. They'd been sitting on the grass, some distance away from the crowd. However, in his dream there was no sign of Lucky, and Crafty was standing close to the barrel, watching as Nell's legs kicked and her body twisted on the end of the rope. At one point a gust of wind blew her ragged skirt up over her head, showing her undergarments. That got another big cheer from the crowd. Then they began to chant:

'*Die, witch, die! Die, witch, die! Die, witch, die!*'

The dream changed. It suddenly became dark, and the blackness swallowed everything but the hanging witch. Crafty was alone in the darkness with Old Nell. Her whole body seemed to be glowing as it twisted towards him, her eyes opening very wide. Her body grew still and even her legs had ceased to twitch. Her neck looked very long and her eyes were bulging slightly. Surely she was dead . . .

But then she spoke to him. '*Do you know what the Shole will become?*' she croaked.

Crafty shook his head.

'*Then I'll show you . . .*'

Now he was standing in a field close to the edge of a wood. It was a bright morning and he could feel the warmth of the sun on his face. Crafty knew that he was still dreaming, but everything seemed very real. The green grass was dotted with buttercups, daisies and dandelions.

Then something caught his eye. There was an irregular patch of darkness right in the middle of the field. At first he thought it was just a cowpat – there seemed to be flies hovering over it. He started to walk towards it, but the nearer he got, the more nervous he became. It was much larger than he'd first thought – twelve feet or so in diameter. As he looked down, his unease changed to fear.

At his feet, something that looked like black tar was bubbling and growing as he watched. The living things hovering above it were not quite like the flies belonging to the Daylight World. There was something warped and unnatural about their tiny bodies. Some had heads that were disturbingly human in appearance.

Crafty had seen similar creatures in the Shole, but the big, black, oily puddle was new. It wasn't the actual Shole, Crafty decided. It was more like some sort of representation of the Shole – like a miniature version of something much larger. The witch was using it to show him something.

There was a sudden slurping noise, and the oily patch expanded rapidly, a tide of slimy darkness rushing towards his boots – just like the Shole when it surged and engulfed whole communities in a matter of seconds.

Crafty turned and ran, and didn't stop until he'd reached the edge of the field. He looked back and saw that the surge had ended, though the black puddle was more agitated than ever.

'*Watch!*' croaked Old Nell's voice in his ear.

Suddenly the black puddle exploded. Globules of black slime were hurled upwards before falling back to earth. Crafty watched the black streaks against the blue sky, and heard the splat as each hit the grass, then flattened out into a small puddle. Crafty's heart sank as he realized what was happening. Each one was now expanding rapidly across the meadow.

'*Do you understand?*' hissed the witch. '*Heed my warning. There will be more than one Shole. Many times more, until the whole world is covered!*'

'Is there a way to stop it?' Crafty cried out in desperation.

'*There may be a way, but there will be a terrible price,*' said the witch. '*Would you be prepared to pay it, Crafty?*'

'Yes!' cried Crafty. 'I'd do anything to prevent that.'

'Then may you get what you deserve!' said the witch.

With a cry, Crafty woke and sat bolt upright in bed, sweating and panting heavily. What a terrible dream! Once again, it was as if the witch had been in the room with him and had spoken directly into his ear.

He felt sure now that this was no coincidence, and that Old Nell was haunting him for a reason. But what was she trying to tell him? Would the Shole explode, each piece falling to earth in a new location, each a seed from which another Shole would spring? Or was there something else at work? The thought of more than one Shole was terrifying, and Crafty was filled with visions of the whole earth being terrorized by dreadful aberrations. Could he really manage to stop it? If so, what was the price he would have to pay?

It took him a long time to get back to sleep.

The following morning the Chief Mancer and Lick came into the Waiting Room together. Both looked concerned but, as usual, no explanation was given. Lucky went off with Ginger Bob while Crafty followed Lick to her room.

She pushed open the door, nodding to Crafty to go in first. He noticed a large bag on the floor next to the gate and wondered what it contained. Lick went across to her desk, opened the top drawer and lifted out a small case. She opened it, removed a locator and brought it over.

'A courier was attacked in the Shole last night,' she told Crafty. 'Now we have a chance to investigate the site of the attack. Thanks to my advice, each courier now carries one half of a locator. If he's in trouble, he pushes it into the ground – if he gets the chance. This change came about because of what happened to your father.'

'So this courier managed to do it?' Crafty asked.

Lick nodded. 'He pushed the locator into the ground as he was attacked. It happened very quickly and he soon lost consciousness. When he came round, he just had the strength to crawl into the Daylight World; luckily he was found by a couple of guards who were patrolling the edge of the Shole, but he died of his injuries almost immediately. So that's where I want you to take us now – the place where he was attacked. The killer might still be around.'

'If he was in such a bad way and ended up crawling out, he can't have been very far inside the Shole,' Crafty said. 'And why didn't the aberration finish him off?' he added.

Lick frowned. 'Yes, it's puzzling. That's why we need to get in there and find out. And now you're not the only one with a weapon!' she announced with a grin, opening the big bag at her feet and pulling out a weapon of her own. It was a crossbow. An arrow was already in place, ready to fire.

'Amazing! Though the arrows are a bit small . . .' Crafty said, peering closer.

'Crossbow arrows are called bolts, and these are tipped with silver alloy,' she said. 'They may be small but they're effective. If we get lucky and find the aberration that killed the courier, this should be enough to deal with it.'

Crafty knew that aberrations were vulnerable to silver, and it didn't take much to do the job. He'd seen crossbows before – some of the castle guards were armed with them – but never one like this. The guards' bows were bulky and heavy. This one was much neater, and made of metal rather than wood. It was also more streamlined and had a leather pouch fitted to its underside.

'I'd like one of those!' said Crafty.

'And eventually you will be issued with one. This is just a test weapon. I came up with the specifications and sketched out a rough design. The castle armourer did the rest. It's very light, and automatically reloads bolts from this pouch underneath.' She tapped it with her forefinger. 'Aberrations can move really quickly, so not having to reload manually could mean the difference between life and death. And, once we develop this further, all gate grubs and couriers will be armed with them. Right,' said Lick, turning back to look at the gate, 'let's get on with it. Take us there, Crafty.'

Crafty relaxed in the chair and tried to ignore the guillotine above him. He felt the cool metal of the locator in his hand and concentrated on the search for the other half. He was immediately successful. The swirling clouds dissolved and he could see into the gloomy world of the Shole. In fact, it seemed even gloomier than usual. Directly ahead a wide path led to a building that looked like a small church, set back amongst a dense cluster of trees.

Silver gates weren't terribly accurate, and they didn't necessarily take you to the exact spot you were looking for.

The buried piece of metal could be twenty or thirty yards away. Now a visual search was needed.

'Where is this?' Crafty asked.

Lick shrugged. 'I don't know, but I think we're somewhere deep inside the Shole – not near the edge, as we assumed. You can tell by the quality of the light. Generally, the further in you go, the gloomier it is.'

'That doesn't make sense,' said Crafty. 'The courier could never have crawled so far.'

'I agree,' said Lick, frowning. 'It's puzzling. But you've taken us to the locator, so let's investigate. Why don't you walk along the path and I'll follow you with the gate.'

It wasn't really a question, it was an order. Crafty didn't like being bossed around, but he liked Lick and it was a sensible course of action. He knew he was lucky to be working with her – he was better off than most gate grubs had been.

Crafty peered out: for some reason he didn't like the look of the path or the grey-stone church at the end, but he buttoned his greatcoat to the neck and carefully eased himself through the gate, feeling in his right-hand pocket to check that the dagger was still there. The aberration might well be nearby.

As he took his first step, his boots crunched on the hard, frosty ground. The air was very cold and already his nose felt numb. Crafty glanced upwards. The sky was dark grey.

Five slow, careful paces brought him to the path. He glanced over his shoulder at the blue circle and saw Lick staring out at him. He glanced left and right into the trees. It was a dense thicket, formed from a mixture of old established trees and saplings. Anything could be hiding in there.

He walked on even more slowly, sensing danger, feeling the hair stand up on the back of his neck. He turned and watched the blue circle wink out. That didn't concern him. Lick was just moving the gate to follow him. It reappeared – this time much nearer; he could see Lick's anxious face. She was holding the crossbow, ready to fire a silver-tipped bolt if necessary.

Suddenly Crafty saw movement up in the trees to his left. It was followed by a terrible shriek. Something big was up there. It looked vaguely human in shape and it was flapping its limbs like a scarecrow in a storm, as if preparing to swoop down on him. It screamed again. There was only one thing to do.

Crafty drew the dagger out of his coat pocket and prepared to defend himself. As the aberration screeched again, he raised the blade. Immediately Lick came dashing through the silver gate and aimed the crossbow up into the tree – but then she shook her head and slowly lowered it again.

Why doesn't she fire? Crafty wondered.

'It's not dangerous, Crafty,' she told him. 'It's a type of aberration called a *flapper*. It was once a human being, but the Shole fused it with the branch of that tree. All flappers do is shriek and flap their limbs – hence their name.'

Crafty stared up at it. 'It's sad to think that was once a person,' he said. 'I wonder how it feels. It must be scared.'

Its head was elongated and completely hairless, but the eyes looked human and seemed to be staring at him. It shrieked again.

'I don't think they remember being human,' Lick told him. 'They probably don't think at all.'

'How do they survive? What do they feed on?' Crafty asked.

'As they're embedded in a branch, the sap feeds them.'

Crafty nodded. It reminded him of what had happened to the Duke of Lancaster.

'Right, Crafty,' Lick told him, all business again. 'Let's get on with it. Carry on walking towards the church.'

She climbed back through the gate into her room and made chivvying gestures.

With the flapper still shrieking up in the tree, Crafty moved forward carefully. He held the dagger ready because he still sensed danger.

As he approached the church, he saw that it was small, just a chapel really. Built of large grey stones, it had a sloping roof but no steeple or tower. Just above the door was a single gargoyle with ears like a bat, sharp teeth and a protruding tongue. It seemed to be laughing but its expression wasn't friendly.

If this was where the courier had been attacked, Crafty thought, looking around, there was no sign of a struggle.

As the flapper screeched again, goose pimples ran along Crafty's arms. Its sharp cry was different this time, sounding almost like words.

Crafty shivered. He was surely just imagining it.

There was another long shriek, and this time there was no mistaking it:

'Run for your life! Run! Run! It's a trap!'

But the warning came too late.

Suddenly everything grew dark; Crafty looked up and saw that the sky was as black as pitch. With a crash, the church door opened wide, a long arm shot out and a hand gripped his shoulder before he could react. He was dragged inside and the door slammed shut behind him. The dagger was dashed from his hand, and something incredibly strong hurled him to the floor. All the air was driven from his lungs. He lay there gasping, stunned by the impact.

It was gloomy in the chapel and there were no pews, just an altar with a single flickering candle – which nevertheless gave enough light to show him how bad the situation was.

Bruised and bewildered, Crafty looked up at the menacing figure glaring down at him.

He couldn't believe it.

It was Viper.

THE FLAPPER

Viper still resembled a human. He had a body, a head and four limbs, and he walked upright. He was dressed in the same white shirt he'd been wearing when Crafty pushed him through the gate. It was tattered and stained. However, his face looked bestial and his eyes were different, the pupils vertical slits. He also had a feral stink – a mixture of manure, wet dog and the coppery tang of blood.

As Crafty stared up at him, Viper's face twisted into a gloating smile and he opened his right hand to show what he was holding.

It was the other half of the locator.

'I attacked the courier close to the northern edge of the Shole,' Viper rasped, 'but I took the locator and came here. I knew it would bring you to me.'

As he spoke, Crafty could see the three rows of deadly needle-sharp teeth jutting up from his lower jaw. He was more than capable of killing and eating a human being, he thought.

Viper pushed the locator into his trouser pocket, then came a couple of steps closer, his movements marked by odd tics and jerks. Crafty scrambled to his knees, his heart thumping and his hands shaking. He wouldn't stand a chance against Viper. Aberrations were super-humanly swift and savage.

Quickly he searched the floor with his eyes, but there was no help there. His dagger was over by the far wall, out of reach.

'I want the girl too,' Viper said, reaching forward to drag him to his feet. 'I think you'll be the means to bring her to me.'

Lick was Crafty's only hope. She had the crossbow. Viper wouldn't know about that. But she couldn't follow him into the church on foot because she couldn't leave the gate unguarded.

He began to panic, but all at once he remembered that she *could* summon guards to defend the gate, as she had when they'd confronted the White Lady. This thought gave him hope – surely this is what she'd do. Then he recalled that Lick couldn't risk bringing the gate into the chapel. It was dangerous in a confined space – especially inside a building. Somehow he had to get Viper outside.

His hopes rose as he realized that this was exactly what Viper intended. Still holding Crafty with his right hand, he opened the church door with his left.

But when Crafty looked around, he saw that the gate was gone.

'She's abandoned you, grub!' Viper gloated. 'I'll fix her another time. In the meantime I still have you!'

But Crafty knew that Lick would never abandon him. She was clever. She'd have a plan. She had some of his hair and could find him outside using the gate. Maybe she was simply gathering reinforcements. *I hope so . . .* Crafty thought.

Still holding his arm, Viper pushed Crafty down the steps and along the path; their boots crunched on the frosty ground. At the point where he'd joined the path, Viper dragged him to the left. Crafty saw more trees ahead of them – a dense copse emerging from the gloom. If Lick was going to rescue him, she had to do it soon; otherwise she wouldn't be able to follow him with the gate.

Now, Lick! Now! Do it now!

Where was Viper taking him?

Come on, Lick! Do it now! he again willed silently.

And she did.

The first thing Crafty knew, there was a *thwack* and then a whooshing sound. Then a groan of pain escaped Viper's lips and he released his grip on Crafty's arm. He spun away and dropped to his knees, a crossbow bolt half buried in his right shoulder.

Lick stepped through the gate and walked towards Viper, her bow still trained on him. 'Walk!' she commanded. 'Get up and go through the gate!'

Crafty glanced round at the gate – and saw the armed castle guards waiting inside.

However, Viper remained on his knees; Crafty could hear him moaning – or was he laughing? – softly. A bolt through the shoulder would hurt, but it wouldn't normally be life-threatening. Still, Viper was an aberration and the bolt *was* silver-tipped. Perhaps he was starting to die, or to go mad?

Lick took a step nearer. 'Walk!' she ordered again, raising her voice slightly.

Viper shook his head but said nothing.

Crafty and Lick exchanged a glance. This was a serious problem. If they tried to drag Viper towards the gate, they would be taking a terrible risk. It was dangerous to go anywhere near him: he was incredibly strong, and Crafty hated to think what sort of damage those rows of needle-like teeth might inflict.

For a third time Lick spoke to Viper, her voice now hardly more than a whisper. 'I'll give you just one more chance to get to your feet and go through the gate. If you don't, I'll fire again.'

Viper simply curled his lip at her and shook his head.

A second later he let out a piercing scream. Lick had put a bolt through his other shoulder. It was a big mistake to defy her, Crafty thought.

She threatened Viper with a third bolt, and that was enough to make him lurch to his feet, stagger towards the gate and clamber through.

The soldiers grabbed him, chained his hands behind his back and bound his arms to his body with leather straps. He sneered at his captors but made no attempt to resist; they led him away, leaving Crafty and Lick alone in her study.

Crafty's heart was racing, but Lick had seemed calm and in control, as usual. Did nothing bother her?

'Weren't you scared, Lick?' he asked her.

'Of course I was, Crafty. I was screaming inside! I feared I wouldn't be in time. A few moments later and he'd have taken you into those trees and I wouldn't have been able to follow.'

'I know. Thanks for saving me.' He gave a sigh of relief. 'And I'd like a crossbow like yours as soon as possible! For now my dagger will have to do. I'd like to go back for it – it's in the chapel,' he said.

Lick nodded. She knew how much the weapon meant to him. That gift from his friend Bertha had saved his life. He felt better when it was in his possession. Once again he sat in the chair, stared into the swirling clouds and concentrated on the dagger. That was enough to move the gate close to the chapel doors. In less than thirty seconds Crafty was safely back in Lick's room with the dagger in his greatcoat pocket.

'Wait here,' Lick told him. 'I'll go and make my report to the Chief Mancer. When I come back, we'll have a little chat. Something really strange happened out there. But at least we've achieved something. If Viper is the killer we've been looking for, then we've put a stop to the murders.'

It was almost half an hour before Lick returned. They sat facing each other across her desk.

'What will they do to Viper – execute him?' Crafty asked.

'That's up to the Duke,' Lick replied, giving him a weary smile. 'I think the most important thing is to find out all we can about him – and what he's been up to. Was *he* the aberration who came through into the Daylight World and killed those gate mancers? He didn't do that this time, did he? He stayed in the Shole.'

'He said he wanted to get his hands on me – and you too. He's looking for revenge, although that doesn't mean he isn't the killer,' Crafty pointed out.

'Well, he'll be questioned and we'll find out eventually. We also need to discover what he knows about the Grey Hoods. And, of course, what happened before he dragged you into that chapel,' Lick said with a frown.

'What do you mean?' Crafty asked.

'Remember how everything went dark just before he pulled you through the door? I wonder whether he's exercising a similar sort of power to Bertha's. I think I should go and talk to him. I need a few answers.'

'Could I come with you? I'd like to hear what he has to say,' Crafty said.

Lick shook her head. 'Sorry, Crafty, but Forensics would never agree to that. It's well outside your remit as a gate grub. Even though I have boffin status, they'll put all sorts of obstructions in my way. It could be days before I get to see him.'

Crafty didn't protest – little did Lick know that his key would guarantee access to the Forensics Room, and to the place where Viper was being confined.

'What did you actually see just before it went dark?' Lick asked.

'It all happened very quickly. I looked up, saw that the sky was black, and then I was dragged into the chapel.'

'That's what I saw too – a totally black sky. It was as if, in an instant, all light had withdrawn from the Shole. We'll need to find out whether that sudden darkness was local or widespread – over the next few days couriers on patrol in the Shole will return to report back to the castle. But some kind of powerful magic must have been at work there. And we need to find out whether it was wielded by Viper or someone else.'

'It must have been Viper,' Crafty said. 'It was timed to distract me so he could drag me inside.'

'True – but was he working alone or did he get help?' asked Lick, thinking aloud.

Suddenly another memory came back to Crafty. 'Oh!' he cried. 'As I approached the door of the chapel, something really odd happened. You know that thing up in the tree? The aberration that kept shrieking?'

'You mean the flapper?'

'Yes, the flapper. Well, it spoke to me. It warned me that there was danger ahead,' Crafty recalled.

Lick looked sceptical. 'Are you sure you didn't imagine it?' she asked. 'It was a dangerous situation and you were under a lot of stress.'

For a moment Crafty felt a flicker of frustrated anger. Why did she always question him? he fumed. But then he calmed down. It was only right that she should do so. He'd also wondered if it had really happened.

'It seemed as if I could hear words in its shrieks. It said something like *Run for your life! It's a trap!* Though I suppose I could have imagined it . . .'

'Well, there's one way to find out!' Lick grinned at him. 'When we get the chance, we'll go back there and check it out.'

THE SHADOW STAIN

The following day Crafty and Lucky were in the Waiting Room playing draughts, expecting to be summoned at any time. And, indeed, soon the far door opened and Lick looked in. Crafty noticed that she was already wearing her greatcoat – something must have happened.

'Got a job for you, Crafty,' she called. 'Bring your coat.'

'Don't touch the pieces while I'm away! No cheating!' he warned Lucky with a grin, before turning to follow Lick.

'I thought you'd be playing chess, not that silly game,' she jibed as they walked down the stone steps. She had been teaching them chess. She had no time for draughts. She didn't think it was challenging enough.

'We do play chess sometimes, but draughts is fun as well,' he replied, pulling on his coat. It looked like they'd both be going out into the Shole.

Down in her office, she drew back the curtain to reveal the silver gate. Crafty stared at the clouds swirling there. He wondered exactly where in the Shole they were going.

'Might as well take the weight off your feet, Crafty,' Lick suggested, 'but we're heading for a fixed location.'

Crafty sat down while she turned the ratchet. When a grub had taken a gate to a point within the Shole, the gate remembered it and could simply be directed to return there. The swirling clouds cleared, and Crafty could see, not too far ahead, the chapel he'd visited the day before.

'I want to take another look at that flapper,' Lick told him. 'I want to see if it communicates with you again.'

'So you don't think that I was just imagining it?'

'I'm keeping an open mind,' she replied. 'Oh, and by the way, it seems that the darkening of the sky when you were snatched *was* just a local effect; it must have been something to do with Viper. So far nobody has reported it happening elsewhere.' She walked across to her desk and brought back her crossbow. 'You first!' she said with a smile.

Crafty stepped through the gate into the gloom and cold of the Shole. He set off along the path, then stopped and looked up. The flapper was high in the tree to his left. Lick took a few steps away from the gate and halted, her crossbow at the ready, guarding the entrance.

The flapper was flapping all right – just as Crafty remembered it. The elongated head was twisting and the limbs thrashing about as if in a strong wind. But it was silent now.

'It's not making any noise at all,' said Crafty, turning to Lick.

'Give it time,' she called from behind him. 'They never stay quiet for long.'

No sooner had she spoken than the flapper began to scream and wail. It sounded like it was in torment.

'Can you understand it?' Lick asked.

Crafty was about to shake his head when the shrieks suddenly resolved themselves into words:

'Help me! Help me! I helped you. Now help me!'

The creature was staring down at him, its eyes very wide, its expression full of anguish.

'It's speaking to me – it's asking for help,' Crafty told Lick.

'Are you sure?'

'Yes. Its words are really clear. I'm definitely not imagining it,' he insisted. 'Can't you hear what it's saying?'

Lick shook her head.

'Take me back with you. Take me out of this terrible place! I'm lonely. I miss my family.'

Didn't it realize that its family would probably have been killed when they were engulfed? Or turned into aberrations too ... But maybe it had some family members safe in the Daylight World, Crafty thought. Perhaps it was just hoping so.

'Is there nothing we can do to help it?' he asked Lick. 'It wants to be brought out of the Shole. It's lonely. It misses its family.'

She looked grim. 'There's nothing we can do, Crafty. It's not like moving the Duke. This tree is far too big to dig up. And if we cut away the branch, the aberration will die.'

Of course Lick was right, but Crafty felt sad that they could do nothing to help it.

'I'm sorry! There's nothing we can do!' he called up to the flapper.

Then it just screeched wildly, and any words were lost in that awful cry.

Crafty felt what he thought were spots of rain on his forehead, but then he looked up at the aberration and a lump came into his throat. It was not rain falling. It was tears.

'It's crying,' he called to Lick.

'Let's go back now,' she said softly.

Moments later they were in her office again, and the gate was filled with dark swirling clouds.

'I thought flappers were supposed to have little awareness or memory,' Crafty said, slumping down in his chair.

'That's what was believed until now,' Lick told him. 'Today has raised some really interesting questions – not least how you were able to understand that creature.'

'Yes – how is it that I could hear the flapper speak and you couldn't?' Crafty asked.

'I'm not sure. Maybe it's one of your Fey gifts – the ability to communicate with aberrations, or at least some of them? We are both Fey, but we won't necessarily have the same gifts.'

That made sense. The Fey developed gifts as they grew up – maybe this was one of his. He wondered if being able to hear the whispering of his brothers was another – though he didn't mention that to Lick. If he ever told anyone about that, it would have to be his father. He owed him that.

'It's strange, isn't it?' said Crafty. 'There's so much about being Fey that I don't know. My father didn't talk about it much.'

'It's not just you and your family. Nobody talks about it,' Lick said with a shake of the head. 'There are so many things we just don't know. For example, when the Shole first manifested itself in the heart of Preston, the usual things happened to those engulfed: they died or they were changed into aberrations. But then, after a few months, something new emerged; a third possibility. Some people were neither killed nor changed. These people were immune and were labelled Fey. But to this day nobody can answer this question . . . Did we Fey already exist before the Shole? Or did the Shole create us?'

'Why would it create people who could do more than ordinary humans to thwart it?' asked Crafty.

'It's a difficult question. That's why most boffins think the Fey were around before the Shole,' Lick told him. 'Some people believe that we're descended from the legendary Fairy Folk, who were supposed to have magical powers.'

Suddenly Crafty thought of Old Nell. Maybe now was a good time to tell Lick about her.

'Do you think that some Fey can talk to the dead in dreams?' he asked.

'I've never heard of that. Why do you ask?' Lick said.

'It's just that I've been having some weird dreams lately. Well, they're more nightmares than dreams. Old Nell talks to me. She tells me things.'

'Such as?'

'That there'll soon be more than one Shole – the whole world will be engulfed.' Crafty frowned as he remembered his horrible nightmare. 'But she said there might be a way to stop it. That I could do it, but I would pay a terrible price.'

'We're already paying a terrible price, Crafty. We're under a lot of strain and we see terrible things. I have nightmares too,' Lick said. 'I'm lost in the Shole and can't find my way out. I'm running, terrified, and a pack of aberrations is close on my heels. I wake up just before they catch me.'

'So you think I've just had bad dreams – nothing more?'

Lick gave him a kind smile. 'Yes, Crafty, I think they're just nightmares.' She paused and pointed at the gate. 'Look, I'd like to try out your ability with a different type of aberration,' she said. 'It's another fixed location . . .'

The ratchet clicked and the clouds cleared. They were close to a group of yew trees. Then Crafty realized that it was a graveyard. He could see tombstones sticking up through the long grass.

'What we're going to see isn't very pleasant,' Lick told him. 'It's called a shadow stain, and it's the remains of a human being. Something similar to a flapper, only worse. According to the records, one of the early gate grubs could talk to them – though he died in the Shole before it could be proved one way or the other. Let's see what you can do.

It's just beyond that first tree, between the first two gravestones.'

Crafty led the way through the silver gate. Lick took up her usual position, her crossbow resting across her arm.

It was really cold and Crafty's breath steamed in front of him – though there was no ground frost here. The air was damp and there were beads of water on the grass. He walked past the first tree, his boots squelching on the soft ground. Suddenly he heard the sound of weeping and saw the aberration between the two tombstones.

It took the shape of a man lying on his back, his trousers and coat almost rotted away. But apart from that it just looked like a stain on the grass, a slight depression in the earth the colour of dark brown mud. Unlike the flapper, it wasn't moving.

But then it stopped crying and spoke to Crafty.

'I'm sorry you found me so upset. I'll be all right in a moment. Don't you worry about me. I just came over all funny and fell over. Would you be so kind as to help me to my feet?'

Crafty looked down at the stain in horror and pity. Now he could see that it *was* moving slightly – or at least the depression in the earth was gently bubbling with water. What could he say to it? It didn't seem to know what had happened.

'I'll need to get help,' he lied.

'Then please hurry. I feel so cold and wet. I just came to visit my wife's grave. Poor Mary passed away last week and I miss her so. Could you find my flowers for me, please? I dropped them when I fell.'

Crafty could see the name on the tombstone on his right: MARY BROWN. The date told him that she'd been dead for almost twenty years.

He turned and walked away, his eyes brimming with tears. On the other side of the gate it was a few moments before he could pull himself together.

'Did it talk to you?' Lick asked. 'All I could hear was a sort of bubbling and rustling.'

He nodded and told her what the aberration had said. She shook her head sadly. 'That's terrible. And there's nothing we can do to help. Hopefully he'll never realize what's happened to him. Maybe he's spent the last twenty years thinking he's just fallen over.'

'Wouldn't it be nice, Lick, if we could just somehow put an end to the Shole, and all the people it's killed just came back to life? And all the people it's changed into aberrations became normal humans again,' Crafty said with a sigh.

'It certainly would, Crafty,' said Lick, sighing too. 'But it's not going to happen. The very best we can hope for now is to somehow put an end to the Shole and stop anybody else being affected. Anyway, cheer up: it looks like you have a gift that might prove to be really useful. I need to think how best we can use it.'

THE GREY LIBRARY

There were no gate-grub jobs that day; Crafty spent his time in the Waiting Room, chatting to Lucky between games of draughts. They managed only one game of chess because they were still hazy about the rules; it ended in confusion, with them repeating the same moves over and over again. As far as Crafty remembered, that meant the result was a draw.

When their time on duty was over, they left to go back to their own rooms as usual. However, it was at least an hour before his evening meal was due to arrive – and suddenly Crafty had an idea about how to fill the time. He would use his key to gain entrance to the Grey Library.

His visit to the Relic Room had started badly. Afterwards, Ginger Bob had suggested that Crafty should let him know whenever he intended to use his key so he could smooth his path. But this was just a library – surely there would be no problem.

Crafty walked along the corridor until he came to a door with a plaque that said:

THE GREY LIBRARY

The key chain had been broken by the guard, so now he kept the key in the right-hand pocket of his trousers. He pulled it out and then rapped twice on the door.

A tall, thin, grey-haired man with spectacles opened the door just wide enough to show his face. It was not a friendly face. He was frowning.

'Don't knock so loudly!' he hissed. 'People are trying to concentrate – this is a library, after all! I'm the librarian. What do you want?'

Crafty showed him the key.

The man's expression changed to one of surprise. 'You'd better come in then. Follow me.'

Crafty followed him into a small room. There was nobody else there – so who had been trying to concentrate? he wondered. There was another door to the right, and just one shelf of books. Each book had a grey cover. He counted them. There were twenty.

'I thought there'd be more books!' he exclaimed. Was this all there was to show for almost seventy years of studying the Shole?

'Of course there are more,' snapped the librarian impatiently, pushing his spectacles up on to the bridge of his nose. 'More than you could read in a lifetime. This is just the index. Are you looking for anything in particular?'

For a moment Crafty was stumped. He really just wanted to browse. But he didn't want to appear foolish. Suddenly he had a moment of inspiration. 'I'm interested in aberrations . . . sub-category . . . bats.'

'Right,' said the librarian, lifting the first book off the shelf and rolling his eyes just a little. 'The vast majority of the library is devoted to aberrations, which is not surprising given that aberrations are the most studied category of the Shole.'

He flicked through the pages and stopped at a section entitled 'Bats'. 'Which particular type of bat are you interested in?'

'Corpse bats,' Crafty told him, remembering the big hairy one he'd seen hanging from a beam in the Relic Room.

The librarian traced his finger down the page. Crafty peered over his shoulder and noted that there were lots of spaces – no doubt so that new books could be added to the index. The librarian's finger stopped. 'Here we are – corpse bats. See that number on the right?'

The number was big – 3,421. Crafty nodded.

'Well, that is the number of the book you seek. Follow me.'

He led Crafty through the other door and then down three flights of steps – so much of the castle lay underground, Crafty reflected. At last he found himself in a long, wide corridor. The ceiling was low, and the tall librarian was forced to stoop. There were torches at intervals along the right-hand wall, and on the left, at head height, a single bookshelf seemed to extend along the wall forever. All the book covers were grey.

He noted the number below each book. The first was numbered 1, the second 2, and so on. The system was simple and would be really easy to use, even though it involved a lot of walking.

On the right, below each torch, stood benches and small tables. As Crafty followed the librarian, he passed a woman and a man, each totally engrossed in reading. He wondered who they were and what they were studying.

They walked on, the tunnel curving to the right so that Crafty could no longer see very far ahead. He realized that they had started at the centre of a spiral and that the tunnel was gradually unwinding outwards.

At last they reached number 3,421.

'Here we are,' said the librarian, coming to a halt and pointing at the book. 'I'll leave you to it. Replace the book when you have finished. The first rule of this library is to have respect for the books. The second rule is to respect the people who use this facility.'

Then he turned on his heel and walked back towards the steps that led up to the index room.

Crafty lifted the book off the shelf, then carried it across to the nearest bench and sat down. He laid it across his knees, opened it at the beginning and began to read.

The name 'corpse bat' is misleading, as this specimen eats fungi rather than dead flesh. A corpse bat rips the throat out of its victim, then uses its wings to scatter blood across the whole body. It then regurgitates spores from its upper stomach and spits them on to the bloodied corpse. Within minutes these root themselves in the body and grow into large, circular fungi, each about the size of a human head. The corpse bat then gorges itself, and roosts during the day, hanging by its clawed feet. When night falls again, it hunts for its next victim.

Crikey, thought Crafty. *I'll be sure not to run into one of those in the Shole –*

Suddenly an outraged voice broke into his thoughts. 'What are you doing here?'

Crafty smiled as he recognized it. He looked up and saw Lick glaring down at him. 'Who gave you permission?'

He saw no point in lying. He took the key out of his pocket and showed it to her. 'The Duke gave this to me. It provides right of entry to any room in the castle. He wants me to note what I see and report back to him.'

Lick sat down next to him. 'I see! Lucky you. And where have you been so far?'

'The Relic Room and now here . . .'

'Hmm. Well, some of those departments aren't going to take too kindly to your presence,' she warned. 'They'll view it as an intrusion. The Forensics people will do anything to keep you out.'

Crafty nodded. 'Tell me about it! At the Relic Room I was pushed against the wall by two burly guards. I've still got the bruises to show for it. The Chief Mancer had to come and make them let me go. Anyway – how are you getting on? Are you any nearer to seeing Viper?' Crafty asked.

Lick shook her head. 'I've filled in the forms, but now they'll keep me waiting.'

'Why don't you go to the Duke? I'm sure he'd speed things up,' Crafty suggested.

'Sometimes it's best to let things take their course, Crafty. It's called diplomacy – keeping people sweet and avoiding antagonizing them. But this has given me an idea . . . You don't care about antagonizing people, do you? Once I've got permission to see Viper, you could come with me using your key. It'll be fun to see their angry faces; there's no way they can blame me!'

Crafty smiled at Lick, came to his feet and carefully replaced the book. 'I'd like that! Yes, please take me with you. I'm going back to my room for supper now. I'm so hungry I could eat a whole cow, hooves and all! Oh!' he said, gesturing towards the long shelf of books. 'Do you think I'd be able to borrow books to read there, or in the Waiting Room?'

Lick laughed. 'Absolutely not! It's a reference library, not a lending library, and the librarian loves his books more than his own children. But you could ask the Duke next time you report to him. If he says yes, the librarian will have to obey.'

'So, basically, forget diplomacy and do what I want!' Crafty said with a smile.

Lick grinned in response and stood up.

'What number is your book, Lick?' Crafty asked her as they strolled back towards the steps.

'Number 27,301,' she said with a smile. 'Read it when you get the chance. I'm sure you'll find it interesting. But I'm going to rewrite it soon and add more of what I've learned.'

'You might want to think of a snappier title than *Towards an Understanding of Shole Aberrations*,' Crafty teased. 'Anyway, a lot of the books in here seem to concentrate on specific examples of aberrations, such as corpse bats . . .'

'That's very observant of you, Crafty. Yes, most of the books in here are works of analysis – they focus upon one particular aspect of the Shole and break it down to document what it is and how it functions. But I am what's known as a *Synthesist* because I put things together. I'm looking at the big picture – the Shole in its entirety. I'm searching for patterns. For example, how do Bertha and her bog fit into the general pattern of the Shole? Are there entities similar to Bertha out there, and what do they have in common?'

Crafty laughed. 'A Synthesist! That's a big word for a little lady!' he said.

Lick immediately stopped and whipped round to glare at him. 'How dare you patronize me!'

He tried to appease her: 'Sorry, sorry – I was only joking!' he said. 'I was just remembering my first meeting with the Chief Mancer – I happened to use the word *practicalities*, and he said it was a big word for a little man!' He could be diplomatic too!

Lick's face changed, and she laughed. It was almost a giggle. 'Yes, *Synthesist* is a Chief Mancer word all right!'

They climbed the steps, then walked through the small room and out into the corridor, closing the door of the Grey Library behind them.

'So what does the big picture tell you so far?' Crafty asked, curious as ever. 'Are you getting any nearer to finding a way to stop the Shole advancing?'

Lick shook her head. 'The more I learn, the worse it gets. I'm finding very disturbing patterns – things that repeat themselves but in slightly different ways, so we can never get a handle on them. I don't think anything from the Shole can be trusted. Not even your friend Bertha.'

Crafty was shocked. 'How can you say that, Lick? She saved our lives – mine more than once.'

'Of course she did, but that doesn't mean she'll always be as kind. Look, I'll tell you more about it tomorrow. Maybe at the briefing.'

With that, Lick walked away, leaving Crafty confused and a little hurt. How could she say that about Bertha? Didn't she trust his judgement at all?

THE GRIM PLOUGHMAN

The following morning Crafty barely had time to nod to Lucky before Lick came into the Waiting Room and sat down facing them. She got straight to the point, picking up the thread of their conversation the previous evening.

'Yesterday Crafty was asking me what I'd learned recently about the Shole,' she said to Lucky. 'I told him that I was studying the big picture, the patterns of behaviour that tend to repeat themselves over the years. And then I said something that probably upset him.'

Crafty raised his eyebrows at her.

She sighed. 'Probably? Fine – I *know* it did. Although Bertha has helped us in the past and seems benign, I predict that her behaviour may well change. She cannot be trusted.'

Crafty took a deep breath and tried to remain calm. He didn't like to hear Lick talk about Bertha like that, but she was clever. She didn't say stupid things. There had to be a sound reason behind it.

'What evidence do you have?' he asked.

'It's not hard evidence, Crafty. I'm just making a prediction based on what's happened in the past. I hope that Bertha will prove to be an exception, but I'll try to explain why I think we need to be very cautious when dealing with her. You know the story of the White Lady –'

'Know it! I've been within spitting distance of her!' Crafty exclaimed.

'Well, here's something you don't know about her. The first time the White Lady visited, someone asked her why she was so kind; why she came out of the Shole to help and heal people. In view of what happened afterwards, her reply is chilling. She said that she just did what the voice in her head commanded . . .'

'You're suggesting that the voice told her to abduct the children?' Lucky asked.

'It's something to keep in mind,' Lick replied.

'So you think that's what Bertha is doing – helping us before a voice tells her to turn against us,' Crafty said. 'Is that why you asked her if she ever heard voices?'

'It is a possibility – and she didn't answer that question, did she?' Lick pointed out. 'She wouldn't talk to me about any voices. So was she hiding the fact that she heard them? We should be prepared for a change in Bertha's behaviour.

'Here's another example,' she continued. 'Aberrations that come out of the Shole seeking human victims are rare –

we call them *excursionists*. Each follows a similar pattern. Another aberration, the *Grim Ploughman*, is another human-shaped aberration; it resembles a man. It came out of the Shole and visited a number of farms on the outskirts of a village called Grimsargh asking for work. Once again that's north-east of Preston. Unlike the White Lady, this aberration was physically intimidating – tall and gaunt, with very large hands. It offered its services as a ploughman. In return, all it wanted was a plate of cold mutton and a hunk of bread.'

'And farmers actually hired it?' Lucky asked, shaking his head in disbelief.

'Yes, Lucky, they did – but this time out of fear. Farms can be lonely places and people often feel vulnerable. Sometimes it's just a farmer, his wife and his children trying to scratch a living out of the soil. The aberration didn't seem to pose a threat so long as it was given work and dinner, so many felt it was better just to give it what it wanted. Anyway, as far as the records show, the aberration worked satisfactorily and was paid accordingly at six farms. At the seventh farm it took a different type of meal by way of payment. It ate the farmer and his wife, then walked back into the Shole and has never been seen again. We have no evidence of a voice directing it, but that might explain its sudden change of behaviour.'

Despite what Lick had said, Crafty couldn't accept that Bertha would suddenly become their deadly enemy, and he said so.

She smiled. 'I'm not sure myself that Bertha will ever prove to be a danger. All I'm suggesting is that we should be cautious. Well, that's enough for today. Just before noon we're going to carry out a combined field operation. The Chief Mancer will explain all about it before we set off.'

With that, Lick left them alone. As soon as she'd gone, Lucky turned to Crafty and raised his eyebrows in surprise. 'I didn't think we'd be doing another of those before they managed to recruit some more gate grubs!'

'Then it must be something really important,' Crafty replied. 'Something worth the risk.'

Lunch was brought to them early; then, at ten minutes to twelve, the Chief Mancer and Lick came into the Waiting Room.

Ginger Bob explained about the combined field operation. It was all news to Lucky, but Crafty had heard most of it from his father. It seemed that the couriers had been tracking the strange bargeman Crafty's father had described, and now, finally, they had some useful information. On the last trip the barge had deviated from its usual routine. It had halted at a warehouse about five miles south of Lancaster, where the bargeman had unloaded two boxes.

'I want you to find that warehouse and bring back those boxes,' Ginger Bob said. 'It should be quite safe at this time of day. There's nothing to fear from the aberrations that usually accompany the barge. They are far away in Preston at the moment. Good luck, Benson and Proudfoot. Now, let's get moving!'

In spite of Ginger Bob's confidence, Crafty had a bad feeling about the job. It sounded like it could be very dangerous.

They went down to the mancers' rooms, Crafty buttoning up his greatcoat and following Lick, Lucky going with Ginger Bob. As usual, Lick pulled back the black curtain and Crafty eased himself into the chair facing the silver gate. As he did so, Lick took something out of her pocket and handed it to him. It was the locator that would enable him to find the place they wanted.

'The couriers placed two within sight of the warehouse,' she told him. 'Lucky has the other one. But hang on until we're ready . . .'

She went over to her desk and pulled the rope that hung from the ceiling above it. Somewhere in the distance a bell rang. Within moments there was a heavy knock at the door.

'Enter!' Lick called, and four castle guards – in full chain mail and armed to the teeth – took up positions facing the gate behind Crafty and Lick. They would prevent anything dangerous from getting into the castle; it made Crafty feel a lot safer.

Now holding her crossbow, Lick gave Crafty a grim smile and then a nod. 'Right, Crafty, take us there!'

He held the locator in the palm of his right hand. It felt warm. He was nervous and butterflies filled his stomach. He looked at the dark clouds in front of him and concentrated. Gradually, through the grey murk of the Shole, he saw the distant canal and, beyond it, a large dark building.

'You lead the way, Crafty. I'm coming with you,' Lick told him.

This gave him confidence, especially as she was holding the crossbow. He already knew that she was a good shot.

They clambered through the gate and trudged in single file across a field. The grass was long and the soil waterlogged, and their boots were soon squelching. Leading the way, Crafty peered ahead, trying to make out the canal between them and the warehouse, then searched for the blue circle of the other gate.

He turned to Lick. 'Where's Lucky?' he asked.

'The other locator is buried on the far side of the warehouse. The courier didn't want to risk being spotted near the canal. Keep going. Don't worry – we won't need to swim across the canal. There's a bridge somewhere ahead.'

They reached the towpath and saw a small bridge twenty yards to their right. Their boots crunched noisily on the cinders underfoot – but any aberration nearby should be asleep. *Keep telling yourself that!* Crafty thought.

As they crossed the bridge, he glanced both north and south along the canal, searching for danger. There was nothing but that calm, narrow stretch of water – though that seemingly innocuous surface could be deceptive. Crafty had encountered an aberration that swam, and had been lucky to escape with his life.

The Shole was even murkier than usual, and to the south he noticed a white mist rising from the canal. It was like a low cloud forming above the water. The weather was warmer today, and Crafty wondered if it was this that was causing the mist. It was always grey and gloomy in the Shole, but he'd never noticed so much mist before.

Now the warehouse was looming up before them; beyond it, to the right, he could see the other gate, a faint blue circle. But where was Lucky? he wondered.

He needn't have worried. Lucky was already leaning back against the huge warehouse door, a broad grin lighting up his face.

'What kept you?' he jibed. Then he turned and pointed at the stout chain and padlock on the door. 'Hope you've brought a key . . .'

'Lucky, run back and tell the Chief Mancer that we need bolt cutters,' Lick commanded.

Lucky's smile slipped and turned into a scowl. Crafty knew that he liked Lick, but he wasn't best pleased to be ordered about by her. Lick didn't mean any harm, but sometimes she sounded abrupt and bossy. Crafty knew she would have sent *him* back, but Lucky's gate was nearer.

Then Lucky smiled again and gave a little mock salute.

'Sorry,' Lick said, surprising them both. 'I should have been prepared for the door to be locked.'

'Don't worry. The courier should have told you!' Lucky replied.

'He didn't get that close to it. Still, there's no harm done. Everything seems calm.'

As Lucky ran back towards the gate, Crafty glanced at the canal again. The white mist was continuing to rise and spread towards them. He felt uneasy. The sooner they got back to the gates the better. It didn't do to spend any longer in the Shole than necessary.

He and Lick waited in silence until Lucky appeared carrying a massive pair of bolt cutters.

Without waiting for Lick's instruction, he placed the open blades of the cutters around the chain and brought the handles together. It seemed effortless – no more difficult than using scissors to snip through string. The chain and lock fell away, but as he turned the big handle of the door, Lick shook her head.

'Lucky, wait until I get into position. Just in case . . .'

Crafty realized that an aberration might be guarding the boxes in the warehouse, waiting for intruders. The courier would have been too far away to see. For all Ginger Bob's assurances, they were dealing with the unknown. Crafty's heart began to beat faster.

As Lick took a few paces backwards and took aim with her crossbow, he drew the blade from his coat pocket. She nodded at Lucky, and he turned the door handle and pulled it towards him. It yielded a couple of inches, then became stuck.

'Help me, Crafty!'

He ran forward to help, reluctantly putting the knife back in his pocket.

The big wooden door was heavy and its hinges had warped so that its base rested on the ground; with difficulty they dragged it open.

First they waited and listened in the doorway. Crafty held his breath, but the warehouse was totally silent. Then, at a nod from Lick, they stepped inside. Crafty took out his blade again.

In front of them they saw a couple of rusty old ploughs, several empty wooden crates and a huge canal barge resting across three trestles. It had a hole in its side and the wood looked rotten. Near the door lay two oblong boxes made of shiny polished wood; they were the size and shape of coffins, one slightly smaller than the other. These were the boxes they sought.

Could they actually be coffins? Crafty wondered. And could the smaller one be for a child?

'We don't want to linger!' Lick said. 'Bring the large box first. We'll take it back to the castle where we can study it properly.'

Just like a coffin, each box had brass carrying-handles. They took one each, but when they tried to lift it, the box wouldn't budge.

'It's too heavy!' Lucky said. 'Maybe it's full of gold!'

'I rather doubt it ⦂ . . Try the smaller one,' Lick suggested wryly.

Even the small coffin was incredibly heavy, but they managed to lift it off the dirt floor, then staggered towards the door, Lick covering them with her crossbow. Crafty glanced back over his shoulder. He couldn't shake off the feeling that something was hiding in one of the dark corners of the warehouse.

But he was wrong. The threat was outside.

*

As they emerged from the warehouse, they realized that the mist had grown much thicker. White tendrils curled around them like snakes, and the bridge and canal were totally obscured.

'The bridge is over there, I think,' Lick said, pointing.

They trudged after her, the box growing heavier by the minute. Crafty was just feeling relieved to hear the crunch of cinder under foot when a figure came striding out of the mist towards them. It was the tall, thin, hooded figure of the bargeman. Lucky dropped his end of the box and turned to flee, but he wasn't quick enough.

He screamed as the bargeman picked him up by the shoulder, struggling helplessly in the grip of that huge hand.

The aberration yanked him towards its mouth. It was wide open, revealing three rows of needle-like teeth.

FIGHTING FOR HIS LIFE

Crafty would never forget that scream. It was like the cry of an animal feeling the edge of a butcher's knife.

He dropped his end of the box and prepared to use his blade, but he knew he would be too late. Within seconds the creature would have torn out Lucky's throat.

Suddenly the aberration gave a deep roar and staggered backwards, a silver bolt sticking out of its left eye. Lick had once again come to the rescue with her bow. But instead of dropping Lucky on the towpath, the bargeman flung him away towards the barge, which floated on the canal beside him.

Crafty cringed as his friend went toppling head first – but there was no sickening crunch, for the barge was covered in canvas. Lucky bounced slightly, fell on to his side and lay still.

'Lucky!' Crafty cried, running forward to help his friend. But suddenly, before he could reach the barge, everything grew dark – just like it had outside the chapel before Viper appeared. When he could see again, the barge and the aberration had vanished.

Dumbstruck, and with a heavy heart, he stared at the place where Lucky had been.

But, as ever, Lick was one step ahead of him. 'Quick, Crafty! Follow me! There's just one chance to save him . . .'

She ran towards the Chief Mancer's gate, and Crafty followed, his mind spinning, a hollow feeling in his chest. He doubted whether the aberration would keep Lucky alive for long.

On the other side of the gate he could see Ginger Bob peering out anxiously. As they climbed through they were greeted by his angry voice.

'Where are the boxes?' he demanded.

An equally angry Lick wasted no time in telling him what had happened. 'If we act now, we might be able to save him, but that creature is very powerful. We need a couple of armed couriers to help us!'

Ginger Bob nodded, still looking far from pleased, and sent one of the guards to get help. Was the loss of the boxes more important to him than Lucky's life? Crafty wondered bitterly.

More precious time sped by – but it couldn't have been more than a couple of minutes before two couriers arrived, long swords at their hips.

Crafty was astonished to see that one of them was his father. Why had he returned to duty so soon? He hadn't mentioned that the last time they spoke. Their eyes met briefly in recognition, but then Lick was pushing Crafty into the chair.

'You're close to Lucky,' she said. 'Find him!'

Once more the silver gate filled with cloud. Crafty concentrated on his friend, trying to take the gate to his location. He felt confident of finding him, but would he still be alive? he wondered fearfully.

The gate cleared, and through the white mist he could just see the canal and the barge again. There was no sign of the bargeman, but Lucky was still lying on the canvas.

Crafty wondered if they were further along the canal, closer to Preston – there was no sign of the warehouse now, even though the mist was no thicker. Only very powerful magic could have moved the aberration, the barge and Lucky like that.

The two couriers climbed through the gate and ran towards the barge. Without a word, Lick and Crafty followed them. Courier Benson eased himself down on to the tarpaulin and gently passed the unconscious boy to his colleague. It all seemed very straightforward, but no sooner had Crafty's father rejoined them on the towpath than there was the heavy crunch of boots on cinders. Then the hooded aberration strode towards them out of the mist wielding a huge double-bladed axe.

The crossbow bolt no longer protruded from its eye, but the wound was a gory mess, with blood and fluids oozing down its cheek. It opened its mouth to reveal the triple row of needle-sharp teeth and, with a bellow of rage, lifted that deadly axe and brought it down straight towards the courier who was holding Lucky.

It would have cut them both in two, but Crafty's father somehow managed to intercept the axe with his sword. There was the clash of metal on metal, but the axe blade was diverted and plunged deep into the ground.

'Get back to the gate! I'll keep it at bay!' yelled Courier Benson.

The other courier hoisted Lucky up on to his shoulder and began to stride towards the gate, but Crafty didn't move. He couldn't abandon his father.

'Go back!' he said to Lick when he realized that she wasn't moving either, but she simply shook her head and stayed by his side.

Once again the aberration lifted the axe, and this time swept it sideways in a scything movement. Courier Benson stepped back, and the sharp edge missed him by a whisker. Then he lunged forward with his sword, the blade biting into the aberration's left shoulder.

The creature staggered for a moment, then wielded the axe like a club, trying to smash the courier's skull. Once again, holding his sword in both hands, Courier Benson blocked the blow and they struggled together at close quarters, axe and sword locked together. The bargeman towered over the courier and began to force him back towards the canal.

Crafty watched in horror. His father was fighting for his life. How could he hope to resist the terrible creature that was driving him towards the water?

He turned towards Lick, who stepped forward and took aim with the crossbow, but then shook her head and lowered it again. 'They're too close, Crafty,' she told him. 'I daren't risk it. I might hit your father.'

Crafty knew what he had to do. Gripping his dagger, he ran straight towards the grappling figures and stabbed the aberration high on the left calf. It bellowed in pain, turned and swung at him with the axe – but Crafty had already danced back out of range.

With the bargeman distracted, his father had a momentary advantage. He used it well. Courier and aberration were right on the edge of the canal. The bargeman swung the axe again, but Courier Benson quickly stepped aside. The creature was carried forward by its own momentum, and a blow from the sword hilt helped it on its way. With a tremendous splash it fell into the canal.

Then all three of them were racing back towards the gate. They were almost there when Crafty heard a thunderous pounding behind them. He glanced over his shoulder to see another aberration galloping after them. It was the bargeman's horse.

And what a horse! It was well over seven feet tall, and instead of hooves its feet had three fingers, each ending in a sharp talon. Its open mouth showed the three deadly rows of teeth, and it snorted as it ran. Steam like dragon-breath spurted from each nostril.

Crafty was spurred on to run even faster, and he reached the gate with seconds to spare. As he clambered to safety, his father waited with his sword raised, ready to fight off the aberration. But they were soon safely inside and the silver gate was full of swirling clouds.

Crafty turned to look at his father, who smiled at him and placed a hand on his shoulder. 'You were brave back there, son. I'm proud of you!' he said.

BACK FROM THE DEAD

For once Crafty arrived at the Waiting Room before Lucky, though his elation soon gave way to anxiety: poor Lucky, still unconscious, had been taken to the Infirmary the evening before and he hadn't yet heard any news of his condition. He must still be in one of the sick rooms.

Moments later Lick opened the far door and came to sit opposite him. Noticing her grave expression, he hardly dared pose the question on his lips: 'How's Lucky?'

'He's awake, but he's got a fever,' Lick replied. 'When the aberration picked him up, its talons cut through his coat into his skin. Still, the doctors think they have his temperature under control now. Of course, we won't be using the gates today. You're the only fit grub we have left and the Chief Mancer doesn't want to risk you unless there's some kind of emergency.'

'Will I be able to go and see him? Lucky, I mean,' Crafty asked.

'Maybe tomorrow, if the fever's abated. Look, I've got a meeting with a group of boffins soon. We can't have our usual session, but I do have time for one question.'

Crafty nodded. 'My visit to the library showed me just how many types of aberration there are – even bats must have dozens of categories. But what about the big groupings like geographical aberrations. How many types are there?'

'Well, let's start with that one,' Lick suggested. 'Geographical aberrations are a new category, and so far the only example is the bog. Then we have what we call *reanimations*. Interestingly, until now only dead humans have come back to life, but that doesn't mean other mammals, birds or insects couldn't do the same. That could happen at any time. The Shole is always throwing up surprises.

'Then we have human hybrids – people partially changed into animal, vegetable or mineral forms. This category includes the feral children we faced in the orphanage and the bargeman. They are very dangerous.'

Crafty thought of his mother and a lump came into his throat. What type of change had she suffered? he wondered. He looked up as Lick continued.

'Then, of course, there are the animals. Most numerous are the canines and those cat-like beasts. Horses are much rarer, though you've seen the bargeman's.

'Well, those are just some of the main categories – there are more but they'll have to wait. I've got to go now or I'll be late for my meeting,' Lick told Crafty. 'But why don't you stay here? I'll be back just after midday. I'll show you a place you might find interesting.'

She gave him a wave and a smile and left him alone in the Waiting Room. He wondered if she was going to take him with her to interview Viper.

With no Lucky to help pass the time Crafty was bored. He played a game of draughts against himself, and then did the same with chess. He really could do with a book from the Grey Library. He remembered that he was due to report back to the Duke on what he'd been up to with the key. The trouble was, since seeing what *might* have been a Grey Hood working in the Relic Room, he hadn't found out anything new. He didn't want to disappoint the Duke but, if there really were Grey Hoods working in any of the other departments, it might be months before he discovered them.

Crafty wondered if that young man in the Relic Room had indeed had a gash over his eye. Had keeping him under observation led to the unmasking of other traitors?

At last his lunch arrived; he was just finishing off his last ham-and-tomato sandwich when Lick came back.

'Are we going to talk to Viper?' he asked. He was looking forward to the interview. Last time he'd been Viper's captive, but now it was the Grey Hood who was the prisoner.

'No. I'm still trying to get permission – it could take a while. However, we *are* going to the Forensics Room, but to witness something else. The team there won't like it, but they can't deny me access because I'm a boffin . . . And they can't deny you because of your key!'

Crafty grinned. 'You're changing your tune!' he jibed. 'I thought you believed in diplomacy.'

Lick grinned back. 'Not this time. This is just too good to miss! While we were rescuing Lucky and fighting the bargeman, the Chief Mancer sent two more couriers back to collect those boxes. The Forensics team are about to open them. I want to be there when they do!'

'So do I!' said Crafty, and they hurried towards the Forensics Room.

When Lick knocked, the door was opened by a surly guard.

'I wish to speak to the superintendent. My name is Miss Crompton-Smythe and I am a boffin,' Lick announced imperiously. 'My assistant, Colin Benson, will accompany me.'

The guard opened his mouth to protest, but when Crafty held the key under his nose he pressed his lips together and frowned.

The man's expression was still cold enough to give them frostbite, but he showed them into a small waiting area, a bare white cube with a single wooden bench. It was cold in that room – no doubt to match the warmth of the reception extended to uninvited guests.

The door closed behind the guard, but opened again a few minutes later. A jovial, florid-faced man wearing a spotless white coat breezed into the room, bowed to Lick and then extended his hand. She came to her feet and shook it briefly.

'How delightful it is to see you again, Miss Crompton-Smythe,' he said, completely ignoring Crafty. 'How much you remind me of your poor deceased mother, may I add. And to what do I owe the pleasure of your visit?'

'Superintendent, I am here with my assistant, Master Benson, to witness the opening of the two boxes that were retrieved from the Shole yesterday.'

Crafty was impressed by Lick's manner. She really did know how to talk to important people and get her own way.

But the superintendent's smile had slipped, and the face was jovial no more – although it did become even more florid. 'Oh, Miss Crompton-Smythe, I really must advise against it. The opening of those boxes could be extremely dangerous. We certainly cannot risk the life of a brilliant boffin such as yourself – or even that of your assistant.'

Thanks, thought Crafty.

But Lick was firm. 'Superintendent, my assistant and I routinely face danger in the Shole. Indeed, we oversaw the removal of the first box from the warehouse, and then came under attack from aberrations. Surely your Forensics Room will be a far less hazardous environment. This is vital to the progress of my study of the Shole. I really must insist that we are present to witness the opening of those boxes.'

'Please, Miss Crompton-Smythe, I beg you to reconsider –'

Lick stood her ground. 'I insist,' she said firmly.

The superintendent gave a little bow and then a big sigh. 'Very well. Please follow me. The team are waiting. As soon as I arrive, the investigation will begin.'

They followed him down two long corridors until they came at last to a door guarded by three men. Inside, another dozen guards were dotted around the large laboratory, their hands on their sword hilts.

In the centre of the room stood a big wooden table, chains dangling on either side – no doubt to bind aberrations. Below, Crafty noticed drainage channels radiating away to deeper gullies in the corners. A sudden chill ran the length of his spine as he realized what they were for.

They were to carry the blood away. This was where they operated on aberrations or took samples of their tissue for further study. It was a gruesome place.

Now, instead of an aberration, there were two boxes on the table: the larger was at least six feet long; the other about two thirds the length. Three white-coated men, one holding a crowbar, had turned to look at the superintendent. All three wore leather gauntlets and surprised expressions. Clearly they hadn't been expecting Lick and Crafty.

However, the superintendent merely nodded at them, and immediately the man with the crowbar approached the smaller of the two boxes and started to lever off the lid. Instantly all the guards drew their swords, ready to face whatever might be lurking inside. There was the sound of crunching and splintering wood, and within seconds the lid had been ripped off and placed beside the box.

The white-coated men peered down into the open box. Whatever was inside was covered with what looked like lead, folded across like four grey petals. They began to pull it back to reveal whatever lay underneath.

'It's a child, Superintendent,' one of them said. 'He is breathing, but whether he is reanimated or changed I am not sure.'

'Then check the teeth!' he commanded.

Crafty was curious. The child was either reanimated – brought back to life after being dead – or was a living child changed by the Shole.

He and Lick approached the table so that they could study the occupant of the box. It was a small skinny boy of about eleven. His eyes were closed, his cheeks were pink, and Crafty could see the rise and fall of his little chest. As he watched, one man touched the boy's mouth and opened it to reveal his teeth. They were not the teeth of a predator.

Bertha was reanimated, and she too had normal teeth, Crafty reflected.

'This one's back from the dead, Superintendent,' the white-coated assistant said.

'Then check the second box.'

Once again, the man with the crowbar set to work. This lid took a little longer to remove, but eventually the box was open and they peeled back the lead lining.

Peering inside, Crafty gasped in astonishment. It was a girl – a girl he had known. He recognized her face, but the other proof was impossible to deny: the purple scar on each leg, just above the knee.

It marked the place where Viper had sliced off her legs with the guillotine.

It was Lucky's friend – the dead gate grub Donna.

THE EXPERIMENTAL
GRAVEYARD

Crafty remembered how upset Lucky had been at Donna's death. They'd been close friends. In the short time he'd known her Crafty had come to like her too.

'Is this one in the same condition?' demanded the superintendent.

'Yes,' the man replied as he opened her mouth to check her teeth; 'another one back from the dead.'

'Her name's Donna,' Crafty blurted out. 'She was a gate grub.'

The superintendent and the lab workers glared at him as if he'd just crawled out from under a stone. He could see the anger in their faces at his presumption in daring to speak.

But Lick put a hand on his shoulder as if to calm him. 'The boy was a gate grub too,' she told them. 'His name was

Bobbie Rickson – they called him Titch because of his small stature. He was killed about four months before Donna. These were the last two gate grubs to die.'

'Then this is a mystery indeed,' said the superintendent. 'All dead gate grubs are buried in the experimental graveyard on the eastern border of the Shole. They must have been exhumed. These are not the coffins they were buried in either – nor are they wearing the uniforms of gate grubs. So why have they been removed?'

Lucky had once told Crafty that gate grubs were buried in their uniforms, but Donna and Titch were now wearing ordinary clothes.

Crafty glanced down at the drainage channels and was suddenly afraid for the two reanimated gate grubs. 'What will happen to them now?' he asked Lick, putting his mouth to her left ear and keeping his voice low.

She gave a slight shake of the head – he realized she wanted him to keep his mouth shut. Then she approached the superintendent.

'Thank you, Superintendent, for letting us see this. Good afternoon – we'll be on our way now,' she said, giving him a warm smile. Turning, she touched Crafty's elbow and led him towards the door.

'We'll go back to the Waiting Room,' she whispered, 'where we can talk in private.'

Reluctantly Crafty followed her. They walked back in thoughtful silence, and took their usual seats, facing each other across the table.

'I'm worried about what will happen to Donna and the boy,' Crafty told her. 'Those channels in the floor are to allow the blood to drain away. Are they going to dissect them?'

'Don't worry, Crafty, they won't cut them,' Lick replied. 'That's the room where specimens are first investigated, but it's also used for autopsies. The channels are there to drain away the blood and fluids of dead creatures that are being examined.'

Crafty nodded but he still wasn't happy. 'So what will happen to them now?'

'There are rules in place to cover live specimens. Forensics will have three days in which to study them. After that they'll be handed over to the Menagerie for further study.'

'If they wake up, will they come back to work as gate grubs? We're in short supply. They could help,' he said hopefully.

Lick looked sceptical. 'I don't know about that, Crafty. That experimental graveyard is only about five years old and no gate grub has ever come back from the dead before. Still, I'll be speaking to the Chief Mancer about it.'

'Do you think the bargeman dug them up?' Crafty wondered.

'Maybe,' Lick said with a frown. 'But they're only the most recent to die. What about the other bodies? Have they been dug up too? Why were they placed in coffins with lead linings? There are lots of questions that need to be answered.'

'Did you notice that Donna had her legs back?'

'Yes,' Lick replied, 'but that's nothing to do with whatever exhumed her. Dead grubs who lose limbs always have them stitched back into place in the hope that, if the Shole revives them, they will be whole again. In Donna's case it seems to have worked. We need to have that graveyard examined. We could send a courier, but it's some way away. Maybe we should use the gate to have a quick look. I'll see what the Chief Mancer thinks.'

'You mean see if he's prepared to risk me – a valuable resource!' Crafty said wryly.

'Yes,' Lick said with a smile.

She left Crafty alone with his thoughts. There were a lot of them, and many more questions than answers. If Donna and the boy woke up, what would they want to eat? Blood and raw flesh? Bertha had ordinary teeth, but that was what she lived on. And what would it be like working with them as gate grubs? And why had the bargeman taken them to the warehouse?

His thoughts were interrupted when the door opened and Lick beckoned to him. He nodded and pulled on his greatcoat.

As they headed down to her room, she explained that they'd been given permission to check out the experimental graveyard. Crafty sat before the silver gate and took the locator Lick handed to him. The clouds cleared to reveal a dismal scene: a woodland glade filled with tombstones, each one the resting place of a gate grub like himself. They would all have died young.

Lick followed him through the gate, her crossbow at the ready. Everywhere in the Shole was dangerous, and this place was no exception. It was also late in the afternoon and the danger was growing by the minute. Crafty glanced back and saw that she was holding something else as well – a thin metal rod with a sharp point. It was about five feet long and had a wooden handle at one end. He wondered what it was for.

'Guard the gate, Crafty!' she ordered, and he took up a position in front of it.

Crafty made a quick estimate of the number of graves – it was around thirty. There was something unusual about the gravestones: they were made of wood, and a single number was carved into each one.

'They don't bother with names then,' he called out bitterly. 'Even when dead, gate grubs are treated badly.'

'There's a reason for the numbers – the higher ones are the most recent,' Lick shouted back. She was close to the graves now. 'And the records back in the castle tell us which number refers to which body. Don't forget that, in the Daylight World, gravestones are really for the benefit of the living rather than the dead. Names and prayers make those left behind feel better. We're in the Shole, aren't we, so the relatives of these poor dead people will never see their graves. Many of them were orphans anyway. I'm looking for numbers thirty-one and thirty-two, the most recent – Titch and Donna.'

Crafty nodded, conceding that Lick was right about the names – though he was horrified to discover that so many grubs had died in just five years. However, as he gazed around he realized that Lick wouldn't need to find the numbered wooden markers. Crafty could see the graves from where he was standing. There was soil rather than grass on top of them. They'd been dug up very recently and the soil replaced.

Then, as Lick approached one of the graves and pushed the thin metal rod down into the soil, Crafty realized what it was for. She was checking to see if the coffin was still there. The rod met with resistance. She nodded and smiled at him. The coffin was there all right. Then she checked the other one.

'Both coffins are still down there,' she said, coming back towards him. 'After they transferred the bodies to the lead-lined ones, they buried the originals again. This could have been going on for a long time. For all we know, all the coffins are empty. Some gate grubs could have been taken years ago. We'll have to dig them up.'

Suddenly they heard the howl of an aberration in the distance. It was enough to remind them that they weren't safe here.

'We've done enough for now. Couriers will need to carry out a thorough investigation. Let's get out of here,' Lick suggested, and they climbed back through the gate into her room.

'Why do you think the new coffins had lead linings?' Crafty asked her as they sat down at her desk.

'That's another mystery,' she answered with a frown. 'But in the past the bodies of kings and lords were sometimes placed in lead-lined coffins. It was supposed to help preserve the corpse.'

'But these are now living bodies again . . .'

'Indeed. What's the lead for?' Lick said, shaking her head. 'Your guess is as good as mine.'

PIGS MIGHT FLY

Crafty found himself alone in the Waiting Room once more the next day. Lucky still hadn't returned to work. When Lick arrived, he asked her how his friend was doing.

She tried to put on a cheerful face. 'The doctors are doing their best, but his temperature has gone up again and the infection is worse. Still, they've had plenty of practice in dealing with wounds sustained in the Shole. They'll beat it in the end, don't you worry. Lucky's in very good hands.'

Crafty bit his lip and sighed; he was still really worried.

'I've got some good news though,' Lick went on brightly. 'I'm to be allowed to talk to Viper. Still want to come along?'

Crafty nodded: he was very curious about Viper, but he also wanted to do something – anything – to take his mind off things. It wasn't just Lucky; he was also anxious about his mother. His father was now back at work. With the cellar full of bog mud, there was no risk of him finding his wife in there, but Bertha had said that she had other hiding places. Courier Benson knew the Shole well. Even if he didn't set out to track her down, he might find her by accident in the course of his work.

To Crafty's surprise, Lick didn't head for the Forensics Room or the Menagerie. Viper was being imprisoned in the castle dungeon – exactly where they'd kept the witch, Old Nell, before they hanged her.

'Viper is a special case,' Lick explained. 'Although he is still under the jurisdiction of Forensics and being studied by them, he's being kept here because it's the most secure place in the castle. He's chained to the floor and there's only one entrance. He'll stay here until they've finished with him.'

They were crossing the castle yard, heading for the big iron gate that gave access to the Witch Well. One guard was standing in front of it, arms folded; others were positioned against the near wall. They certainly weren't taking any chances with Viper.

'I thought Forensics had to hand live specimens over to the Menagerie after three days,' Crafty said. 'Shouldn't he be transferred there tomorrow?'

'In Viper's case the Duke has overturned the usual rules. The severity of his crimes – the murder of the gate grubs as well as his membership of the Grey Hoods – means that he may well be hanged, but for now they're trying to learn all they can.'

Lick stopped in front of the guard. 'I'm here to see the prisoner,' she announced, and handed him a folded piece of paper.

He made a big show of unfolding it with exaggerated care and then studying it closely. Crafty suddenly wondered if he was short-sighted. Maybe he was – though it wouldn't look right for a big tough guard to wear spectacles!

The guard nodded without smiling and handed the piece of paper back to Lick.

'Thank you. And my assistant will be accompanying me,' she said.

'Oh no – it didn't say nothing about that,' said the guard. 'Your authorization only admits one.'

At that, Crafty produced his special key. 'This was given to me by the Duke. It gives me the right to enter any room in the castle,' he told the guard.

For a moment he seemed ready to protest, frowning and making a strange noise in his throat as if he was choking. Then his left eye twitched three times and his face turned the colour of beetroot. However, at last he lifted his bunch of keys from his belt and inserted the biggest one into the lock.

The guard hadn't bothered consulting anyone else this time, so Crafty wondered if word had spread that he had the backing of the Duke. That was both good and bad. Good because he wouldn't be hassled when trying to use his key; bad because other departments such as the Menagerie – which he planned to visit soon – would be expecting him. It would give them the chance to hide anything they didn't want him to see.

He and Lick were now walking down the steep steps into the Witch Well, the deep dungeon where witches were kept. The guard remained at the top, and Crafty heard the key turning again. They were locked in with Viper.

The light was gloomy but there was an unsteady glimmer from below. The air seemed to grow colder with each step down, until at last they reached the stone floor of the dungeon. The big cell was lit by a single flickering wall torch. It smelled just as bad as the last time Crafty had visited. Then, he'd seen before him a bundle of dirty rags with a leg protruding. It had been the witch's leg, fastened to a ring set into the floor.

This time Viper was sitting cross-legged, looking straight at them. His back was straight and he seemed alert, though he still wore the same stained white shirt. Through the rips in that tattered shirt, Crafty could see that Viper's shoulders had been bandaged. They must have removed the crossbow bolts. For now, they wanted him alive and able to answer questions.

But he was securely confined. Not only was his leg fastened to the ring in the floor; both wrists were attached to new rings set into the wall behind him. Crafty estimated that if he got to his feet, he wouldn't be able to take more than a step towards them.

Still, he and Lick kept their distance. They certainly didn't want to get within range of that dangerously strong body and the wide mouth with its three rows of sharp teeth.

'I'm here to ask you a few questions,' Lick told the aberration. 'It would be in your best interests to answer them as truthfully and accurately as you can.'

Viper opened his mouth and smiled at her, showing all his deadly teeth. Then his eyes locked on Crafty and his grin grew even wider. 'What a pleasure to meet you two again,' he said. 'I won't be answering any of your foolish questions, but I do have some things to tell you – things you won't like. You won't like them at all.'

Lick was about to say something, but Viper continued with hardly a pause.

'Very soon, far sooner than you think, this castle will be engulfed by the Shole. But that won't be all. No doubt preparations are already being made to leave. Am I right?' he said, staring hard at Lick.

She didn't answer, but one glance at her face told Crafty that Viper had hit a nerve. Preparations to evacuate the castle must have already begun.

'Yes, clever little Miss Crompton-Smythe, as you well know, all the departments are packing and preparing to move east. But that won't achieve anything. It doesn't matter how far you flee. After the castle is engulfed, the next surge will carry the Shole on for hundreds of miles. Soon the whole world will be part of it.'

'And pigs might fly!' Lick retorted.

'They might indeed, for the Shole is a law unto itself, and dark wonders will come forth and inherit the earth. You and the Castle Corpus are inept, blundering fools. I'm just giving

141

you a little assistance, warning you about the night of your doom. Now I shall give you a sign so that you will know I speak the truth. At midnight I will cast off my chains and leave this dungeon. Soon afterwards, the castle will be claimed by the Shole!'

Crafty and Lick were once more in the Waiting Room, facing each other across the table. Lick had tried to ask Viper a few questions, but he had simply stared silently back at her.

'Are preparations really being made to evacuate the castle?' Crafty asked her.

She nodded. 'It started after the last big surge that covered the canal. Equipment and samples are slowly being transferred east to Clitheroe Castle. It's mostly done at night so as not to cause alarm. If the city folk knew, they would panic. Many have fled already; the rest are relying on the Castle Guard to defend them against the Shole. But, as you saw, they're starting to lose faith and are slowly turning against us. And the Grey Hoods aren't helping – they're stirring things up, as usual.'

'Could Viper be right about it happening very soon?' Crafty wondered. 'I know you're trying to find a way to predict these surges. Have you got anywhere with that?'

'No, Crafty, but we do believe that the next one will come sometime during the winter – that's why we're already evacuating parts of the castle. I'm sure Viper is just trying to scare us – though I will certainly make a report to the Chief

Mancer. As for him escaping from that cell tonight – as I told him, there's more chance of pigs flying. It's just not going to happen.'

But when the guard took Viper's breakfast down to him the following morning, the dungeon was empty.

THE MENAGERIE

Crafty heard the news when Lick came to the Waiting Room. Instead of their usual fifteen-minute session, she told him all she knew about Viper's escape.

'The dungeon was empty. The chains had been snapped. It was as if he'd simply broken free and vanished into thin air. There's only one way out – up those stone steps. But there's a locked gate and a guard at the top. He didn't go out that way.'

Suddenly Crafty knew how Viper had escaped. There could be only one explanation.

'Someone or something in the Shole has a silver gate – or something like it!' he exclaimed. 'They used it to get into the dungeon and take Viper back with them.'

Lick grinned at him. 'Great minds think alike!' she said. 'I put that very idea to the Chief Mancer earlier this morning. I think we were wrong about the killer too. We thought that something from the Shole had found a way to use *our* gates and get into the castle. But you're right, Crafty – they must have a gate of their own. And a very special gate it must be too. Our gates can't take us to places within the Daylight World – but theirs can.' She sighed. 'Well, I'm off to another meeting – this time with the other boffins *and* the Chief Mancer. Things are moving fast now.'

'What do you mean? Now that Viper's escaped, are they taking his warning seriously?' Crafty asked.

'It's still considered unlikely that his prediction is accurate, but we're taking no chances. It's almost certainly going to happen before the end of the winter. You stay here, Crafty, and I'll come back and let you know what your duties will be . . .'

'My duties?'

'Of course – when the castle's engulfed, you'll have a big part to play. People like the Chief Mancer will go east and operate from the new base, Clitheroe Castle. But we Fey will stay here and fight the Shole under the command of the Duke.'

Crafty nodded, momentarily silenced, but then, as Lick prepared to leave, he realized that he hadn't enquired about Lucky. 'Any improvement?' he asked her.

She smiled at him. 'Yes, his fever has finally broken, but he's very weak and it will be a while before he's fit to return to work. Anyway, stay here. I'll come back and see you after the meeting – though I'll be a couple of hours.'

A couple of hours was all Crafty needed to take a look at the Menagerie. He knew Lick wanted him to stay put, but this was too good an opportunity to miss.

He knocked on the door, showed his key and was admitted by a thin man in a white coat, who looked impatient. The man didn't bother to introduce himself but gestured irritatedly towards the large hallway where other men in white coats were stacking cages. Clearly people must know about Crafty's key if he was being waved through so freely.

Crafty looked around. Growls and whines came from the cages and there was a stink of urine.

'As you can see, we are busy moving specimens,' the thin man told him. 'I can't forbid you to enter, but the timing of your visit is extremely unfortunate. Try not to get in our way!'

With a frown and a bad-tempered shake of his head, the man stalked off, leaving Crafty near the door. No doubt the specimens would be moving east before the castle was engulfed, he thought. In spite of the welcome he'd received, he decided to have a quick look around anyway.

There were three passageways leading away from the hallway; choosing the one on the left, he hadn't taken more than five paces before he was barged aside by a man carrying a box. 'Walk on the left! Keep to the left!' he was told angrily.

Crafty doubted it would make much difference: there was barely enough room for two people to pass anyway. How on earth would they get large cages through?

When he reached the end of the corridor, his question was answered. They didn't: SMALL SPECIMENS said a sign over the door. The large room contained dozens of specimen boxes. These weren't cages like those in the entrance hall.

Each had a glass side for observation like the ones he'd seen on his visit to Forensics, but while those specimens had mostly been dead, these were very much alive.

The first case contained what looked like a giant ant. It was as big as Crafty's fist, and no sooner had he put his face to the glass to peer in than it scuttled towards him and started to scratch right in front of his eyes. Crafty jerked his head back so quickly that he overbalanced. Scrambling to his feet, he reflected that it was just as well he hadn't met the creature in the Shole.

Most of the specimens here were insects that had grown much bigger than those found in the Daylight World. But then he came to a case containing half a dozen creatures that weren't just larger but had been changed in other ways. He remembered seeing something similar before, when he was collecting samples by the canal after a surge – and also hovering above the oily pool in his nightmare – though these were larger. They had eight legs and resembled spiders, but the head looked almost human, with a nose, a mouth and eyes, and expressive faces. They came close to the glass, as if to inspect him. Most of them were frowning, but one seemed to be grinning. It was not a friendly grin.

Crafty headed back to the hall and this time took the central corridor. This was much wider and led to a door with a different sign: LARGE SPECIMENS.

This room was gloomy, lit by only a couple of wall torches, and the stink was overpowering. It was lined with huge cages rather than glass display cases. He peered into the first, and saw something sleeping, half buried in a heap of dirty straw. He couldn't make out what it was, but he could see its body rising and falling with each breath. It was at least twice the size of a human.

In the next cage was something that reminded Crafty of a One-Bite. It resembled a large, sleek dog with two horns protruding from its narrow forehead. Whether it was indeed one of those or just something very similar, he couldn't tell. But it was asleep in a corner.

Why were all these aberrations asleep? Crafty wondered.

His thoughts were interrupted by the sound of something moving in a cage in the far corner. Maybe it was awake, he thought.

When he reached the cage, Crafty realized that he was mistaken. The creature was asleep, but a big man in a white coat streaked with fresh blood was taking chunks of raw meat out of a large sack and pushing them through the bars into the next-door cage with a stick.

The man paused and his brow wrinkled with a scowl as he noticed Crafty.

'Why are all the aberrations asleep?' Crafty asked him.

'You might be able to come in here with that key, grub,' the man snarled, 'but it doesn't mean we're obliged to answer any of your stupid questions!'

'Sorry for asking,' Crafty said with a shrug. 'I was just curious.'

He turned to leave, but the man had decided to answer his question. 'They're sleeping because we put something in their food to keep them docile. They're less trouble that way, and much less dangerous!'

'Thanks for telling me,' Crafty said politely. Then he thought of another question. 'Are these large specimens being moved out of the castle? That won't be easy.'

To his surprise, the man answered again. 'A few of the smaller ones might be, but some are far too big to transport. I don't know what's been decided, but it would be best to put them out of their misery – kill them here. That's what I'd do. I wouldn't want to leave such dangerous creatures alive. Of course, the two humans are dead already; their bodies have to be destroyed so they can't come back. Burn them in the ovens – that should do the trick.'

Crafty's heart plummeted at those words. The man must be referring to Donna and Titch!

With another scowl at Crafty, the man slung the blood-stained sack over his shoulder and headed for the door. Crafty was inclined to follow him, but decided to check out a few more cages. All he saw were more large creatures, mostly hidden by dirty straw.

But then he came to a cage where the aberration was asleep like the others, but lying on top of the bedding, in plain view.

It was Donna.

THE RELOCATION

Crafty could have reached through the bars and touched her. She was now wearing the uniform of a gate grub, but it was crinkled and dirty.

Crafty felt a surge of rage. Why had they done this? Forensics had handed her over to the Menagerie and they'd just put her in a cage. And where was the boy from the other coffin – the one called Titch?

He'd hoped that both grubs would be returned to duty, but that didn't seem to be the plan. They'd been drugged like all the other aberrations here. And would they be considered too big or too dangerous to move? Would they be killed here? Crafty wondered angrily. It wasn't fair.

Still, it was no use complaining to anyone in the Menagerie: the authority he'd been given along with the key had clearly led to a lot of resentment.

There was only one way he could possibly help Donna and Titch.

He had to go and see the Duke.

As he reached the foot of the central steps, Crafty glanced around the Ducal Chambers. The last time he was here, apart from his escort, he'd been alone with the Duke. Now there were a couple of dozen men and women, some in white coats, working in silence. Were they boffins like Lick? he wondered. Others were writing at tables. It was evident that they were making preparations for when the Shole engulfed the castle.

Crafty looked up at the Duke, who smiled and beckoned to him. Crafty gave a deferential bow and began to climb the steps. He halted when his head was just lower than the Duke's.

'Well, Crafty, have you come to report on your recent visits to the departments? You've certainly stirred up some hornets' nests there! I've been expecting you. Did you find anything of interest?'

'I'm sorry, sir, but so far I've found no new evidence of activity by the Grey Hoods. May I ask what happened to the young man from the Relic Room? Was he truly a member of that cult?'

'When he reported for work, he did indeed have a gash over his left eye. He is still working there, unaware that we are watching him closely. As a result of that surveillance, we have so far identified two other possible Grey Hoods working in the Relic Room. Arrests will be made very soon. So well done, Crafty. I am sure you will soon discover more!'

'I've just been making preliminary visits, sir – I intend to return until I find out more. But today in the Menagerie I did discover something that disturbed me . . .'

Crafty gave the Duke a quick summary of the situation and ended by begging him to spare Donna and Titch. 'We're really short of gate grubs, sir, and their help could make a lot of difference.'

The Duke stroked his beard and his eyes became glazed, as if his mind was far away. Then he looked straight at Crafty; it was clear that he had made up his mind.

'You have to understand, Crafty, that some of my decisions are very painful, but must be made for the good of the Castle Corpus. Indeed, our very survival depends on these difficult choices. The preliminary interrogations of the two dead gate grubs did not go well. They were hostile and considered to be extremely dangerous. Consequently, they were medicated to make them more manageable and –'

'Please, sir, let me talk to them,' begged Crafty. 'Maybe they were frightened and weren't thinking clearly. After all, it would be the same if I was killed and then brought back to life and locked in a cage! It must have been really traumatic for *you*, sir, when you were changed by the Shole. Perhaps at first you were angry too, and said things that you didn't really mean – things that you were later sorry for having said?'

A number of expressions flickered across the Duke's face, some of which Crafty couldn't read – though one of them was surely anger. He had interrupted the Duke and been far too outspoken in reminding him of his own terrible experience. Now he dreaded hearing the Duke's response.

'Some of the specimens may have to be destroyed,' the Duke replied, 'but, once again, for a boy of your age you have shown great wisdom. After you helped rescue me from the Shole and I was returned to the castle, I was indeed angry and undoubtedly hurt people who were only trying to help me. You could well be correct about those two gate grubs, but we cannot take any chances, so I will give the order for them to remain confined and medicated but not destroyed if the Menagerie staff are forced to abandon the castle. Does that ease your mind, Crafty?'

It was not what he had hoped for, but it was better than nothing and would do for now. 'Yes, sir, it does. Thank you for that. Thanks for listening to me.'

The Duke dismissed him with a wave of the hand, and Crafty descended the steps and left the Ducal Chambers. It might just have been his imagination, but it seemed that the Duke had suddenly grown a little cooler towards him.

Lick was already back in the Waiting Room, drumming her fingers impatiently on the table.

'What kept you? Where have you been?' she demanded, the irritation evident in her voice.

Crafty told her everything that had happened in the Menagerie, ending with his conversation with the Duke.

'You did the right thing,' Lick said. 'I think those two grubs deserve a chance to prove themselves. But do be careful how you speak to the Duke. From what you say, I think you may have overstepped the mark. Don't forget that he has royal blood in his veins and is used to being obeyed, not challenged. He has the power of life and death over us all! The Duke's under a lot of pressure at the moment – he gets angry when things go wrong.'

Crafty nodded. Lick was right. 'What happened at the meeting?' he asked. 'Anything that affects me?'

'Not directly, but I'll find out more tomorrow. The move to Clitheroe Castle is well under way. It's south-east of here, in the Ribble Valley. Some of the Castle Corpus have gone ahead – including some couriers, your father for one. They are needed to support the communities trapped in the Daylight Islands.'

The Daylight Islands were surrounded by the Shole; the people there had to be supplied by couriers. Without that routine support they would have starved.

For a moment Crafty felt hurt – his father hadn't come to say goodbye – but then he put his sensible hat on and realized that he must have been sent away at short notice and hadn't had time.

'Once the Shole engulfs the castle, we Fey will be running it,' Lick continued. 'Most of us will be based in the Ducal Chambers with the Duke – they're going to strengthen the main door – but at least one Fey will be assigned to each department. The couriers will be responsible for wider security around the castle and beyond.'

'How many Fey will be here in total?' Crafty asked.

'About sixty. That includes the couriers not needed in Clitheroe. There won't be many of us to defend the castle, but we'll just have to do the best we can.'

Lick paused and reached under the table. 'And now I've got a surprise for you, Crafty . . .' And she placed a crossbow in front of him.

Crafty was delighted!

'Pick it up,' she said with a smile. 'It's for you. Now, come with me and we'll see what you can do.'

Filled with excitement, he followed her to the archery range, a big flagged yard behind the main castle buildings. There was a row of wooden targets and, with Lick's guidance, he began to fire at the one on the left. His first shots went wide, but soon he was firing bolts close to the centre. One even found the bullseye.

'Try and get some practice in each day,' Lick advised him. 'We could be engulfed at any time. That bow could mean the difference between life and death.'

That night Crafty found it hard to sleep. He couldn't get Viper's warning out of his head.

Had he just been trying to frighten them and appear important? Or did he *truly* know that the castle was about to be engulfed?

NO LONGER FULLY HUMAN

When Crafty finally got to sleep, he was plunged into another nightmare.

He was standing in the cobbled street outside the castle, facing down the hill. Overhead a gibbous moon bathed everything in its silver light. Before him, racing up the slope, was a black wall of turbulence like a giant wave surging towards him. But this tsunami was the front edge of the Shole.

People were running away from it up the hill; Crafty wanted to run too, but he took a deep breath and stood his ground. He was Fey, and being engulfed would not harm him. There would be aberrations within the Shole that certainly could, but a newly engulfed area was relatively safe, even at night.

However, the fleeing citizens of Lancaster were not so fortunate. Most would begin to die the moment the Shole touched them. They screamed in terror as they fled: men, women and children running for their lives. A child tripped, falling headlong on to the cobbles. His mother turned back and tried to pull him to his feet – but she was too late.

Crafty wished he could help them, but there was nothing he could do. There were too many and it was happening too quickly. The Shole swept over them and they fell to the ground, screaming. Seconds later it engulfed him. There was a moment of darkness as a cold wind buffeted him; then the moon vanished. It was night and he could see little, but he could hear the screams and cries of anguish around him. Some were already fading to whimpers as the Shole did its deadly work.

Then, all at once, he felt cold breath against his face and a voice whispered in his ear. It was a voice he recognized – that of the dead witch, Old Nell.

'Wake up, Crafty. Quick. Quick!'

When Crafty opened his eyes, he gasped with relief. He was safe in his bed – though a grey light illuminated his room and it felt unusually cold.

Had it been more than a dream?

He shivered. It was *really* cold in his room.

Suddenly he heard distant screams outside his door; it sounded as if people were being massacred. Had the Grey Hoods broken into the castle? Were they fighting with the guards? Or was it something even worse?

Crafty felt sluggish and his temples throbbed. Filled with a growing sense of urgency, he forced himself out of bed and strode across towards the narrow window that looked down over the city towards the Shole.

The view confirmed his worst fears. The sky was a very dark grey and everything looked murky, as if a grey mist was obscuring the city. And he could no longer see the dark wall of the Shole that divided it from the Daylight World.

Crafty shivered and turned back – and saw that his bedroom was filled with mist too. He could barely even make out the bed. Beyond his door the distant cries continued, but they were growing weaker, slowly changing into the whimpers he'd heard in his nightmare.

He no longer felt sluggish. His mind was clear, his heart racing in terror. What they had long anticipated had finally happened.

The castle had been engulfed.

Crafty dressed quickly. He had to report to the Ducal Chambers and help guard the Duke. All the Fey within the castle would be gathering there.

His mind raced as he considered what the engulfment meant; he went over the immediate dangers. It might take some time before any aberrations started to move towards the castle, he thought – but then he realized that the Shole would have already done its deadly work. With a shiver of horror, he understood that those who were not Fey would already be dead or dying: the Chief Mancer, along with the Castle Guard and most of the departmental staff. All those people would surely be gone. The same would be true of the inhabitants outside the castle walls, but on a much larger scale. Houses would now be occupied by skeletons, the melting flesh forming pools of slime on the floor. Those not slain immediately would now be changing into aberrations that would most likely be feral and dangerous.

Crafty pulled on his boots and then buttoned up his greatcoat against the cold. He checked that his dagger was safely in his right pocket and then picked up his crossbow. He hadn't expected to be needing it so soon. It had one pouch of bolts slung beneath it, but he had no spares. It would have to do.

As he was about to open the door, he froze. There was something outside. Something big sniffing at the door. He kept perfectly still, hardly daring to breathe. Whatever it was sniffed again, then padded away. It sounded as if it was walking on all fours. It had to be an aberration – but what was it doing here? Surely the creature couldn't have been changed so quickly? But it wouldn't already have come from deeper in the Shole either, would it?

Crafty listened with his ear to the door. All was silent, so he opened it carefully and peered down the gloomy corridor. It was deserted. There were no more screams – just an ominous silence. Crafty was about to set off for the Ducal Chambers when he realized that there was somewhere else he needed to go first. Lucky was in one of the sick rooms. He was still ill and would be vulnerable. Lucky was his friend and, whatever the danger, he couldn't leave him behind.

Cautiously he set off along the corridor and reached the first set of steps. He descended slowly – and came across the first of the many dead he would surely encounter. The Shole had already killed the guard and was now swiftly working on his dead body. The face was half melted. Slime and water were beginning to pool beneath him, and there was a sweet stink of vinegary rot. Crafty's stomach spasmed and he had to hold his breath and swallow to stop himself vomiting. The eye sockets, now filled with a pink jelly, stared up sightlessly and the hands were already fleshless, the bones covered in yellow slime.

Crafty moved on quickly and descended another short flight of steps before continuing along the lower corridor towards the Infirmary. Mist swirled around his knees.

There were a dozen small sick rooms – Crafty hadn't been allowed to visit Lucky so he had to try one after the other: the first two were empty, but there were groans coming from the third. Was it Lucky? he wondered.

He eased open the door and glanced inside. The man before him was kneeling on the bed and moaning as if in pain, his head twisting from side to side. He seemed to be staring at Crafty, but it was evident that he couldn't see him. He couldn't see anything.

Two short twigs had sprouted from his eyes; they had formed fat green leaf buds that were starting to open. The man was being changed by the Shole.

There was no way Crafty could help him. He knew that it would be best to kill him – that was what any courier would do without hesitation now that the castle had been engulfed. The man on the bed was no longer fully human. He was being changed by the Shole into an aberration that might be dangerous. But Crafty couldn't bring himself to do it. Instead he closed the door behind him and continued with his search.

The next room was empty, but the one beyond contained another of the slimy dead. He closed the door on the corpse quickly.

At last he found Lucky sitting on the edge of his bed. He was dressed in just a thin nightshirt and was shivering violently.

'What's wrong? What's wrong?' Lucky asked, peering up at him anxiously. 'Oh! It's you, Crafty!' he said, lurching to his feet. He took a step and staggered, and Crafty caught him before he could fall.

'I'm so cold!' he said. 'The room's spinning. I need to get back into bed . . .'

Lucky might be feeling cold, but he was clearly still burning up with a fever. Lick had said he was getting better but he must have taken a turn for the worse.

'No. You can't do that. You can't stay here. The Shole's engulfed the castle,' Crafty told him. 'We need to get to the Ducal Chambers. Here – take my coat . . .'

Crafty put his crossbow on the bed and, after tucking his dagger into his belt, removed his greatcoat and helped Lucky into it. Using one arm to support Lucky, he picked up the crossbow and moved towards the door, his friend leaning on him heavily.

Out in the corridor he heard a screeching from somewhere overhead and saw a flapper embedded in the high stone ceiling. Most humans were changed by the Shole quite slowly, but flappers took their new form within minutes. He couldn't make out its face, but its four limbs were twitching and flapping in the manner that gave the aberration its name.

However, the screeching quickly resolved itself into words that Crafty could understand.

'Light a candle! Light a candle, Mother! Please light a candle. I can't see!' it cried.

Crafty was puzzled by that because there was a torch on the wall just behind it. It gave out a strange red glow and was spluttering smoke into the corridor, but there was enough light to see by.

'I'm afraid of the dark! I'm afraid. Please, Mother, light a candle so that I can see.'

No doubt it was one of the castle guards changed by the Shole; it thought it was a child again – though that didn't explain why it couldn't see.

Still supporting Lucky, Crafty went on, and slowly the cries of the flapper faded away – though now, suddenly, his heart lurched at the sight of a large black dog along the corridor on his left, no more than thirty paces away, its breath steaming in the cold air. It was sleek like a greyhound but more muscular, and its narrow head had two horns jutting forward. It was one of the dangerous aberrations called One-Bite. Was it this that had been sniffing at his bedroom door? Was it the creature he'd seen in the Menagerie? If it had escaped, then other aberrations could have done the same, Crafty realized.

It growled and loped towards them, showing its three rows of sharp teeth. A single bite, Crafty knew, could be fatal.

He had only had that one short practice session with the bow: his aim had been good and he'd shown some talent – Lick had certainly thought so – but he'd been aiming at a static target, whereas the One-Bite was moving fast, its muscles rippling, saliva dripping from its open mouth.

Everything seemed to happen very slowly, as if time had slowed down. Crafty took away the arm supporting Lucky and felt his friend toppling to the floor. But there was no choice – he needed both hands to operate the bow properly. He took a deep breath and then let it out, aimed at the aberration, his hands trembling slightly. He pulled the trigger and released the first bolt.

To his dismay, it passed a handspan above the creature. At least he didn't need to reload: the next bolt was pushed up by a spring and he heard it click into place.

He fired again.

He missed again.

This time he'd been closer, but not close enough. Time was still passing very slowly: Lucky was now lying on the floor, but the dog aberration was much closer. Crafty could clearly see its hungry slavering jaws.

Suddenly time lurched forward again, and the beast was bounding straight for him, its jaws aiming for his right leg.

There was another click as the next bolt locked into position. This would be the final one – he wouldn't have time to fire any more.

His last chance.

ONE MORE MYSTERY

Crafty released the bolt, then watched it hurtle towards its target and bury itself in the shoulder of the One-Bite. It wasn't a fatal wound. Crafty's heart jumped with fear as he realized that he hadn't done enough.

The bolt didn't bring the aberration down, but the creature staggered, gave a yelp of pain and lurched aside, missing Crafty's leg by inches. He turned and watched with relief as it continued along the corridor, turned a corner and disappeared from view. For once the aberration hadn't lived up to its name.

Crafty quickly reached down and pulled Lucky to his feet. He didn't seem to have been hurt by the fall, but he looked bewildered. Crafty started to help him down the steps to the ground floor. At its foot was the long corridor that led to the various departments and the Ducal Chambers.

'Keep going, Lucky,' Crafty said, trying to encourage him. 'We're almost there!'

Getting his friend down those steps proved difficult: another dead guard lay across them, and the stone was slippery with melted flesh. Lucky seemed almost unconscious now, a dead weight.

Then, at last, they were moving along the corridor, passing the Forensics Room and the Grey Library. All the doors were closed and there were couriers outside the Menagerie and the Ducal Chambers. The Menagerie door had been boarded up – sealed with long planks of wood.

Still struggling to support Lucky, Crafty approached the nearest courier – the one outside the Menagerie – to ask for help with his friend, but the man snarled, drew his sword and pointed it at Crafty's throat.

'Keep your distance and keep moving!' he growled.

'We're gate grubs and my friend is ill,' Crafty protested. 'I need help.'

'I can see that. Keep moving. They'll deal with you in the Ducal Chambers,' he said, gesturing with his sword.

Crafty understood. They were taking no chances. No doubt they'd been warned to look out for humans in the early stages of transformation.

As he struggled on, he saw two dead bodies outside the door of the Ducal Chambers. The guard glared at him and Lucky, and he too drew his sword.

'Stop! Wait there!' he commanded. 'State your names!'

'I'm Colin Benson and this is Pete Proudfoot. We're gate grubs reporting for duty,' Crafty answered.

'What's wrong with your companion?'

'He was in the Infirmary,' Crafty explained. 'I went to get him and bring him here.'

The guard eased his sword back into its scabbard, then reached round to rap on the door. It opened and another courier came out. It was Captain Clayton.

He looked them both up and down and grimaced. 'Well, let's get you both inside,' he said decisively.

He picked Lucky up as if he was a baby and carried him inside. Crafty followed at his heels. 'There's an aberration loose in the corridors,' he told the captain. 'I think it was a One-Bite!'

'That's not the only aberration at large,' he replied, not bothering to glance over his shoulder. 'Many escaped from the Menagerie before we managed to seal it. For now, the only safe place is here in the Ducal Chambers.'

As they entered, Crafty glanced about the large room. Half a dozen men and women were seated at the tables. The Duke was positioned in his container at the top of the steps as usual, and was talking to a man in a white coat. Neither of them looked at Crafty.

The chamber looked very different now. Everything was gloomy, the torches struggling to penetrate the murk, their flickering light a baleful red. There were four braziers, one in each corner of the big room, but they seemed to make little impact on the cold and were putting out more smoke than heat, adding to the murky atmosphere.

Then Crafty noticed something new: a large square space marked by four sturdy wooden corner posts with a chain linking them. Was it to keep people out? If so, why? Crafty wondered.

'Follow me!' Captain Clayton barked.

There were lots of questions that Crafty wanted to ask him. How many had been killed by the Shole? Were the departmental heads all dead? He was grateful that his father had gone east to Clitheroe, out of danger.

However, the captain was clearly in a hurry, carrying the unconscious Lucky through into what seemed to be an anteroom. Before becoming the Ducal Chambers, this area had been known as the Pessimists' Room. But each departmental 'room' was really a warren of rooms – specialist areas that could be accessed from the ground-floor corridor. This was no exception. Three long dim corridors disappeared into the distance, while two flights of steps led to lower floors.

The captain nodded to the first one. 'Down there!' he said curtly. 'Third door on the left. You'll be working with Miss Crompton-Smythe. I'll get your friend to the doctor.' And he turned, with Lucky still over his shoulder, and headed back the way he'd come.

Crafty went down the stairs and rapped twice on the door. Lick opened it almost immediately.

'Where have you been?' she demanded. 'I've been worried about you.'

'I woke up just as the castle was being engulfed,' Crafty told her. 'Then I went to get Lucky and bring him here.'

'Is he all right?'

Crafty shook his head. 'He's very feverish. He was either asleep or unconscious so Captain Clayton has taken him to see the doctor.'

'Don't worry, Crafty. He'll be in good hands. Anyway, this is my new room,' Lick said as he followed her inside. 'It's smaller than the other one, but we'll just have to make the best of it.'

There was a single torch on the far wall, a blood-red light flickering across the walls and floor. Sealed packing cases filled half the room, leaving just enough space for a small wooden desk, a single chair and, in the far corner, a silver gate complete with guillotine and chair, the latter fitted with leather straps to restrain a gate grub when making a snatch.

'Is that the gate we usually use?' Crafty asked.

'No, but it's even better for what we need now. I've been experimenting, and have tweaked the components of the gate, so it's more precise. This gate allows us to walk into buildings if they're spacious enough and we use a locator. I've checked it thoroughly, ready for when the castle was engulfed.'

Crafty marvelled at how prepared Lick had been – and how clever she was with her experiments. He wondered how many other things she was working on. She didn't always let him into her confidence.

Lick continued. 'So now we can go anywhere inside the Shole, including a few of the larger spaces inside the castle – lots of locators are already in position for that. Everything we need is in this desk drawer,' she said, tapping it with her fingers.

'That's amazing, Lick! So can we go outside the Shole as well – into the Daylight World? Or even to the Daylight Islands?' Crafty asked. If that was the case, they'd be able to send help directly to the people trapped in areas surrounded by the Shole. It would lift a burden from the shoulders of the couriers.

Lick shook her head. 'So far we've found no way to do that, though I hope we'll be able to in the future. Our main point of contact with the new headquarters will be through a silver gate there. You saw the chained-off area opposite the Duke's throne?'

Crafty nodded.

'That's where the gate will open once it's been tested. It's brand new and is about three times the size of a normal gate. That will make it easier for bringing in provisions – as you know, porter magic is unreliable in newly engulfed areas.'

Once again Crafty was impressed. It was clear that the boffins were making real progress – though he was sad to find that Lick had been keeping him in the dark.

'Viper was right, wasn't he?' he said to her. 'Not only did he escape, he's now been proved correct. The castle *was* engulfed soon afterwards.'

'I'm afraid he was,' Lick admitted. 'Some of the aberrations clearly know more than we do. They're even more dangerous than we thought.'

'So where are we going?' Crafty asked, settling himself down in the chair facing the gate.

'We're not going anywhere for a while, so make yourself comfortable, Crafty. I'm just going to bring you up to speed – there are a few things you need to know.'

Lick went and got the chair from behind her desk, placed it next to him and sat down.

He swivelled round in his seat to face her. 'Before I forget: there was a flapper embedded in one of the corridor ceilings,' he told her. 'I could hear what it was saying again. It seemed to think it was a child and was blind. It was asking for its mother.'

Lick looked grim. 'Flappers are embedded in whatever is nearby when they're engulfed. It happens very quickly – within minutes, rather than the hours or days it takes for a human to change into an aberration. If they're embedded in a tree, they retain most of their faculties and can survive for as long as the tree does, because a tree is alive and its sap provides them with nutrients. The ones embedded in stone don't last long. They can absorb water and sometimes minerals from the stone, but in a week or so they wither away and die. Most are blind – but a few seem to have exceptional vision, although so far nobody has been able to explain why. Another mystery to be solved. At least they're not dangerous – and, believe me, dangerous aberrations are already on the prowl. Soon after the castle was engulfed, someone released most of the aberrations in the Menagerie and –'

'Yes – we saw a One-Bite in one of the corridors!' interrupted Crafty. 'I managed to shoot it in the shoulder and it ran away. I thought they were all sedated.'

Lick gave an exasperated sigh. 'There was one worker in the Menagerie who was Fey,' she told him. 'He was found with his neck broken – he hadn't had time to feed them the doctored food. We think that someone or something used a gate to get into the Menagerie, slew the one person not killed by the Shole and then started to release the aberrations.'

'So they didn't manage to release them all? What about Donna and Titch?' Crafty asked anxiously.

'I was coming to that,' Lick said with a frown. 'Whoever it was must have been interrupted by a patrol. The guards killed some of the aberrations that were still loose in the Menagerie, then sealed the door to keep the others inside. Donna was – and is – still in her cage, but I'm afraid we don't know where Titch is. Maybe Donna knows. And that's where you come in, Crafty. In about an hour the couriers are going into the Menagerie to sort things out. They have orders from the Duke to kill every aberration in there.'

Crafty opened his mouth to protest, but Lick held up her hand to silence him and spoke first.

'We'll be going in with them. You know Donna, don't you? You're the best chance she and the boy have. It's your job to talk to her: if she responds and remains calm, the couriers won't kill either of them. Instead they'll be shackled and brought back here until we can make a proper evaluation. They have a chance, and you have the Duke to thank for that. It seems that he's still listening to you, Crafty. We have a chance to save Donna and the boy – let's take it!'

A Turn for the Worse

Crafty buttoned up his greatcoat – which had been returned to him – as he and Lick followed the seven couriers down towards the Menagerie. The air was now icy cold.

The couriers were led by Captain Clayton, and were all armed with the new crossbow designed by Lick. Three of them were carrying torches that sputtered fitfully and gave off a lot of acrid smoke. Lick and Crafty were carrying their bows too. There was a good chance they'd need them.

When they reached the door, two of the couriers knelt and took aim while another used a heavy crowbar to rip away the planks. There was a lot of crunching and splintering – which Crafty knew would alert anything at large inside.

They pulled the door open and moved into the chamber where Menagerie staff had previously been stacking cases, ready for the move to Clitheroe Castle. There were still a few piled in the corner.

Captain Clayton raised his hand. 'Silence!' he commanded.

They listened for danger, but there was nothing to be heard. No doubt any aberrations had been given warning by the noise the couriers made and had moved deeper inside the Menagerie.

The captain led the way down the central passageway to the door bearing the sign: LARGE SPECIMENS. He turned and looked at Lick. 'Miss Crompton-Smythe, I think it safer if you wait here while we deal with anything loose inside. Once it's clear, you can come in.'

Lick nodded and the captain went in, leaving two of his men behind to guard the door; one held a torch, the other held his crossbow at the ready.

Within five minutes, despite their thick greatcoats, Crafty and Lick were stamping their feet and shivering, their breath steaming in the cold air of the Shole. Beyond the door they could hear shouts and the occasional eerie cry – no doubt as bolts or swords ended the life of an aberration.

They must have waited for at least half an hour. At one point there was a growl from somewhere down the dark corridor, reminding them that there was danger all around. Some of the aberrations were loose in the Menagerie's labyrinth of rooms and passageways. They would be getting hungry.

At last the door opened and the captain beckoned Lick and Crafty towards him. 'I can't guarantee that we got them all, so stay vigilant!'

They followed him inside, leaving the two couriers on guard. As he filed between the cages, Crafty saw that some of the aberrations were watching them through the bars. They were alert now, some growling in anger or fear and pacing back and forth, showing their teeth. He knew that the couriers would start killing the ones in the cages later. He was determined to make sure that Donna and Titch weren't amongst them.

When they reached Donna's cage, Captain Clayton put his hand on Crafty's shoulder. 'Make it quick, young Benson. The sooner we're done and out of here the better.'

Donna was kneeling on the straw facing Crafty. Her face and arms were streaked with dirt and it looked like she'd been crying. He knelt down in front of the cage.

'Crafty! Crafty!' she cried as he approached, her voice brimming with emotion. 'I'm so glad to see you. Can you get me out? Please! Please! I can't bear to stay in here any longer.'

'Ask her if she knows what happened to her,' the captain commanded from behind Crafty. 'We need to know that she's thinking clearly – that she's held on to most of her humanity.'

'Of course I know what happened to me!' Donna wailed, shuffling closer to the bars and gripping them tightly. 'As I climbed back through the gate, Viper used the guillotine to cut off my legs. I died, and the Shole brought me back to life. That was bad, really bad, but worse has happened since I was brought here. They treat us like animals – they poke us with sticks – and then they beat poor Titch!'

'What?' cried Crafty, horrified.

'At first he was with me, but then someone poked him so he spat at him through the bars. Then they pulled him out and dragged him away. They were beating him – I could hear him crying with pain. He could be dead for all I know.'

Lick had remained silent while Donna spoke, but now Crafty heard her give a little sob. Glancing sideways, he saw that tears were running down her cheeks.

'Someone will pay for that!' growled the captain. 'If those guards are still alive, they'll wish they weren't.'

'Viper was here too,' sobbed Donna. 'It was minutes after we were engulfed. He looked different, but it was Viper all right, and he had some of the Grey Hoods with him. They were letting aberrations out of their cages. He didn't free me though. He said he'd return to deal with me later – he was going to eat me. Is Viper an aberration too? He certainly looked like one.'

Crafty nodded, but the captain spoke before he could explain.

'I've heard enough. Get her out!' he commanded, and one of the couriers stepped forward and unlocked the cage.

Crafty went to support Donna on one side while Lick took the other. Following the captain, they picked their way between the cages. Donna was limping and she kept grunting with pain.

'Are you hurt?' Lick asked.

'It's my legs,' she explained. 'They hurt where they were cut and there's little strength in them.'

'They'll probably start to feel better when you're free to walk about more,' Crafty said. 'Being confined in a cage can't have done them any good.'

Suddenly there was a shout ahead of them. 'We've found him, sir.' A courier was approaching with a small unconscious boy in his arms. 'He seems to be breathing but we can't rouse him.'

'It's Titch!' cried Donna.

For a moment Crafty wondered if the captain would allow Titch to be brought out. After all, he couldn't pass the test as Donna had. But the captain just nodded at the courier and gestured that they should move on.

However, when they got back to the Ducal Chambers, instead of taking Donna and Titch to see a doctor, as Crafty had hoped, the captain led the way to a cell deep within the Chambers.

'We don't have to go in there, do we? What have we done wrong?' Donna wailed.

'It's for your own good,' said Captain Clayton. 'Since the engulfment, a lot of people in this castle have died. Technically, you and the boy are aberrations, so this is partly for your safety. Some of the survivors would kill you soon as look at you, girl. Until we get a chance to evaluate you and make a decision about your future you'll have to stay here.'

And with that, Donna was pushed into the cell and the unconscious Titch placed on the floor beside her. Crafty's heart sank as the door clanged shut behind them. He could see that Lick was dismayed too; her eyes were brimming with tears again. It may have been for their own good, but it still seemed that Donna and Titch were being treated very shabbily.

Crafty and Lick returned to her study and sat down, staring at the gate. Neither spoke for a while. Crafty knew that Lick couldn't do anything about the situation, but he still had questions.

'Donna said that there were Grey Hoods in the Menagerie just *after* the castle was engulfed. Surely that means they're Fey.'

'That's likely. A few *must* be Fey. Some people think that most witches are Fey too. That would explain how they're able to carry their dead into the Shole in the hope that they'll come back to life. You know, hearing about Viper's actions makes me even more certain that he's the killer.'

'Could be,' said Crafty. He didn't mention Old Nell, but it suddenly struck him that she was another possible killer. The White Lady, Viper and now the witch. Which one could it be?

They both fell silent again, but after a while Crafty could hold his tongue no longer.

'It's not fair!' he grumbled, shaking his head. 'Donna and Titch don't deserve to be imprisoned again. Lucky and Donna were close friends. If he knew how she was being treated, he'd go crazy!'

Lick avoided his gaze. He sensed that she didn't want to look him in the eye. Then he sensed something else. She was holding something back.

'What's wrong?' he asked. 'What is it? Tell me, please.'

Finally Lick turned to face him. Fresh tears were running down her cheeks. 'It's Lucky,' she said. 'I couldn't bring myself to tell you this earlier, but I can't put it off any longer – you have to know. He's taken a turn for the worse. There's nothing the doctor can do. There's no easy way to say this, Crafty – Lucky is dying.'

DOWN INTO THE BOG

Crafty couldn't believe what he was hearing.

'No! No!' he protested. 'There must be some mistake. That can't be right.'

'I'm so sorry, Crafty. The poison from the aberration's talons has spread through his blood – it's almost reached his heart. There's nothing more that can be done for him.'

'Isn't there another doctor? A different treatment?' he asked desperately.

Lick shook her head. 'The doctor treating Lucky is the best we have – he's an expert on diseases and poisons from the Shole. He's also the Duke's personal physician. There is nobody else who can give Lucky better treatment. I'm sorry, Crafty,' she repeated. 'I wish there was something more we could do.'

But Crafty's brain was working fast, and suddenly he knew what had to be done.

'There is one person who *might* be better than your doctor at treating diseases from the Shole. Let's ask Bertha. Maybe she can help.'

'Maybe . . . but have you ever seen Bertha display any medical knowledge?' Lick asked, her voice sceptical.

'No, but it's worth a try, isn't it?' Crafty said. 'She's so knowledgeable about the Shole.'

'Sorry, Crafty, but I think you're just grasping at straws –'

'I'm not!' protested Crafty.

'Don't raise your voice at me!' Lick said angrily in return.

He took a deep breath to calm himself down. 'I really do think there is a chance that she can help. Bertha told me that in her home beneath the bog she keeps things from her own time – and other things she's found since: brooches and amulets containing magic. We've seen how she controls the bog too – she might be able to use her power to help Lucky.'

'Even if she could, it might be dangerous to approach her. You know I'm concerned that Bertha might be like the White Lady and the Grim Ploughman: helpful at first, but then obeying a voice in her head telling her to kill you.'

'And *you* know that I trust Bertha. Even if there is a slight risk, I want to take it. It's the only hope for Lucky. Otherwise he'll die for sure!' Crafty exclaimed.

He realized that he'd raised his voice again, but instead of ticking him off Lick buried her face in her hands. She often did that when she was deep in thought, with a difficult decision to make.

'OK, we'll do it!' she said eventually, lowering her hands and coming to her feet. 'But this time I'm going to take my crossbow through the gate.'

Crafty frowned. 'Bertha won't like that –'

'Tough! She can like it or lump it. I'm not going to take any chances, and neither are you. Right – take us to her!'

Lick swivelled Crafty's chair round until he was facing the silver gate, and then he began to concentrate on Bertha. Lick waited, her foot close to the pedal that worked the guillotine. She didn't often do that, but Crafty knew she was right to be extra cautious this time. Things were growing more and more dangerous. Anything might be waiting for them within the Shole – maybe even Viper.

The dark swirling clouds cleared and Crafty could see the edge of the bog. It looked extremely calm. He stepped through the gate and Lick followed, cradling her crossbow. She waited in front of the blue circle while he walked slowly forward.

As he reached the bog, there was a disturbance on the surface to his right. Seconds later the crowned top of Bertha's head broke through as far as her nose, her green eyes staring up at him. Then her whole head emerged and she gave him a warm smile, which instantly reassured him. Lick's reference to the Grim Ploughman and the White Lady had unnerved him more than he'd realized. The thought that Bertha might suddenly transform from a friend into something malignant and dangerous was terrible. The smile had reminded him that they were friends: she had saved him from certain death in the past. If only she could save Lucky.

Bertha stepped out of the bog, mud sliding off her body until not a speck remained. Her hair was dark and glossy, as if freshly washed. Crafty saw her glance over to where Lick stood guard in front of the gate, and her expression became wary.

'It is good to see you, Crafty. But is there danger nearby? I sense no threat at all, but your friend Lick is armed,' she said, frowning.

'She is just being cautious,' he told her. 'We aren't always aware of the presence of danger like you are. Lick likes to be prepared.'

'Then what is it you want? Does she wish to ask me further questions?' Bertha asked.

Crafty felt uncomfortable as he remembered that the last session of questioning had ended very suddenly when Lick had asked Bertha if she ever heard voices. Bertha hadn't replied. She had simply left – he hoped it wasn't because she was hiding the truth.

'There are no questions this time, but I want to ask for your help, Bertha. The castle has finally been engulfed by the Shole and my friend Lucky has been hurt. A creature grabbed him by the shoulder and its talons punctured his flesh. He became ill and seemed to recover, but now he's deteriorated further and is burning up with a fever. The poison is spreading to his heart and our doctor can do nothing. He's dying. Is there any way you can help?' Crafty asked.

'Which type of creature hurt him?' Bertha wanted to know.

'It was the tall bargeman – the one who leads a horse and barge along the canal.'

Bertha frowned. 'I know a little about that creature – it's best to keep your distance and avoid meddling in his affairs. To heal a wound that *he* has inflicted will not be easy. Still, I will try. You will have to come with me as I search for a cure. I have medicines, but some are so potent that they are as likely to kill as to cure. All would certainly kill an ordinary human, but as both you and Lucky are Fey you will have a greater tolerance. I need to check for harmful side effects.'

Crafty didn't like the sound of that, but how else could he help Lucky? 'Where will we go?' he asked.

Bertha pointed downwards. 'Below, to my home in the bog.'

Crafty looked at her doubtfully. 'Will it be safe for me? How will I breathe if I'm covered in mud?' he asked.

Bertha looked hurt. 'I would never knowingly lead you into danger, Crafty. Don't you trust me?' she said.

Even after Lick's warnings he *did* still trust Bertha, though none of what she wanted him to do sounded good. But if this was his only chance of saving Lucky, he had to take it.

Crafty turned back to face Lick. 'Bertha might be able to help!' he shouted. 'I have to go down into the bog. Wait for me. I'll be back soon.'

He saw the look of dismay on Lick's face, but before she could say anything he turned back to face Bertha. She held out her hand; it felt very warm in his.

'Keep up with me, Crafty,' she told him.

They headed into the bog. After three steps Crafty knew that there was nothing solid underneath him to support his weight, but still they continued.

'Make sure your mouth is closed – it's best if you hold your nose and close your eyes,' Bertha advised him.

He just had time to do that before they took their seventh step together. It was like falling off a cliff. They plunged into the bog feet first.

Crafty's heart lurched, and darkness sucked him down.

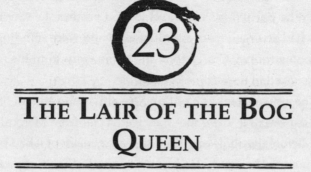

THE LAIR OF THE BOG QUEEN

Crafty's heart was in his mouth, and his fear increased with each second of their fall. They continued to hurtle downwards, and he felt himself enclosed by warm, oddly frictionless mud that did nothing to slow their descent. He was still gripping his nose and holding his breath.

His eyes were squeezed tightly shut and he could feel the mud sliding across his face. How could Bertha's home be so deep? he wondered. They were still falling, and the need to breathe was growing stronger with every second. But Crafty knew that if he let go of his nose, the mud would surge up his nostrils and down into his lungs. He began to feel close to panic and gripped Bertha's hand even more tightly.

But then, thankfully, they began to slow down, until at last they were hardly moving. Finally they came to a halt and seemed to be standing on something solid. Bertha took three steps forward, pulling Crafty with her. He felt the mud sliding off him, and then there was cool air on his face. When he opened his eyes and looked around, he saw that they had emerged from a wall of mud and were standing in a gloomy tunnel. Crafty took his hand away from his nose and sucked in a welcome breath.

The air was dank but not unpleasant, with a hint of brine and seaweed. He knew that they weren't far from Morecambe Bay. Before the Shole engulfed this area, much of it had been sea marsh. He could also hear the sound of running water. His eyes were already beginning to adjust to the low light, and when he looked down he saw that he was standing in a shallow stream that came halfway up his boots.

Bertha turned to look at him. 'Come, Crafty!' she said. 'It's not far now.'

As he followed her along the tunnel, the light began to improve and he could see more of his surroundings. And what he saw he found disturbing.

The water that ran past his boots was a light shade of red; it looked like diluted blood being washed from a wound. He also sensed movement beneath his feet and saw that the whole tunnel was expanding and contracting as if taking slow, shallow breaths. It was as if the bog was alive.

Looking down at his clothes, he saw that his greatcoat, which should have been plastered with mud, was only slightly darker in colour, as if damp. The mud had fallen away just as easily as it did from Bertha. It was clearly not ordinary mud.

The tunnel narrowed and ended in a stout wooden door. Bertha opened it, and Crafty followed her through into a large open space. He stared about him, attempting to make sense of the structure.

The outer walls were constructed of wooden palings, tall split tree trunks. If built on the land above, he would have called it a stockade. Crafty wondered if it was the kind of defensive structure that the Segantii, Bertha's tribe, had used long ago. It had walkways and ramparts, but they were built against a solid wall of mud. And above, where there would have been sky, was a cavernous roof made of solid rock. Was all this to prevent other aberrations from moving through the mud to invade Bertha's lair? Crafty wondered. Was she under assault by enemies?

'Why do you need such a large space, Bertha?' he asked.

'It is similar to the one where I lived when I was alive. The walls are a defence to keep things out. The space is to give me room to store my collection,' she replied.

The light was brighter than ever, but it had no single source – or at least not one that Crafty could see. It was as if the air itself glowed with a soft lambent radiance.

Within the stockade were a number of large square buildings also made of logs. Bertha led him towards the smallest of these, right in the centre of the space. Inside there was no furniture, but the walls were lined with wooden cupboards. This must be where she kept the things she collected.

'Sit down,' Bertha said.

The floor was covered in yellow straw, but it was dry, and Crafty made himself as comfortable as he could, sitting cross-legged.

Bertha spent a few moments searching through the cupboards, then sat down opposite him. She was carrying three small earthen bottles, each fitted with a cork, and a small glass jug containing a pale blue liquid.

'These are the only three concoctions I have that might cure your friend without doing irreversible harm,' she told him, indicating the bottles. 'Hold out your hand, palm downwards. I'm going to see how you react.'

Obediently he held out his right hand, and Bertha popped the cork out of the first bottle, then allowed a single drop of liquid to fall on to the back of it. Then her green eyes stared into his as if awaiting his reaction. She didn't have to wait long.

Crafty felt the drop make contact with his skin. For a moment it felt cool, then it quickly became hotter, until the back of his hand was burning. The pain was intense and he could hardly breathe. He cried out in agony, and would have lurched to his feet in shock, but Bertha seized his hand firmly and poured the blue liquid over it.

'Take a deep breath. The pain will ease,' she promised.

His eyes were watering, but he didn't want a tough warrior like Bertha to think that he was crying, so he took a deep breath and the pain did indeed begin to ease. Within moments it had subsided to just a dull throb.

'Your bad reaction has proved that we can't use that one. Are you ready to try the next?' she asked.

Crafty nodded, though rather warily.

'Let's use your other hand,' Bertha suggested.

He lifted his left hand and she tried a drop from the second small bottle. This was worse than the first! Immediately the liquid began to bubble, and steam rose up from the back of his hand. Crafty cried out in pain and tried to rub at his skin, but Bertha was even quicker to administer the blue liquid. Within moments he was breathing normally again and the pain had eased to almost nothing.

'I'm sorry, Crafty, but this is the last chance,' she said, easing the cork out of the third small bottle. 'Let's use your right hand again . . .'

Crafty held his breath. *Please let this be all right!* he said to himself. If this was as bad as the others, then there was no hope for Lucky.

The liquid felt cool, like the first drop of rain from a shower at the end of a hot, sultry day. He cringed, anticipating the pain, waiting for the burning to begin, but all he felt was a faint hot itching. It wasn't pleasant, but it was bearable.

'It's all right!' he cried happily.

'Are you sure? Don't forget there will be more than that one drop applied to your friend's skin . . .'

'There's a bit of an itch and the back of my hand feels hot, that's all. And that could be a reaction to the first bottle, couldn't it?' Crafty said hopefully.

Bertha nodded and gave him a smile. 'It could. So this one should be safe,' she said, pushing the cork back in and handing the bottle to Crafty.

He thanked her and put it in his greatcoat pocket.

'The medicine is not meant to be taken internally – he mustn't drink it. It should be rubbed into the wound and on to his chest over his heart. It should be done three times, with an hour between each dose. That should combat the poison.'

'You really think it will work?' Crafty asked.

Bertha shrugged. 'I hope so, but we can't know for sure. All three would have counteracted the poison, but the side effects of the other two would have killed your friend. You should get back. The sooner the treatment begins, the better.'

She led the way out across the stockade towards the door. Soon they were walking back down the tunnel. Then, suddenly, Bertha paused.

'I have something to tell you, Crafty. Something you won't like, but must be said . . .'

She stared hard into his eyes. Her own seemed larger than ever. 'Your friend Lick asked me a question recently – one that I chose not to answer. She asked me if I heard voices inside my head.' She paused. 'The truth is, I do hear a voice. And it tells me to do things . . .'

Crafty's heart lurched inside his chest. This was terrible – it meant that Bertha might be dangerous after all – though he tried not to panic.

'What does the voice tell you to do?' he asked, his own voice coming out as little more than a croak.

'Earlier, when I met you on the edge of the bog, the voice told me to drag you down into the mud and kill you. It promised me that your flesh would be tender and sweet – better than anything I'd ever tasted before.'

Crafty's knees began to tremble. He suddenly felt really scared. Was it his imagination or was the light in the tunnel growing dimmer?

He was suddenly very afraid of what Bertha was about to do.

LIKE A TRAITOR

She continued to look at him intently.

'It tells me to do things I do not wish to do. So of course I refused, Crafty. You are my friend and I would never hurt a hair of your head.'

Crafty felt very relieved, but his legs were trembling – he hoped Bertha hadn't noticed.

She went on. 'But others do listen to that voice. We who dwell within the Shole – some of us listen to the voice and obey it; others go their own way and disregard what is said to them.'

Crafty nodded. He was anxious to get back to the surface and help Lucky, but there was one more thing he needed to know.

'Whose voice is it?' he asked. 'Who speaks inside your head? Do you know?'

'It is the voice of the Shole, Crafty. The Shole is alive, and it is greedy to absorb more and more life. It will not cease to expand until it covers the whole world! You are attempting to halt its progress so you must be eliminated.'

Crafty had heard something similar from the witch, Old Nell. She too had warned him that the Shole would cover the earth.

'There is a more immediate threat too,' Bertha told him. 'The voice has commanded all aberrations to attack the castle. The first wave will reach you tonight. More will come later, and it will get worse each night. You must leave now – warn everyone and save your friend.'

Crafty was shocked. What about Donna and Titch? he wondered. They were still in their cell. Would they obey the summons and try to kill anyone they came into contact with? His mother would also receive that same command. Would she be able to resist like Bertha had?

But even as he considered these questions, Bertha was seizing his hand and turning to face the tunnel wall, warning him to close his eyes and hold his nose. He did so, and immediately they took three steps forward into the wall of mud. Crafty felt it close around him, and they lurched upwards.

Soon they were rising up through the bog, more slowly than on their descent, and as the moments passed his need for air became increasingly desperate. But just as he was beginning to panic again, he felt his face break through the surface, and there was cool air on his face. As he stepped forward, still holding Bertha's hand, he sucked in a deep breath and opened his eyes. He could see the blue circle of the gate directly ahead, and an anxious Lick standing in front of it, still cradling her crossbow.

'Farewell, Crafty,' Bertha said to him. 'Take care. You should abandon the castle and retreat further into the world beyond the Shole. It is coming, and it is unstoppable.'

With that, she stepped back into the bog and was lost to sight. He knew that she had given him good advice, but he couldn't leave the castle. And he hoped that she was wrong about the Shole.

As he headed towards Lick, he saw a mixture of anger and relief on her face.

'I thought I'd never see you again!' she cried. 'I've been waiting for you for hours – I was just about to give up.'

How could that be true? Crafty stared at her in astonishment. 'It seemed like only five minutes to me,' he replied. 'Surely I've not been gone that long.'

But then he looked around. There was much less light than previously. It seemed to be late in the afternoon.

'You took a terrible risk there!' Lick accused him. 'You put yourself – and me – in danger!'

'I know, and I'm sorry, but it was worth it,' he replied, reaching into his greatcoat pocket and pulling out the small bottle. 'This should cure Lucky!'

They stepped back through the gate, and Crafty gave Lick a quick summary of all that had happened – especially what Bertha had said about the voice in her head and the attack on the castle.

Lick looked grim. 'Right – I'll take this to Lucky's doctor right now and get his treatment started. I can't say I'm totally happy about using it when we know that Bertha might be influenced by the voice, but it's been tested on you – and it really is Lucky's only hope. Then I'll report to Captain Clayton and the Duke about the other things you told me. Stay here!'

With that, Lick left the room and Crafty settled down to wait. So much had happened since the Shole had engulfed the castle that morning, and he was glad to be able to relax for a few moments.

But as soon as he did so, new worries crowded into his head. The sensible part of him knew that Bertha's final piece of advice had been sound. It made little sense to attempt to defend the castle now that it was engulfed. How could they hope to win? If they stayed here, many of them would surely die – and they were the last of the Fey who were trained to do this kind of work. Wasn't it better to preserve these lives? Surely a much better tactic would be to retreat into the Daylight World and continue the fight from Clitheroe Castle. So why didn't they?

Then Crafty became aware of a terrible thought lying deep within him. It made him feel awful just to consider it, but he couldn't get it out of his head: the only reason they couldn't leave the castle was because the Duke was bound to it by his roots. That was the real reason why they had to stay. If they left him, they would all be free to save themselves.

Just thinking this made Crafty feel like a traitor, but the idea wouldn't go away.

It was well over an hour before Lick returned. She greeted Crafty with a smile.

'You were reckless and took a big risk, but I'm glad to say it paid off,' she said, sitting down. 'The doctor has just administered the second treatment, and Lucky is already responding. His fever is down, his vital signs are much improved and he is seemingly out of danger.'

Crafty grinned back at her. 'That's great! It was a risk, but I knew that Bertha would help us. Still, there were a few scary moments – especially when she told me about the voice in her head ordering her to kill me.'

'Hmm, indeed. I know you've already given me the general outline, but could you now go over the whole thing again in detail?' Lick asked him. 'Describe *everything* you saw and *precisely* what Bertha said.'

Crafty was happy to do just that and he left nothing out. He knew that Lick had an amazing brain and might learn things that he would have missed. As he spoke, she made detailed notes.

When he'd finished, she thanked him and they sat in silence for a while as she digested the new information and continued to jot things down. Meanwhile Crafty was thinking about his new fears for his mother – and Donna and Titch, who would almost certainly be seen as threats. Any chance of getting them released was probably over – but he hoped they wouldn't be hurt.

'The crucial piece of information is that Bertha is able to resist the voice,' Lick said at last. 'If only we knew why she's able to do that . . .'

She didn't elaborate but got to her feet. 'Come on. We have to be in the Throne Room in five minutes. The Duke is going to make an important speech and he wants everybody there.'

Crafty followed her to what she described as the Throne Room. He'd never heard it called this before but realized that it was an accurate description. As they entered, he smiled secretly to himself. He looked up at the Duke; his 'throne' was really a giant plant pot covered by a large purple cloth that was fastened around his waist and swept down to the floor. On the one hand Crafty saw that it was funny; on the other, it was tragic and sad. The Duke would never walk again. He could never leave this place because his roots had grown down through the base of that huge soil-filled pot, deep into the foundations of the castle. He was only a young man – it all seemed very cruel.

About fifty people were standing facing the Duke, whispering to each other. Many of them wore white coats – either boffins or departmental representatives, all of them Fey. Crafty recognized one of them as the ginger-haired Doon; he was wearing his usual grin as he muttered something to a colleague.

Doon worked in Forensics. He was a few years older than Crafty, a Scot from the north, far beyond Lancashire – though Crafty hadn't known he was Fey. He was an acquaintance of Lucky's and they'd once met him down in the city, where he'd given them information about a killer who'd supposedly come through the gates.

That situation had been bad enough, but their present predicament was much worse. They faced an attack by perhaps hundreds of aberrations who were coming to massacre everybody in the castle.

Crafty saw the couriers and Captain Clayton in front of him. He had never seen so many gathered together in one place.

As he and Lick took a place on the right, he noticed that the room seemed gloomier than ever and wondered if that was because it was now early evening and, somewhere overhead, far above the Shole, the sun had already begun its decline. He'd rarely been in the Shole after dark because it was then at its most dangerous. Everyone in the castle would soon be living through those perilous hours of darkness.

Directly behind the throne was the chained-off area, where the large new silver gate would materialize, linking the castle with the Daylight World. *That could be an escape route . . .* thought Crafty. But once again he tried to block that treasonous thought. Why did he keep thinking such things? It wasn't right.

The Duke raised his right hand for silence, and an immediate hush fell upon the gathering. Then he began to speak. His voice was low but it filled the room, and each of his words was crystal clear.

'A few of you are already aware of what I am about to say, but for the majority this will come as a shock. I'm afraid there is no way to mitigate that. The Shole has always been a terrible threat, but now we face unprecedented danger.

'Not only are we engulfed – swallowed by its foul miasma – but we have just learned that a large number of aberrations are moving towards the castle, intending to kill every last one of us. The first wave will reach us tonight, but even if we survive the dark night ahead, that will not be the end. On each subsequent night more will arrive, and the danger of being overwhelmed will increase each time.

'But we will resist and defeat our enemies. We *must*! And I am sure that your courage and skills will carry us to victory. The coming night will be divided into two watches so that half our company is on guard while the other sleeps. But when the attack begins, we must all fight. Each of you will receive your orders from Captain Clayton. Now – try to enjoy your evening meal and be sure to fortify yourselves for what lies ahead.'

The speech was over, and everyone bowed to the Duke and began to move towards the far door in silence. Crafty and Lick followed, and soon found themselves in a communal dining room with a single long table, where they sat down opposite each other. Plates and cutlery were already laid, and soon servers came down the table ladling out potatoes, carrots and thick slices of beef topped with a rich steaming gravy. In spite of the circumstances, Crafty reflected, they still had food on their plates and were able to eat in comfort. That was the result of good planning, concentrating the vital facilities of the castle into the Ducal Chambers, which could be defended. But Crafty wondered how long this could last. If they did manage to hold off the aberrations, food might soon have to be rationed.

Wasting no time, they both tucked in. Around them, everybody was silent, too busy filling their mouths to chat. All they could hear was the clatter of knives and forks. It was a long time since Crafty had eaten and he was really hungry. The food was just what he needed.

'This is delicious!' said Lick. 'I pity the poor Duke . . .'

'Why?' he asked.

'He can't eat like we do. He gets his nutrition from the soil. All he can do is wet his lips with water.'

Crafty had never really thought about him not being able to enjoy proper food. It made him feel even guiltier about the treasonous thoughts he'd had.

The Duke was an inspirational and resourceful leader. Despite Crafty's misgivings, perhaps it was right to make a stand here. Lancaster Castle was not only a redoubt and the centre of the fight against the Shole, it had symbolic importance.

So long as the castle held, they could surely prevail in the struggle ahead.

A SCREAM OF TERROR

'Tonight we'll be patrolling the castle in pairs,' Lick told Crafty when they'd finished eating.

'Me and you together then?' he asked.

She shook her head. 'No, I have something else I need to do tonight. I think you'll be paired with one of the couriers.'

'I wish my father were here – then I could patrol with him. That would make sense . . .'

'Sorry, Crafty, but that would make no sense at all. He's the last courier they'd ever pair you with. Think about it: in dangerous situations your father would be concerned about protecting you. That could affect his judgement.'

Crafty nodded. Lick was right. His father would protect him at any cost.

People were leaving the dinner table. 'You need to come back to my office and collect your bow,' Lick told him as she pushed her chair back under the table.

Crafty followed her to her room and picked up his crossbow. She also gave him another pouch of bolts, showing him how to attach it to the weapon.

Then she sat down in the chair facing the silver gate. 'I'm going to try a few things with the gate, check out some of the locators within the castle,' she explained. 'Good luck, Crafty. See you in the morning when we've got the first night over with.'

He nodded at her and smiled. She was trying to appear confident, but he could read the nervousness and uncertainty in her expression. There was no guarantee that either of them would be alive come morning.

With that grim thought, Crafty returned to the Throne Room to report to Captain Clayton.

The captain was waiting by the door. The chamber was almost empty, but for a couple of armed couriers at the foot of the steps to the throne and a boffin talking to the Duke.

'Sorry I'm late, sir,' Crafty said to him.

'You're not late, Benson – but another thirty seconds and you would have been,' the captain told him sternly. 'The others have been paired off and gone on patrol. The rest have been told to sleep until the second watch. As you're the last, you'll come with me.'

With that, the captain turned on his heel and led the way along the corridor at a furious pace. Crafty struggled to keep up. He noted that the captain wasn't carrying a crossbow but wore a thick leather belt over his greatcoat; two scabbards held long swords.

Soon it was clear that they were heading up to the battlements. As they climbed the stone steps, Crafty could hear screeching and shrieking from various points along the walls – guards who had been changed by the Shole into flappers. None of them would last very long, embedded in stone rather than living wood. This time he couldn't make out any words – just sad cries of pain and distress. He wondered how much the changed guards remembered of their former lives. As he peered through the gloom of the Shole, he saw at least a dozen, most flapping their limbs – but then he glimpsed one that wasn't moving. As he got closer, he at first assumed that it was some new type of aberration. Vaguely human in shape, it was covered in spines, like a hedgehog.

Then Crafty realized the truth. The spines were arrows fired by couriers irritated by its disturbing cries. They had silenced it forever.

High on the battlements, the air was colder than ever and it was almost fully dark, with just a faint glow in the misty sky over Morecambe Bay to the west.

'Do we know how far the Shole has expanded this time?' Crafty asked.

'As a matter of fact, we do. A courier went out to check. It's reached just north of the river.'

Crafty opened his mouth to ask another question. He wondered how many of the Castle Corpus had survived. Were the Chief Mancer and all the heads of departments dead? He had never been exactly friendly with the Chief

Mancer, but he hoped he was alive somewhere. However, the captain put a finger to his lips. 'That's enough questions. It's more important to use our ears rather than our voices!' he hissed, and led the way towards the southern battlements, where they had a view over the town towards the canal.

Crafty was surprised to find that they could see the canal again. When the castle was still in the Daylight World and it had been engulfed by the Shole, it had been invisible; now it seemed to be glowing slightly.

'Is the canal shining, sir, or is it my imagination?' asked Crafty, unable to keep his curiosity at bay.

'Yes, Benson, but keep your voice down! It *is* glowing. One theory is that it's because minute organisms have been changed by the Shole to emit light – although the canal doesn't glow every night. It's a puzzle for our boffins to solve.

'Now, I'm sure your young eyes are better than mine,' he continued, 'so look down into the city between the canal and the castle. Tell me if you see anything odd – any movement – anything at all.'

Visibility in the Shole was never good; tonight coils of mist obscured parts of the labyrinth of cobbled streets below. Crafty started on the near bank of the canal and let his gaze cross from left to right, then right to left, scanning the streets, moving up the hill towards the castle walls. There were glows behind some of the windows – probably just torches that hadn't been extinguished. They'd burn out soon, leaving only dark rooms where the dead lay.

Suddenly he thought he saw movement. He stared at the place, but saw nothing more. 'I thought something moved on the corner of Blades Street, but I was probably mistaken,' he said.

'Maybe you did see something and it ducked out of sight,' the captain suggested. 'Don't forget that not everything down there will have been killed outright. A few people and animals will be in the early stages of change. But what we are *really* looking for is more general movement – several things advancing towards the castle together. Keep looking . . .'

Crafty did as he was ordered, and twice more saw movement; once he glimpsed a flickering light in a window. At last Captain Clayton was satisfied that the enemy were not yet in sight and they moved towards the north-facing battlements. Danger was unlikely to come from this direction, but the captain explained that they might be encircled before the attack began – that way the aberrations could approach from all sides.

Crafty was ordered to search again, but again saw nothing of significance.

Suddenly Captain Clayton turned towards him and said: 'I've heard quite a lot about you, Benson – mostly good things.'

Crafty looked up at him in surprise.

The captain continued. 'I'm aware of the part you played in helping your father to fight off that aberration on the canal bank, and that it's you we should thank for the timely warning about the attack tonight. You also found and helped to rescue your father and another courier.'

Crafty hadn't expected to receive such praise, but he knew he couldn't take all the credit. 'It's really to Bertha, the Bog Queen, that we all owe thanks,' he replied.

The captain nodded, but seemed displeased by Crafty's comment. 'In my opinion, all aberrations should be wiped off the face of the earth. But maybe we should make an exception for that bog creature,' he said with a frown. 'She's helped us before, but this time I hear you took a great risk and went down deep into her lair. So don't be modest. As well as giving us a timely warning, you've saved the life of young Proudfoot. I think you might well have the makings of a courier. Think it over. You might be better employed joining our ranks and training for that rather than grubbing for gate mancers.'

The captain's talk of wiping all aberrations off the face of the earth made Crafty fear for his mother and Donna. And he wasn't sure he wanted to stop working with Lick and Lucky and become a courier. He thought it unlikely that he would be released anyway. Gate grubs were in very short supply. Fey were rare, and few of them were able to use a silver gate.

The rest of the watch passed without any sign of the expected attack. It was very cold up on the battlements and, despite the thickness of his greatcoat, Crafty became chilled to the bone. At last Captain Clayton dismissed him, sending him down to Dormitory Two, which was just beyond the kitchens that had recently been installed in the Ducal Chambers.

As he walked along the lower corridor, Crafty came across Doon. They stopped and greeted each other.

'I didn't know you were Fey, Doon,' Crafty said.

'Well, I must be, laddie, otherwise I'd just be a rusty bucket full of slime and a stained sack of bones by now,' he replied with a grin. 'Either that or I'd be running across the ceiling with eight legs and a gob full of razor-sharp teeth!'

Crafty grinned back at his joke.

'Where's your friend Lucky?' Doon asked.

'He was hurt in the Shole. He's been very ill, but he's getting better now,' Crafty told him.

'Aye, it's a dangerous job ye young grubs do. I'm sorry to hear that he was hurt. Pass on my best wishes when next ye see him,' Doon said, turning and continuing on his way.

Crafty went down two flights of stairs and passed the door to the little kitchen, where a couple of cooks in white aprons were at work. They would be preparing breakfast, he thought, feeling hungry again.

He soon found the dormitory. The first watch had just left and he was one of a dozen new arrivals scrambling for a bed – except that they weren't the kind of beds he was used to.

He was looking at a row of hammocks, each strung by rope between two wooden poles. A sailor would have been at home, but Crafty could see the others having problems. He watched a man struggling to climb into a hammock, which immediately dumped him out; he fell to the floor with a groan. And even if Crafty could successfully climb into one, were there any left?

The sergeant with the moustache came across to intercept him. 'Over there!' he barked, pointing to the hammock at the end next to the wall. 'Take off your coat and boots but don't bother getting undressed. You might be summoned to fight at any time.'

It was gloomy in the dormitory, and very cold, so Crafty kept his coat on and just took off his boots, placing his crossbow next to them. He managed to clamber into the hammock and lay on his back while it swung from side to side before settling down. It was quite comfortable, but his head was full of worries about his mother and he couldn't sleep – but suddenly he had a new concern.

As one of the Fey, he would hopefully develop gifts that might help him fight the Shole. But it seemed that the ability to hear a flapper and a shadow stain was rare. He was able to understand two types of aberration. What if he heard another, more dangerous voice? What if the voice that was commanding aberrations to attack the castle tried to bend him to its will? Would he be able to resist?

Bertha had resisted. He would have to do the same. He would have to find the strength from somewhere.

At last he sank down into sleep, and was soon plunged into a series of dreams. The first one took him back to a happier time, before the Shole had engulfed their house. He was living there with his mother and father and his two older brothers, Brock and Ben. It was dark, and he was standing in the back doorway, watching the glow of his father's pipe as his parents sat out in the garden. They were holding hands and whispering to each other. He knew they had really loved each other, and he had been happy because they were happy. He felt loved and wanted in the dream. It felt good to be alive.

Suddenly the scene changed: it was daylight, and the dream became a nightmare. Crafty was playing in the garden with his dog, a Border collie called Sandy. He threw a stick over the hedge and his dog leaped after it. Then his father came to the door, shouting and pointing. The dark wall of the Shole was racing towards the house.

Everything grew dark, and now he began dreaming about Old Nell again. He was very close to her glowing shape as she swung on the end of the rope, her eyes bulging like two angry boils that were about to burst. As she twisted towards him, she spluttered and coughed. Then she spoke, her voice hardly more than a croak.

'Listen well! Heed Old Nell's warning! The voice of the Shole commands us all to attack the castle and kill anyone who dwells inside. Fanged creatures have obeyed and move towards ye now. The first will arrive in about a minute. Wake up and prepare to fight for your life! Unless ye flee, your days are numbered, boy. Don't say I ain't warned ye!'

Crafty woke up sweating and trembling at the witch's warning. He thought he heard footsteps walking away from his hammock, but when he looked there was nobody there.

Why did he keep dreaming about the witch? he wondered. What use was a warning when you couldn't do anything about it? He had been ordered to stay where he was.

In the dream the witch had repeated Bertha's warning. The idea of the voice commanding aberrations to attack the castle was a worry, but Bertha had forewarned him about that. No – he was worried about those at risk. What would happen to Donna and Titch? They were still inside their cell. Would they obey the summons and try to kill anyone they came into contact with?

His mind returned to his dream: when his home was engulfed by the Shole, he had made it back into the house, but his dog hadn't. When he'd first used a silver gate, Sandy had bounded towards him, terribly changed: she was far larger and had those three rows of razor-sharp teeth. However, she hadn't hurt Crafty; she still remembered him. Was she still out there now, racing towards the castle with the horde of aberrations?

Worse, much worse, his own mother was out in the Shole. He was still tormented by the memory of her voice speaking to him from the cupboard in the cellar – telling him that she was changed and didn't want to be seen – and that she never wanted to see either Crafty or his father again.

Don't you ever come back. I've changed so much that even your poor dead brothers don't know me. Even they are afraid of me. Go now, while you still can. I'll always remember you.

Bertha had resisted the voice's command, but would his mother be able to do the same? If she was part of the attack, she might be killed by one of the defenders. He might even find himself confronting his own mother!

And what about Brock and Ben? They were dead – they'd been buried in the cellar, their graves marked with huge stones. Of course, Bertha had swamped the cellar with mud to stop his mother going back there and being ambushed – and if they were dead, surely they wouldn't care. But all the same, Crafty didn't like the idea.

He turned to face the wall, but the hammock began to swing violently, threatening to tip him out. He lay back slowly, but he knew that, after his nightmare, he would find it hard to get back to sleep.

Crafty could hear the man in the next hammock snoring. The dormitory was dimly lit by a single torch in a wall bracket near the door. He glanced carefully over his shoulder, causing the hammock to rock again. The sergeant with the moustache was standing in the doorway. No doubt, if danger threatened, he would be the one to wake everybody up and organize the castle's defences.

It was then that Crafty heard a noise. It didn't come from anywhere in the long dormitory. It came from somewhere there should be *no* sound – from beyond the stone wall next to him. They were well below ground level and he was facing the outer wall of the castle. There should be only soil and rock beyond it. Yet there was a noise, and it was getting louder.

It was a sort of grinding, vibrating noise that set his teeth on edge, as if something abrasive was moving along the outer wall, scraping against the stone. Could nobody else hear it? The man next to him was still snoring; the others were probably asleep as well. And maybe the sergeant was too far away?

But what *could* move out there? What could possibly push its way through soil and rock?

Now the noise was fading, as if its source was getting further and further away.

Should he get up and tell the sergeant? Crafty wondered. The man would think he was crazy. But what if he didn't tell him and something happened? He would be responsible. His conscience forced him to get out of the hammock. He did it clumsily, almost losing his balance and falling over, then headed towards the doorway.

The sergeant saw him coming and met him halfway. 'Nobody is to leave this room – not until the captain says so. If you're looking for a chamber pot, son, there's a line of them over there,' he said, pointing and giving a little smirk.

'I heard something moving on the other side of the wall,' Crafty said, also pointing, but in the other direction.

The sergeant stroked his moustache, shaking his head and smiling in a condescending manner. 'We're below ground. What you heard was just in your dreams, son. Get yourself back to bed.'

'I wasn't dreaming,' Crafty insisted. 'I could hear something scraping along the outside of the wall. It was moving that way, towards the kitchens.'

The sergeant's face lost its supercilious smile and grew annoyed. He opened his mouth to tell Crafty off – but he never got the chance.

There was a sudden thud, and then a boom that made the floor shake.

It was followed almost immediately by a high, thin scream of terror.

It came from the direction of the kitchens.

THE GIANT GREY WORM

That first scream was followed by another. Something was clearly happening in the kitchens. Something bad.

The sergeant stepped past Crafty. 'Rise and shine!' he shouted at the top of his voice. 'Boots and coats on. We've got trouble!'

Crafty ran back to his hammock, tugged on his boots and laced them up. He checked that his dagger was still in his pocket, then picked up his crossbow and ran back to stand in front of the sergeant. Only one person had beaten him to it – a courier.

Another cry came from the direction of the kitchens. The sergeant glanced at the rest of the men, who were still getting dressed. One was still struggling to get out of his hammock. The sergeant shook his head and rolled his eyes.

'We can't wait,' he said. Then he shouted to the other men, 'Follow us to the kitchens! Be armed and ready!'

Turning to Crafty and the courier, he said, 'Let's go!' and they followed him out. The two cooks were no longer in the small room where the vegetables were prepared, and the door leading directly to the kitchen was wide open.

The sergeant readied his bow and led the way cautiously inside. The place seemed deserted. Had the two cooks run away? Crafty wondered. Was it they who had cried out? What had scared them?

Directly ahead were draining surfaces stacked with cutlery and dishes; beyond were three large ovens, and behind them was a big empty area and what Crafty thought must be the outer wall of the castle. However, he suddenly realized that it wasn't empty at all: there was a noise from behind the furthest oven. It was a sort of slithering, scraping sound.

The sergeant led the way round behind the oven, and they saw a big hole in the wall; fragments of stone and soil were scattered across the floor. Something big had breached the stone wall. Something monstrous had just forced its way into the castle!

And it was now squirming its way into the kitchen. It looked like a giant grey worm; twelve feet of it was already clear of the hole, its segments rhythmically expanding and contracting as it oozed forward. It was covered in black lumps like huge warts.

They stared at the giant worm for a moment before something else drew their gaze. Ahead of the worm, a nightmarish figure was heading straight towards them. It was an aberration – something that had once been human.

It had two arms and two legs, but its head had been changed into something terrifying and hideous. The top, where the hair should have been, was like a shiny black shell. Below that, instead of a face, there was a mass of tentacles, bulging eyes and what looked like writhing, multi-segmented legs.

Before Crafty could even take aim with his bow, the sergeant had put an arrow straight through the creature's chest. It fell headlong, just in front of the sergeant's boots.

Suddenly Crafty noticed that it was wearing a white apron. His brain struggled to make sense of that. Surely this was one of the cooks he had seen earlier. But when a human changed into an aberration – apart from a flapper – it could take hours, days or even weeks. This was too quick. Far too quick!

Then something happened that made all three of them step back a pace. The hideous head suddenly scuttled away from its body: the cook wasn't an aberration after all. He was a victim. The back of his head was a mess, the scalp eaten down to the bone.

Crafty glanced across at the giant grey worm oozing its way into the kitchen. Its body was soft but it had managed to break through the wall – he'd heard it earlier, scraping away at the stones. All at once he realized that what he'd thought were black warts were in fact hard-shelled insects like the one that had attacked the cook, and as he watched they began to detach themselves and scuttle down on to the floor. The giant worm had merely carried them through the soil, like a horse carrying an armed warrior; in this case it was a very big horse and lots of warriors.

The aberration that had eaten the cook's scalp was now crawling towards the sergeant. Crafty aimed his bow and fired at it, but the bolt bounced off its hard carapace without doing any damage. The courier's arrow was also on target, but again had no effect.

The sergeant then showed them how he had earned his stripes. In one fluid motion he dropped his bow, realizing that it was of no use against his attacker, and drew one long sword from its scabbard. He didn't try to chop the creature in two, but pushed the point of his blade under its shell and flicked it up into the air. As it fell, he used his sword tip again – this time to impale it. Then he hurled it away so that it fell helpless on its back, legs in the air; he stabbed down hard into its soft underbelly and it lay still.

Crafty turned to see more and more aberrations dropping off the worm and scuttling towards them. The other courier stepped forward to join the sergeant, quickly proving equally skilful with his sword.

Crafty wasn't sure what part he could play. His dagger was far shorter than a sword and would bring his arm within reach of legs and tentacles. His bow was useless against those hard shells, and some aberrations were evading the probing swords and heading straight for him. He was relieved when more couriers, led by Captain Clayton, appeared, wielding their swords against the aberrations.

Crafty glanced round and saw that other men from his dormitory were hanging back near the doorway. He didn't blame them – some were armed only with clubs, and surely even the stoutest of those wouldn't do much against those hard protective shells.

Then he realized that there *was* something useful he could do: his crossbow might have an effect against the worm. Its body looked soft and its big oval mouth toothless. It might not pose a threat in itself, but it could carry smaller creatures in a further attack against the castle. He couldn't see any eyes, but there were two purple circular depressions on what might have been a forehead. They were filled with short hairs that moved rhythmically. Maybe they sensed things – movements? sounds? – and helped the creature to navigate its way through the soil.

He aimed carefully and fired. His first bolt was low – about six or seven inches below his target – and disappeared into the soft grey body. The worm showed no reaction. Still, his second bolt found its mark, and this time the creature gave a terrible cry that rattled the stacked plates and cutlery. Crafty's third bolt found the second 'eye', and the creature convulsed and began to retreat into the hole it had created. Just before it disappeared from view, another arrow found the concave circle on the left side. It had been fired by someone standing just to his right. He turned and saw Lick lowering her bow.

'Good shot!' he told her.

'Almost as good as yours,' she replied.

By this time all the aberrations in sight had been dealt with. Captain Clayton and the sergeant were approaching the hole into which the giant worm had retreated. Crafty and Lick followed, stepping round the dead creatures. However, the soil had closed up behind the worm and there was nothing to see.

The captain turned and raised his hand to get the attention of those facing him. 'Well done!' he said. 'You were brave and effective. The anticipated attack on the castle came in an unexpected way, but we have repulsed it.'

Despite the captain's encouraging words, Crafty was starting to feel anxious. It was true that they had successfully defended themselves against the attack, but it had almost seemed too easy. Was that the best the Shole could do, or was this first night still not over? Were there further dangers to face before dawn?

The answer came almost immediately.

They heard a loud scream from the direction of the Throne Room. It was filled with fear and agony – a mind pushed far beyond what it could bear. It could only mean that a second attack was under way.

They raced along the corridor and up the steps towards the Throne Room. As they entered the chamber, they all stared up at the source of that terrible cry.

It was the Duke.

A Chance of Survival

His head was arched back, exposing his throat, and he was tearing at his hair and still screaming, hardly pausing for breath.

A courier was on guard at the foot of each set of steps and Crafty couldn't see any threat. On the Duke's left, a man in a white coat seemed to be trying to speak to him, but he was too distraught to reply.

'That's the doctor – the one who's treating Lucky,' Lick told him.

The doctor shook his head and began to descend the steps, leaving the Duke still screaming. Then he turned and addressed Captain Clayton.

'When it first began, the Duke was coherent,' he explained. 'That was before the pain became too severe. He said he was being eaten alive: something was chewing at his roots.'

'It could be something similar to what we've just dealt with!' said the captain, pointing to the giant container under the Duke's body. 'We need to get those panels off and check inside.'

Crafty wanted to help, but Lick placed a restraining hand on his arm. 'These people are experts. They know what they're doing,' she said. 'It's better to leave them to get on with it.'

So they watched from a distance as three men in white coats went about their business quickly and efficiently. Firstly, they removed the long purple skirt that flowed down to cover the huge container – they could now see that it was probably about eighteen feet high and twelve across. *That's a lot of soil*, Crafty thought.

Were there aberrations hidden inside it, their teeth chewing on the Duke's roots? Crafty shuddered. He looked up again and saw that the doctor was attending to the Duke again. The cries had been reduced to a pitiful whimpering peppered with occasional shrieks. No doubt he'd been given something to relieve the pain.

As he watched, Crafty saw that the giant pot was made not of terracotta but of wood shaped into curved panels that could be removed one by one. The men began to unscrew these panels, starting about a third of the way up and working downwards. As they did so, soil started to flow out on to the floor so that the tangle of white roots within became visible. One of the men worked with a spade, shovelling the soil away from the base of the pot, thus allowing more soil to descend. As more and more panels were removed, releasing a further torrent of soil, Crafty began to fear that they had made a mistake. Why had they started at the bottom? he wondered. Wasn't there a risk that the whole container would collapse, bringing the poor Duke tumbling down? But then he looked more closely and saw that the four broad vertical planks that shaped the container were linked by thin circular metal hoops. It was constructed like a gigantic barrel.

Two couriers, swords at the ready, took up positions behind the men removing the panels, ready to deal with the aberrations that were attacking the Duke.

The men worked quickly, sweat dripping from their foreheads and chins. At last they reached ground level and halted to discuss the situation with the captain. Crafty could see that the roots went deeper, right down through the floor, and a terrible thought came into his head. The bottom of the container was now empty of soil, and so far not one of the insect-like aberrations had been found.

The Duke had once told Crafty that his roots went very deep – right down beyond the foundations of the castle. What if this was where the aberrations were attacking him? How could anyone possibly get down there and deal with them all?

He told Lick his fears, and she nodded and went to talk to the captain. After a few moments she returned to Crafty's side.

'The captain thinks it's a possibility, but first they are going to remove a few panels further up, just in case some of the little beasts are hiding there.'

It took another hour before the captain was satisfied that the container was empty. He talked to the doctor, and then to Lick. By then the Duke's whimpers had returned to high-pitched, agonized cries.

Many of those who, drawn by the Duke's screams, had gathered in the Throne Room now quietly slipped away. Crafty didn't blame them. It was hard to be in the presence of someone who was in so much pain. The only people now in attendance, apart from Lick, the doctor and Crafty, were a few of the couriers.

Suddenly, despite the risk, Crafty knew that there was only one way to put an end to it. The risk to the Duke's life would be great but there was no other way. On impulse, he went over to join the discussion. 'Sir, I think I know what must be done,' he told the captain.

Captain Clayton raised his eyebrows. 'I'm glad somebody does . . .' he said.

Crafty took a deep breath. 'We must cut off the Duke's roots at floor level and free him.'

'Impossible!' cried the doctor. 'The shock would kill him!'

'It might,' agreed Crafty. 'That's a risk. But I think he is probably dying anyway – being eaten alive by those aberrations. At least this way he might have a chance.'

'Benson, I know you were there when the Duke was freed from the Shole,' said the captain. 'He survived what you did then. But this situation is very different.'

Crafty nodded, glancing at the place where the tangle of roots disappeared into the ground. 'Yes, sir, we dug around the roots to release them, and any that we cut through accidentally were very small. These are thicker but, providing we don't sever the central taproot, there is a chance that the Duke could survive. My mother sometimes did the same with plants. She said they were very resilient.'

'The taproot may go deep underground,' said the captain.

'It may and it may not,' Crafty replied. 'It's at the centre, hidden by the other roots, and we can't tell until we cut them away.'

'I will *not* be responsible for this madness!' the doctor protested.

'Extreme situations call for extreme measures,' said Captain Clayton, glaring at him. 'Could you administer a strong dose of medicine – one sufficient to render the Duke unconscious?'

'I could, but in his weakened condition that could pose another threat to his life.'

'Then do it!' the captain commanded. 'I will take full responsibility.'

Shaking his head as if what he was instructed to do was crazy, the doctor picked up his black leather bag and climbed the steps.

'I'll go and get what we need,' Lick said, heading towards her office.

Soon after the doctor had administered the medicine, the Duke stopped screaming and the Throne Room fell silent. Crafty, the captain and the other couriers waited uneasily for Lick to return.

She soon came back carrying two sharp-bladed pruners similar to the ones Crafty had used to free the Duke in the Shole. She handed one to Crafty and, without a word, they knelt side by side and set to work snipping through the roots, as close to the floor as possible.

At first, they worked slowly and carefully but soon speeded up as they realized the scale of the task at hand. At last they had cut through the outer roots and pushed them aside to reveal the heart of the root system. Crafty gave a sigh of relief and Lick smiled hopefully. They could see the thick central taproot, which stopped several feet short of the floor.

'We don't need to cut through the taproot to free the Duke,' Crafty said, looking over his shoulder at the captain.

The Duke had a chance of survival.

As Crafty and Lick were working, a large blue circle had appeared in the chained-off area. The new silver gate was finally working. It was three times larger than the ones Crafty had previously worked with. Now the captain approached it and began to talk to the man standing there within the gate. Crafty saw that it was Ginger Bob, the Chief Mancer.

He was very pleased and relieved to find that the Chief Mancer had survived. Despite his pomposity, Crafty liked him and recognized the vital contribution he had made to the resistance to the Shole.

But, as he watched, the gate suddenly winked out. The captain shook his head and frowned. He returned just as they were snipping through the final roots that bound the Duke to the earth.

'I'm afraid the new gate isn't stable,' he told them. 'It keeps failing – they're working hard to fix it. As soon as they do so, we're going to get the Duke out of here – back to the Daylight World. He'll have a better chance of recovery where we have more medical resources.'

Crafty and Lick stepped back to allow the couriers room to work. They tied a thick rope around the rim of the container, then threw the end over an iron beam that crossed the ceiling. Four couriers took up the strain as they carefully lowered the container on to its side. They first packed the upper part of the container with soil, then, with the doctor supporting the Duke's head and body, gently rolled it towards where the gate had been. Suddenly the blue circle reappeared and Ginger Bob beckoned them forward.

They worked quickly, probably afraid that it would wink out again. The container was too large to fit through sideways, so they then turned it until the roots were facing the gate and dragged it through.

The Duke's face was very pale. His lips were twitching as if he was trying to say something, but his eyes were closed. The ends of the severed roots had turned black; Crafty hoped they weren't dying. The tips of the roots protruding above the soil had also changed colour, but from white to a pale green. Maybe that was a good sign.

After a few moments the Duke disappeared from sight through the gate, and the doctor followed him through.

Crafty wasn't optimistic about the Duke's chances of recovery. Behind his back some people had jokingly referred to him as the Wooden Duke – though he'd insisted on staying and fighting the Shole even after the castle had become engulfed; he'd wanted to become known as the Iron Duke.

That would no longer happen. Crafty was sad about this, but there was a small part of him that was relieved. Now it made no sense for any of them to remain in the castle. Hopefully they would all go back to the Daylight World and fight the Shole from there.

However, the captain's next words put an end to that idea.

'You two go and grab something to eat – there are some sandwiches in the kitchen – and then catch up on some sleep,' he told Crafty and Lick. 'You'll need to be at your best tomorrow night. Benson, you'll be on first watch.'

Crafty glanced around and saw that the Throne Room was much lighter. What passed for morning in the Shole had finally arrived.

Tomorrow night would come soon enough, and then they would have to face another attack by aberrations.

What form would it take this time?

SOME FORM OF PLANT

Crafty and Lick left the Throne Room together. He was desperately hungry and tired, but first there was something he wanted to do.

'Do you think Lucky is well enough for a visit?' he asked.

'Why not?' said Lick with a smile. 'The doctor's not here to forbid it, and a brief visit should do him no harm. He probably needs cheering up!'

They found Lucky sitting up with a pillow at his back, wrapped in a thick dressing gown. He had a chequered wooden board spread out on his knee and was playing draughts against himself.

Crafty was delighted to see his friend looking so well. Their breath was steaming in the ice-cold air, wisps of mist coiled like snakes around the bed and strange shadows twitched in each darkened corner of the room – yet here was Lucky, playing a game as if nothing was wrong.

'I thought I'd taught you better than that,' Lick mocked him gently. 'You need chess to exercise your brain.'

'But I *am* exercising my brain!' Lucky retorted with a grin. 'I'm playing both ends of the board!' Then his gaze flicked towards their crossbows and his eyes widened. 'I like the look of those! When do I get one?'

'As soon as you're up and about. I have one waiting for you,' Lick told him.

She and Crafty sat down, and Lucky pushed the board aside. He was eager to know what had been happening. 'They tell you nothing in here,' he complained. 'The doctor says that I can get out of bed tomorrow, but I'll have to take it easy. So? What's been going on?'

Between them, Crafty and Lick gave him a run-down, concluding with the night's events. What neither of them mentioned was that Donna and Titch had returned to life and were now being held in a cell. Crafty remembered how close Lucky and Donna once were, how upset he'd been when she had been slain.

'It's definitely best not to tell him anything about Donna for now,' Lick said after they'd left the sick room.

'Great minds think alike!' Crafty joked grimly. 'Perhaps we should go and visit Donna now. It might make her feel better to see that someone's concerned about her.'

'Don't overdo it, Crafty. I'm really tired – I've been up all night and so have you. Let's grab some sandwiches and then some sleep – I'll meet you in the Throne Room in about four hours. We'll go and see her then.'

Crafty felt that Donna could do with a visit sooner rather than later, but he was exhausted and pushed his feeling of guilt aside.

They went off to their separate dormitories, and this time, as soon as Crafty had dragged himself into his hammock, he fell straight asleep.

Crafty was usually good at waking up when he wanted to, and this time was no exception. He woke to hear a dormitory full of snoring men.

There was no soap and no towels, but using water from a bucket by the door he sluiced himself down as best he could, then headed for the Throne Room to meet Lick, taking his bow with him. Even though it was still what passed for daylight in the Shole, it was always best to be prepared.

No sooner had he reached the doorway than he sensed that something strange was going on. Five people were facing someone sitting just where the Duke's container used to be. He also noticed that the blue circle of the gate was no longer there. Was it still unstable or had they just shut it down for a while?

As he approached the group – Lick, Captain Clayton and three other couriers, including the sergeant – the hairs on the back of his neck began to rise. And then he saw why. Viewed from behind, the person in the middle appeared to be the Duke. He was wearing a short green tunic that came down to the floor but he wasn't moving. And nobody was speaking. Lick and the couriers were just staring down at him.

But how could this be possible? Crafty wondered. Had they brought the Duke back already, and replanted him at floor level?

Then, as he moved to Lick's side, he saw the seated figure from the front and gasped in astonishment. A spike of fear went through his heart. It was the Duke in every detail. Yet it wasn't the Duke. It was some form of plant that had grown from the severed roots.

The eyes were closed as if in sleep, but everything looked like the Duke's, including the hair and fair beard and the hands that lay limp on the floor. But when Crafty studied him more closely, he could see that although all the colours seemed correct – from the beard to the golden buttons on the green tunic – everything was formed from some form of plant. The buttons appeared to be buds, and the tunic could never be removed because it was connected to the body like green bark. Looking at the Duke's face, Crafty realized that the skin had a greenish tinge.

'Ah, you're here, Crafty,' Lick said, turning to him. 'Well, to fill you in, it seems that a large bud started to form several hours ago and then grew at an astonishing rate until it became a replica of the Duke.'

'It's an aberration,' said Captain Clayton confidently. 'I think it best if we destroy it immediately.'

Crafty detected a faint smell that made him wrinkle his nose. It reminded him of a dead rotting horse he'd once stumbled across in a wood. Then another memory came to him – the scent of a flower grown by his mother.

'I think it does represent a possible danger, Captain,' Lick said, 'but don't forget that the Duke, whom we've just returned to the Daylight World, is also an aberration. We have a chance to learn new things about the Shole here. Surely this is too good an opportunity to miss.'

The captain didn't reply; he just continued to stare down at the aberration. 'You can have a few hours to study it, Miss Crompton-Smythe, but I want it destroyed before dark. The night will bring new threats. We don't need to be worrying about this thing as well.'

Crafty was as fascinated by the aberration as Lick; he couldn't take his eyes off it. Then, as he watched, a sudden change occurred. The plant seemed to shudder. It was cold in the Throne Room, and the braziers had burned low. The warm breath of everyone present was steaming in the cold air. Now the aberration was breathing too, but with one significant difference. Its breath had a faint green tinge to it.

Then it opened its eyes and looked at them.

29

FOUL GREEN BREATH

Everyone but the captain took a step backwards. The aberration was smiling slightly and sweeping them all with its gaze.

Then it spoke. 'Ah! It is good to feel so well again,' it said in a voice just like the Duke's. 'Step a little closer, Captain Clayton, and make your report. Tell me all that has happened while I have been indisposed.'

Crafty expected the captain to refuse. After all, just moments ago he'd been wanting the thing destroyed before nightfall. Yet now he obeyed as if it was the real Duke.

Crafty listened in astonishment as he gave a summary of all that had happened up to the point where the Duke had been taken through the gate into the Daylight World.

'I have no further use for my former body,' said the aberration when the captain had finished. 'It is an empty shell and will quickly wither away and die. Yet I will live on

235

in this strong, healthy new one. I feel reborn and ready for the fight. I would speak to you privately so that we can discuss our plans for the defence of the castle.'

'Yes, your grace,' said Captain Clayton, dismissing the others with a wave as he stepped closer to the aberration.

Crafty and Lick moved away and watched them from a distance.

'This is astonishing,' said Lick.

'Yes . . . and it's also scary. Do you think it really *could* be the Duke, regrown from his roots with all his memories and faculties intact?' Crafty asked.

Lick shrugged, but kept her eyes on the aberration. 'It's a possibility. The Shole is a strange place. Who knows what an aberration is capable of? But this could also be something else . . . Look, Crafty, I know I promised to visit Donna with you, but would you mind if I stayed here? I want to keep an eye on things.'

'Of course,' he said.

'Give her my regards, and please tell her and Titch that we hope to get them released soon.'

Crafty turned and headed for the cell where Donna was being held. As he walked, he mulled over what had just happened.

The captain had addressed the aberration as 'your grace'. This was the most formal mode of address for the Duke and, as commander of the couriers, Captain Clayton was the only one who ever really used it. It surely meant he believed that he really was talking to the Duke.

But what had changed his mind so quickly? Whatever it was, Crafty wasn't sure he felt as confident.

There was no guard in attendance outside the cells, so Crafty walked straight through the anteroom. There were four cells, but Donna and Titch were the only prisoners. Donna was in the first cell on his left; Titch was in the far one on the right. It seemed as if they'd been deliberately placed as far apart as possible. He peered through the bars into the gloom. Both appeared to be sleeping – he could see the gentle rise and fall of their chests.

All at once Crafty noticed a big bunch of keys hanging on the far wall. No doubt one of them opened the cell doors. He approached Donna's cell and called her name softly. Eventually she turned over and saw him. Her eyes widened and she came over to the bars, looking a little unsteady on her feet. He wondered if that was because her legs had been cut off by the guillotine. Maybe she would never walk properly again. Of course, being confined like this wouldn't help.

'Crafty? Have you come to let me out at last?' she said, peering up at him hopefully.

'That's up to Captain Clayton. He's in charge. Don't worry, I'm sure they'll let you out soon,' he told her.

She shook her head and gripped the bars so hard that her knuckles turned white. 'I don't think so. It's terrible in here – they're so cruel. Yesterday they didn't bring me any food at all – nothing but a few sips of water. And last night, when they thought I was asleep, I overheard two guards talking about killing me. They said I was an additional danger and they'd never risk letting me out.'

'But that's just empty talk, Donna,' Crafty reassured her. 'Anyway, it's not their decision to make. The captain will decide. And Lick says hello. We'll both ask him to let you go.'

But Donna wasn't convinced. 'The captain has a reputation – he hates aberrations, and that's what I am now. It's a wonder he hasn't had us killed already. Why don't you ask the Duke? He might listen.'

'I would if I could, but strange things have been happening, Donna . . .' Crafty told her everything that had occurred, ending with the strange puzzle of the replica Duke.

Donna shook her head. 'That can't be right,' she said. 'Surely it means there are two Dukes. And the captain now believes this new aberration is the real one? That's very strange – I wouldn't trust it at all.'

'Yes, I agree, Donna. There's something sinister about it –'

Suddenly there was the sound of a bugle, a long, sustained note, repeated twice more. It came from the direction of the Throne Room.

'That's the captain's signal. Everyone able is being summoned to the Throne Room,' Crafty told Donna.

'Does that mean there's danger?' she asked.

'It could mean that. Or he may just want to tell everyone what's going on.'

'Where's Lucky?' she wondered suddenly. 'Why hasn't he been to see me?'

'He's been ill, Donna – he was hurt in the Shole – but he's nearly better now. He'll come and see you soon.'

Donna started to cry. 'Please let me out, Crafty! Please don't leave me in here a moment longer. Look – the key to my cell is on the wall,' she said, pointing to the big bunch hanging there. 'It would only take two seconds to unlock the door!'

Crafty felt very sorry for her, but he knew he couldn't do that. 'It's too dangerous. I can't. And I don't just mean because *I'd* get into trouble. If you were loose in the castle without the captain's permission, you'd be hunted down and killed. I'm sorry, Donna, I have to go. But I'll come back as soon as the meeting is over – I promise.'

Suddenly there was a howl from the other cell, and Crafty looked across to see Titch gripping the bars tightly, his face distorted with anger.

'Out! Out! Out! I want to get out *now*!' he shrieked, his face almost purple with rage.

The boy looked demented, Crafty thought with alarm. If Captain Clayton saw him like that, he'd never be freed.

'Titch needs to calm down, Donna. Behaviour like that could jeopardize his release. See if you can reason with him.'

Donna looked sceptical. 'I'll do my best, but you know he had another nickname that nobody used to his face. They called him Twitch because he was excitable and could act a little strangely. He seems worse than ever now.'

'Just do your best,' Crafty replied, then said goodbye and left the small prison, with Titch still shouting angrily.

He wasn't confident about getting the captain to release either of them, but he would certainly give it a try. He was aware that even letting Donna out was not totally without risk. Perhaps she too heard a voice, like the aberrations approaching the castle?

He seemed to be the last to arrive in the Throne Room. People were standing just inside the doorway, blocking his view, but he could hear the Duke addressing the gathering. He moved closer to get a better look.

By peering over the shoulder of a courier, he could see Lick, the captain and the sergeant. They were sitting on the floor, very close to the Duke. To his huge surprise he saw that all three had their eyes closed. Then he noticed that the sergeant was drooling, a long silver thread of saliva dripping slowly from his chin. There was something very wrong . . .

'Come closer!' commanded the Duke in a loud booming voice, and those ahead of Crafty shuffled forward. He himself felt very uneasy and actually took a step backwards.

All at once he realized that the Throne Room was filled with a faint green mist. Was it the aberration's breath? Had that caused Lick, the sergeant and Captain Clayton to fall asleep? Crafty wondered. A moment later his theory was confirmed.

With a tremendous roar that vibrated through the soles of Crafty's boots, the aberration exhaled a big dark green cloud. It rose up to the ceiling before sinking and spreading to fill the Throne Room. Those who were standing dropped in a heap as soon as it reached them; Crafty heard a loud crack as one courier's head struck the floor.

He immediately took a couple more steps backwards so that he was just outside the doorway, but the green mist was creeping towards him – and he was the only one still standing. He was drawing attention to himself.

The aberration turned towards him. 'Come forward! It is a command. Obey your Duke!' it cried.

Then there was another roar and a whoosh as it breathed out another cloud of foul green breath – this time directly towards Crafty.

CASTLE LOCATORS

Crafty turned and ran.

At first he ran blindly, desperate to escape the aberration's poisonous breath. Then he slowed and came to a halt while he got his own breath back. Thinking hard, he turned round and headed back towards the sick room, the terrible implications of what had just happened starting to become clear in his mind.

When Crafty reached Lucky's room, he found him still sitting up in bed; this time he was playing chess.

He looked up and smiled. 'I took Lick's advice,' he said, his smile widening. 'Maybe it's not too late to start exercising my brain more!'

Suddenly his expression changed as he noticed the look on Crafty's face. 'What's wrong?' he asked.

'Everything! It couldn't be worse . . .'

Crafty sat down on the edge of the bed and quickly described all that had just happened in the Throne Room.

'It'll be dark soon,' he concluded. 'Then the next wave of aberrations will attack the castle. Most of our forces are unconscious. Some might even be dead!'

There was little hope of help from outside – although there must have been communication between the two castles. Maybe some couriers were on their way with messages from Clitheroe – perhaps even his father might come, though this was a very faint hope.

Lucky immediately climbed out of bed and began to get dressed. 'There are two defenders left – me and you! We won't give up without a fight!' he declared, his face filled with determination.

'Maybe the odds are slightly better than that,' Crafty said. 'There might be four of us . . .' And he went on to tell him about Donna.

'So,' he finished, 'Donna and this boy called Titch could help too.'

'I can't believe it!' Lucky cried, and his face lit up with happiness. 'I can't believe Donna is back from the dead. Is she all right? Have you spoken to her?'

'Well, she and Titch are locked in cells, but I know where the key is,' Crafty said.

'What is she doing in a cell?' Lucky asked, his expression changing, his face growing red with anger. He scowled at Crafty as if it was his fault.

'When she came back from the dead, she was automatically classified as an aberration. They don't trust her,' Crafty explained.

'They don't trust Donna? Are they stupid or what?'

Crafty told Lucky about the voice that was commanding aberrations to attack the castle. 'She could be hearing that too. It could control how she behaves and might tell her to harm us. It'll be risky to release her. And that boy Titch looks quite crazy.'

'Then it's a risk we'll just have to take!' Lucky said, tugging on his greatcoat. 'Let's go and let her out.'

Crafty would have let Donna out anyway, but he realized that things had reverted to the time when he had first begun work as a gate grub. As far as Lucky was concerned, he had the greater experience and would give the orders.

The decision taken out of his hands, he led Lucky to the cells. As they approached Donna's cell and Lucky grabbed the bunch of keys from the wall, she cried out: 'Lucky! Lucky! I knew that *you* wouldn't let me down!'

Her tone of voice suggested that she thought that Crafty *had* and he felt rather hurt.

He glanced at Titch, who was curled into a ball on the floor of his cell. His fingers were bleeding, and he was biting his nails frantically and muttering to himself. Could they risk letting him out too? Crafty wondered.

At the fifth try Lucky found a key to open Donna's cell door. Crafty tensed, not sure what to expect. Would Donna attack them?

She rushed through the door towards Lucky, and Crafty held his breath, reaching into the pocket of his greatcoat for his dagger . . . But Donna simply folded herself into Lucky's arms. They hugged each other tightly as she wept with happiness.

'What a pong!' Lucky laughed as he held her at arm's length. 'You need a good scrub from head to toe!'

She grinned back. 'I might be a bit smelly, but I could never be as bad as your stinky feet!'

Crafty kept his distance. This looked and sounded like the Donna of old, but he wasn't taking any chances. She pulled away from Lucky and stared at him. He thought she might blame him for not letting her out earlier. Instead, she gave him a warm smile.

'Thanks for bringing Lucky to release me,' she said softly, her face becoming more serious. 'Does the captain know? Or is this without his knowledge? Will I be in danger?'

Crafty gave her a quick summary of what had happened in the Throne Room. 'As far as I know, we might be the only ones in the castle who are still conscious. And in a few hours a new attack will begin,' he told her.

'What about me? What about me!' cried a voice, and all three looked across at Titch, who was now gripping the bars and staring over at them, his eyes wild.

Without consulting either Crafty or Lucky, Donna grabbed the bunch of keys. She found the right one quickly and let Titch out. They hugged each other, Donna bending down as he was only half her size. Crafty and Lucky exchanged a look. Crafty still wasn't convinced about Titch and Lucky seemed uneasy – the boy's eyes were twitching to and fro. He looked demented.

'Now we need weapons,' Donna said decisively. 'Bows like yours, and swords as well. We'll get them from the armoury. Bring those keys, Lucky!'

The armoury was just a few doors away. As Donna led the way, Crafty noticed that she walked with a slight limp, though she was still able to move pretty fast. They came to a stout iron door, but one of the keys allowed them to enter. Inside, the walls were lined with weapons – mostly long swords and spears, but there were a number of crossbows, each armed with a full clutch of bolts. Donna, Lucky and Titch grabbed those first, and Crafty quickly demonstrated how to use them.

'Once you fire, the next bolt moves up into position automatically,' he told them. 'You can get a lot of shots off really quickly.'

'Great. We should take a sword each as well,' Donna said.

Crafty was eyeing something else and he pointed them out, his mind racing as he considered the best way to proceed. 'Maybe we'd be better off with those instead,' he suggested.

'Axes?' asked Donna in puzzlement.

They were long-handled, double-bladed war axes, made to be wielded by large muscular warriors. The four gate grubs were small and light – especially Titch. Axes would surely not have been their weapons of choice.

Crafty nodded and smiled. 'I've just thought of something,' he said.

'Another of your crafty ideas, is it?' Lucky said, grinning back.

'There are only four of us,' Crafty continued, 'so how can we hope to patrol the battlements, then respond to an attack successfully – especially if it comes from more than one direction at once? We need help. So let's go and get it.'

'From the people in the Throne Room?' Donna asked.

'Where else?'

'What about the thing breathing out that green poison?' Lucky wanted to know.

'We distract it,' Crafty said. 'If possible, we destroy it. That aberration grew from roots and is mostly made of wood. That's why we need the axes.'

'Go on,' said Donna. 'Tell me more.'

'First we need to find out if you three are capable of hitting a barn door from ten paces,' he said, tapping his own crossbow. 'We'll need extra bolts, and then we'll head for the practice range.'

They gathered up all the weapons and ammunition, then set off for the range behind the castle yard, safe within the walls. As they walked, Crafty kept glancing from side to side. There were still aberrations loose in the castle. Only the Ducal Chambers were guarded.

Crafty sent a few bolts into the centre of a target, just to show how it should be done. Lacking his experience with the crossbow, neither Lucky nor Donna were as accurate; still, even if neither found the bullseye, they were consistently hitting the target. However, Titch was a revelation. He had an excellent eye and his bolts joined Crafty's in the centre of the target.

Crafty led them to the corner of the dormitory where there was a pile of blankets and sheets on the floor. They were intended for use in case there weren't enough hammocks to go round. 'If we soak these sheets with water and wrap them around our heads, covering our mouths and noses, it might keep out the worst of that green mist. We shouldn't be in there very long anyway,' he explained.

So, using the water from the large jug near the door, they saturated the sheets.

'Can I get this straight? We just charge in and, while two of us attack the aberration with our crossbows and one with an axe, the other drags the couriers out?' asked Lucky.

'Something like that, but to use one of the big words that Ginger Bob likes so much, we'll need a bit more finesse.'

'*Finesse?*' Donna and Lucky chorused, while Titch just opened his mouth and gaped in puzzlement.

'Yes, a bit of subtlety to gain the advantage of surprise,' replied Crafty. 'We'll use a silver gate.'

'What? Inside the castle?' Donna asked incredulously. 'It's dangerous to use a gate in a confined space. If a gate were to collide with something solid like stones or brick . . . It doesn't bear thinking about.'

'It's always risky, but it can be done. Lick's tweaked the gate and positioned locators within the castle. Under the circumstances I think it's worth taking the risk. Let's go to her room and I'll explain in a little more detail.'

So, adding the wet sheets to their burden, the four gate grubs set off for Lick's new room inside the Ducal Chambers. They dumped everything on the floor while Crafty tried to open the desk drawer. It was locked, but he didn't let that put him off.

He picked up one of the axes and eased the thin sharp blade into the gap between desk and drawer. He twisted it and, with a crunch, the drawer flew open.

'Lick's not going to like that!' Lucky exclaimed.

'If things go well, she'll thank us. If they go badly, it won't matter anyway,' he said.

This was very true. If they failed, then they would all die when the aberrations attacked – including those lying in the Throne Room.

Crafty turned back to the desk drawer. Inside were several boxes, each clearly labelled. He found the one marked CASTLE LOCATORS, placed it on the desk and lifted the lid. He was hoping to find more information to help him, and he wasn't disappointed.

Before him were seven of the small cylindrical locators, each with a number. There was also a small piece of paper, which he unfolded to find a sketch of the ground floor of the castle, with seven places clearly marked with small stars. He knew that the other halves of the locators were buried at these points. Lick had probably tested them all, so they should be safe enough.

One of the locators lay just beyond the Throne Room but still inside the Ducal Chambers, close to the inner door. That was perfect. They could move the gate near the door, out of sight of anyone or anything within the Throne Room.

Unfortunately there was no locator in position for the final place he wanted the gate to be – as close to the aberration's back as he could possibly get so as to take it by surprise. He would just have to reach it using the skills he had developed as a gate grub.

And without a locator it would be extremely dangerous.

31

FEAR AND FURY

Crafty thought quickly. If he told the others about this, they would insist on going themselves. They had the greater experience, so they would pull rank. But Crafty had seen the aberration that resembled the Duke; he had smelled the faint sickly odour of rot that it gave off. He knew he had the best chance of getting close.

He would have to be doubly careful when moving the gate. Not only did he have to take the aberration by surprise, but he risked harming Lick, the captain and the sergeant, who were sitting facing it. If he collided with them, he might even kill them.

So, taking two locators out of the box, he fibbed to his friends, knowing that only one would be of any use.

'These will do the trick!' he said, forcing a smile on to his face and placing a locator in each pocket of his greatcoat.

Then he explained exactly what his plan involved.

*

Crafty sat in the chair facing the silver gate. They had moved their gear close by. Lucky and Titch were already holding their crossbows. They were to be the main distraction. Donna had an axe. She would be coming with Crafty.

They had each wrapped a wet sheet around their heads, allowing the ends to hang down their backs. Titch's was trailing on the floor behind him. It was uncomfortable, but these sheets could mean the difference between life and death.

'Ready?' asked Crafty, his voice muffled.

The others nodded, and he stared at the swirling clouds within the silver gate, gripped the locator with his left hand and concentrated. Instantly the clouds cleared to reveal the stone wall of the Throne Room.

Clutching his bow, Lucky led the way through, Crafty and Titch following. The plan was for Donna to remain behind until the gate moved again. She was holding the double-bladed axe, ready for action.

As the three of them moved towards the doorway, Crafty noticed that a little of the green mist had seeped through. They peered round the door into the Throne Room, where they could just see the prone couriers through the dense mist. None of them were moving. Had they all died from the effects of the aberration's breath? Crafty pushed that thought out of his mind and studied the creature. It seemed to be unaware of their presence. Was it asleep? Not for much longer! he thought.

He brought his crossbow up to his shoulder and took careful aim. There was the usual thwack of the bolt leaving the bow and the whoosh of its passage through the air. His first shot was on target – right in the centre of its forehead. That certainly woke it up. It cried out in pain and tugged the arrow free, then glared at them; again Crafty felt the vibration through his boots as it forced out a jet of green breath.

He heard Lucky and Titch let off the first of their bolts, but he was already running back towards the gate. Those two grubs would continue to fire at the aberration, distracting it from what he and Donna were doing. He jumped through the gate, sat down in the grub seat, took a deep breath and concentrated. This was the difficult part.

His mind focused on the aberration, imagining its sickly stench in his nostrils, conjuring in his mind the view from behind it. He had a moment of doubt and fear. If he got this wrong, the gate might damage Lick and those around her. Crafty took a deep breath and thrust that thought to the back of his mind.

For a moment nothing happened and the dark clouds continued to swirl through the gate. He tried again, concentrating even harder, and this time, to his relief, the clouds cleared and they were in exactly the position he'd hoped for.

Crafty had told Lucky and Titch to cease firing the moment they saw the blue circle of the gate, and to remain in view just beyond the doorway, still trying to distract the aberration.

Donna went through the gate fast, already lifting the axe for the first blow. Crafty followed but took only the blade from the pocket of his greatcoat. His job was to drag people back through the gate into the safety of Lick's room.

The axe was heavy, but Donna wielded it as if it weighed nothing at all. She struck the aberration a terrible blow, the axe biting into its back, where its body joined the roots. The creature threw back its head and screamed. Donna continued her attack, striking a second furious blow before Crafty was even fully through the gate.

'Treason! Treason!' the creature shrieked. 'I am your Duke!'

Crafty ran past it towards the sergeant, the captain and Lick. They were still sitting with their heads slumped on their chests. He couldn't tell whether they were breathing, but all three had drool coming out of their mouths. As he approached them, he wondered who he should take first.

What if he only got the chance to pull one of them to safety? He might not have time to save more – for now he saw that the aberration, its face twisted in fury, had reached round to seize the axe. Donna was struggling to pull it free.

Looking down again, Crafty agonized over the decision he had to make: maybe he should take the captain first – a leader who might help them survive and eventually triumph; the sergeant was a good fighter too. But instead it was Lick that he half dragged, half carried towards the gate. Lick was clever – her brain might make all the difference. That's what he told himself. But deep down he knew that he'd chosen her because she was his friend.

Crafty got her back into the office, pushed her on to her side so that she wouldn't choke if and when she started to come round, and then went back, intending to retrieve the sergeant. But, instead of going through the gate again, he hesitated. Donna was still struggling to get the axe back, but now the creature had seized her wrist with its other hand, and was dragging her towards it. It was made of wood – it must be incredibly strong.

Crafty realized that he had to help Donna first, so he picked up another axe. It was very heavy, but fear and fury lent him strength.

With his first blow he chopped through the wooden left hand that was holding Donna's wrist. With his second he severed the right hand close to the shoulder, freeing her axe. The aberration screamed, writhed and tried to hit them with its stumps, but now they both went to work chopping into it as if it was a tree trunk. Chips of wood flew everywhere, and soon the thing ceased to twitch and became still. They had defeated it!

However, they couldn't rest on their laurels. They immediately set to work dragging the sergeant and the captain through the gate. Crafty glanced around Lick's office and, to his relief, saw no sign of the poisonous mist. Lucky and Titch started to help, pulling those nearest the door out into the corridor.

Even with all four of them working, it took over an hour to get everyone safely out of the Throne Room. By then the green mist had dispersed so they'd cast aside the wet sheets.

Finally they could rest; they were standing close to the remains of the aberration, grinning and feeling pleased with themselves, when Lucky suddenly made a dreadful discovery.

He was no longer smiling. As he pointed, his finger shook and his expression was one of dismay. The aberration had been so badly damaged that it no longer resembled the Duke.

But in spite of this, new buds were starting to form.

The creature wasn't dead.

32

DUSK UNTIL DAWN

They soon took care of that new growth with their axes, but this was no longer a permanent solution. That mass of roots below the castle was still alive. And as long as this was so, the aberration would continue to regenerate. Those roots posed a constant threat.

Within an hour the first of the aberration's victims started to revive. Unfortunately the doctor had gone through the silver gate with the real Duke and hadn't returned – though they found a medical orderly who was soon strong enough to help those who were still recovering. There was a lot of coughing, spluttering, and runny eyes and noses, and some of the victims were sick; the air quickly filled with the stink of vomit. The orderly also found that two had died.

Thankfully, despite her proximity to the aberration, Lick was one of the first to recover.

'You took a chance,' she accused Crafty once she was on her feet, 'moving the gate into the Throne Room without a locator . . . Yet another risk, Crafty!'

'What?' cried Donna. 'You mean there wasn't a locator there? You lied to us!'

'I did, but I did it for the best of reasons,' Crafty said, feeling angry. 'I'd been close to that thing pretending to be the Duke. Neither you nor Lucky had. I thought I had the best chance of getting close to it. And it worked.'

Before anything more could be said, Captain Clayton approached them. His hair was dishevelled, the front of his uniform was stained and he smelled of vomit. He also looked furious.

'You two!' he said, pointing to Donna and Titch. 'Back in the cells, both of you. You shouldn't have been released without my authorization.'

Donna scowled and Titch gave a hiss that was more animal than human.

'Sir, you were in no position to authorize anything,' Crafty told him, trying to keep his voice even. He knew better than to rile the man.

But then Lucky jumped in angrily, without showing the slightest respect. 'That's stupid! You want to lock Donna and Titch up again?' he roared. 'They helped to save you and all these people. We couldn't have done it without their help!'

'Know your place, boy!' Captain Clayton snapped. 'One more word from you and you'll be locked up too.'

It was Lick who saved the day. Before Lucky could make things any worse for himself, she came up and put her arm round his shoulders. 'Captain, I'm sure Lucky is sorry and doesn't mean to give offence. However, what he says is true. They released Donna and Titch because they needed their help, and they both proved themselves to be trustworthy. They saved many lives, including yours and mine.'

The captain was silent for a few moments but then let out a long breath. 'Fine. In that case they are now on probation and I place them under *your* careful watch, Miss Crompton-Smythe. And what about you, boy?' he said, glaring at Lucky. 'What do you owe me?'

'An apology, sir,' Lucky said, realizing what was expected. 'I'm sorry for speaking to you in that manner, but I spoke the truth.'

The captain still didn't look happy with him, but he nodded, turned on his heel and went to speak to the orderly.

Night came only too soon. This time there would be no chance to sleep: there weren't enough fit people to staff two watches. The sick rooms were filled with those still suffering the after-effects of the poisonous green breath. There was to be only one watch lasting from dusk until dawn and, once again, Crafty was paired with the captain.

He saw that Lick and Lucky had been ordered to team up with Donna and Titch. Crafty knew that it was because the captain didn't trust the two reanimated grubs. Even after what they'd done, Crafty didn't either. If the voice spoke inside their heads, commanding them to turn on their friends, they might not be able to resist.

He followed the captain up on to the battlements, where their breath steamed in the cold air. Only the couriers, with the addition of Lick, Lucky, Donna, Titch and Crafty himself, were defending this part of the castle. Those fit enough to fight, from cooks to boffins, were to remain in the Ducal Chambers; if there was a breach in the defences, they'd do their best to defend those who were still incapacitated.

'Use those good eyes of yours again,' came the abrupt order from the captain. 'What do you see?'

Crafty stared south into the darkness of the city, with its narrow streets and huddled houses. There were a few faint lights showing, but nothing was moving towards the castle.

'It's just like last night,' he responded. 'There are things down there all right. I can see glimmers of light, but no clear threat.'

'The attack might come from underground again – though we can't be sure of anything,' the captain said. 'I've given orders for that aberration in the Throne Room to be pruned back hard every half-hour – just in case.'

They headed for the north-facing battlements, and Crafty scanned the area leading towards the river. But again nothing was happening.

The captain spoke again. 'At first, Benson, I thought you were a loose cannon . . . You know what that means?' he asked.

'I think it's a gun that does more harm than good,' Crafty replied.

'Exactly. The phrase refers to a ship's cannon that should be fired at the enemy, but breaks loose and maims or kills those on deck. However, I've changed my mind. You're not a loose cannon. What you are is a maverick.'

Crafty looked embarrassed. 'I'm afraid I don't know what that word means, sir. Is it worse than being a loose cannon?'

The captain smiled. 'No, just the opposite – it's far better. A maverick is someone with an independent mind who behaves in an unorthodox manner. That's exactly what you are, Benson. And between you and me, that's exactly what makes you *very* suitable to serve as a courier. We aren't like the Castle Guard, with their strict rules and chains of command. In our job we often work alone and need to make instant decisions. Resourcefulness and initiative – that's what you have, Benson. I believe you have a nickname?'

'It's Crafty, sir,' he answered.

'Yes, and you certainly lived up to it when you helped rescue your father and the other courier: I was told all about it. You came up with a plan and carried it out using guile. You were ruthless, and did what had to be done without looking over your shoulder for anyone's permission or approval. I like that. I think you were born to be a courier. As soon as this crisis is over I'll be having a word with the Chief Mancer. I'm sure he'll agree to your transfer.'

Crafty groaned inwardly. He didn't really want to be transferred away from his friends. The captain had said something similar the previous night. *He's like a dog worrying a bone!* Crafty thought. *He just can't let go of it.*

However, before he could work out how to turn the captain down there came the warning call of a bugle. The only other courier who used one was the sergeant. It was a cry for help.

The captain started running towards the sound, and Crafty followed him down the stone steps to the ground floor. The bugle sounded again – this time much nearer. They sprinted along the corridor, past the Throne Room, the Forensics Room and the Relic Room, until they came to an open door at the far end. Crafty had passed the room before. It didn't have a plaque on the door and he'd often wondered what it was.

Two couriers were standing just inside, both holding torches above their heads. Crafty saw that one of them was the sergeant, an axe in his other hand, the bugle tucked into his belt. He peered into the room and saw that it was some sort of storage area, with large boxes stacked against the far wall – but the floor was covered with dry yellow straw and there was something in the centre that didn't belong there. Something dangerous.

The human figure was standing perfectly still – but it wasn't another version of the Duke. It was dressed in a black cloak and a hood formed from bark, but from the waist down it was a tangle of dark fibrous roots. The head was bowed, the hood obscuring the face, and the arms hung at its sides. There was something strange about those arms, Crafty thought. He couldn't see any elbows, and they extended right down into the straw.

'It's grown from the Duke's roots like the other one, sir,' the sergeant told Captain Clayton. 'So far it's dormant. Best to chop it up before it does any harm . . .'

'Yes, go ahead, Sergeant,' ordered the captain.

'Hold this,' he said, handing his torch to the other courier. Gripping the axe with both hands, he licked his moustache, then advanced towards the aberration with a determined expression on his face.

As he did so, the aberration lifted its head and stared at him. Its face was very pale, its pupils vertical slits.

Crafty recognized that face immediately. It was Viper's.

Then the aberration spoke:

'What fools you are to meddle with me. And you, grub, I thought you'd know better by now!'

THE MONSTER

Crafty expected the aberration to exhale a poisonous green mist, but instead it did something horribly unexpected. The poor sergeant never had a chance.

The aberration's arms had been hidden in the straw; now, suddenly, Crafty saw how long they were. Its left hand, tipped with sharp black talons, rose up and grasped the sergeant by the neck, lifting him right up to the ceiling. He made a terrible choking sound and dropped the axe. Blood spurted from his neck and ran down his body, dripping on to the straw. Then he gave one last shudder, and was still.

Crafty took aim quickly. There was the thwack and whoosh as the bolt left his crossbow to thud deep into the aberration's left eye. It dropped the sergeant's body and let out a shriek, its arms whirling overhead. Wasting no time, Crafty sent a second arrow into its other eye, and then a third into its forehead.

'Good shooting – now hold your fire!' commanded the captain, collecting the axe from the straw, and then chopping into the aberration, sending chips of wood flying everywhere. Finally he landed a terrible blow which split its head almost in two. Within moments the arms stopped thrashing and the creature lay still, apparently lifeless.

However, Crafty knew that it would almost certainly regenerate. The root system beneath the castle was vast. How many more aberrations would grow from it? Even now other threats could be forming underground. Would they have to keep up a constant search of the castle?

The creature had used Viper's face too. Why? He felt sure that his enemy was elsewhere, still in his own body. It had sounded exactly like Viper, he thought. Was Viper's mind inside it? Had his consciousness looked out through the eyes of the aberration that had developed from those roots? Surely that must be so because it had known who he was!

Crafty and the courier joined the captain, who was now gazing down at the body of the sergeant. 'He was a good, brave courier; a man who could be relied on. We'd worked together for almost twenty years and I considered him a friend as well as a colleague. He will be missed,' he sighed, his eyes glistening with tears.

He turned to face the other courier. 'Jameson, you'll be acting sergeant from now on. Your first task will be to search the ground floor of the castle in case any more aberrations are growing.' He handed him the axe. 'You know what to do when you find one. Take two couriers with you and make sure they're armed with crossbows!'

Then, as the new sergeant strode away, the captain turned and put a hand on Crafty's shoulder. 'That was quick, accurate shooting, Benson. You blinded the thing so that it couldn't see me coming. Without that I'd never have got anywhere near it.'

Suddenly they heard approaching steps, and another courier came into the room; he was gasping for breath, and glanced quickly at the dead sergeant before making his report: 'The enemy are moving towards the castle, sir! And there are a lot of them.'

'Back to the battlements,' Captain Clayton commanded, leading the way.

Crafty gazed south over the city. What he saw filled him with horror and dismay.

Down in the maze of cobbled streets, faint lights were moving up the hill towards the castle. It was more like the steady soft green and yellow light from glow-worms than the flicker of torches. Yes, they were actually emitting light from their bodies. Then, as his eyes adjusted to the dark, Crafty saw other shadowy creatures bounding ahead on four legs. These gave off no light, and his heart lurched as their distant cries told him that they were the cat-like beasts that usually occupied the dwellings around Winckley Square in Preston.

He had been chased by them more than once before. They were large and fierce, with the triple rows of sharp teeth that belonged to many of the predatory aberrations. One had almost caught Donna as she climbed back through the gate; it was this that had given Viper the excuse to use the guillotine.

Crafty could hear their savage cries getting nearer and nearer, the pack now bounding out of the narrow cobbled streets and racing up the grassy slope towards the castle walls.

One of the couriers took aim with his crossbow, and an arrow whooshed down into the darkness.

'Save your arrows for later!' commanded the captain. 'Those creatures won't be able to climb the walls and there's no way they can get through the portcullis and the main gate. But there'll be aberrations that *can* climb. They'll be your targets.'

That was sensible, thought Crafty, as the howling beasts circled the walls beneath them. They had sharp talons and could probably scamper up trees, but there was no way they could climb a sheer stone wall.

But what were those other glowing creatures ascending the hill behind them? As they drew nearer, Crafty shuddered with fear. They were roughly human in shape, but more muscular, and covered with fur. Their arms were very long, their fingers almost touching the ground. Without hesitation they headed for the walls and began to climb.

More couriers were now coming up on to the battlements. They would certainly be needed. Then Crafty spotted his four friends; Donna looked terrified, and he suddenly realized why.

She wasn't afraid of the aberrations climbing the southern wall of the castle. It was the howls and shrieks of the circling cat-like beasts that terrified her: that was the last sound she'd heard before she clambered through the silver gate to face the guillotine.

As Crafty watched, concerned, Donna shivered, took a deep breath and composed herself. Then, along with his other three friends, she aimed over the wall and fired down on the aberrations below.

He picked his own target. He thought he'd struck it on the shoulder, but it hardly faltered, continuing straight up the wall. With a thwack and a whoosh, he sent another bolt into it, and this time it paused and looked up at him. It glowed a sickly yellow, and its face looked demonic, with long sharp fangs curving up on either side of its nose. The aberration had once been human; now it had changed into a ravenous predator that wanted his flesh and blood. As it held Crafty's gaze, saliva dripped from its open jaws and he saw a sly intelligence in its eyes. It was almost as if it was saying, *I'm coming for you, boy!*

He hit it with a third arrow, this time in the throat. It shrieked and fell off the wall, hitting the ground hard. It lay there on its back, arms and legs writhing, still alive but no longer a threat.

However, some of the enemy were advancing very quickly. To his left, Crafty saw one creature pull itself up on to the battlements. There were four or five arrows buried in its chest and shoulders, but it was still moving, growling and roaring out its hatred. It seized a courier by the head, lifted the poor man off his feet and threw him over the wall. He fell screaming to his death.

Now, before it could hurt anyone else, the captain raised his long sword with both hands and hacked at the creature with the same skill he had just displayed with the axe. Another courier came to join him, and within moments the aberration lay dead at their feet.

However, looking over the battlements, Crafty saw that more and more were now scaling the walls. Surely there were too many to hold off? The cat-like beasts were still circling below, but now he saw something different: two aberrations with horns and more dog-like bodies. These were One-Bites, standing staring up at the castle battlements, as if waiting for something.

Then, his eyes drawn by a gleam of white light, Crafty spotted an aberration that was scarier than anything he'd seen so far. The White Lady was standing under a tree gazing upwards. She was still dressed in a long white dress that shone even more brightly than the glowing aberrations scaling the walls. Crafty had cut off her hair, and he remembered how the severed ends had dripped blood, but it had already grown back, and now it fell luxuriantly over her shoulders, coiling away through the grass like a sinuous silver snake.

Suddenly she moved her head slightly and he realized that she was looking directly at him. Their eyes locked, and he felt a chill of horror and fear. She would never forget what he had done to her. She would want revenge.

It took a great effort to drag his eyes away, but now he saw that a great horde of aberrations were climbing the hill and moving towards the castle, shadowy figures of all shapes and sizes. This was the threat that he needed to deal with first, Crafty told himself.

He selected another target and, in rapid succession, fired three arrows into it, but still it continued to climb. He looked around. Surely, he thought, the captain must see that there were too few of them to defend the castle. Was it cowardly to leave in order to fight another day?

Crafty couldn't imagine that things could get any worse, but they did.

All at once he heard the cry of a flapper; the sound was ear-piercing, and the shrieks quickly resolved themselves into words:

'Watch the sky! Watch the sky! Bats! Bats!'

'There's danger from above!' Crafty shouted to those around him. although they were too busy holding off other attacks to heed his warning.

Something huge and dark, with black wings and a body covered in brown fur, swooped down upon the courier next to Crafty. There was a splash of blood, and the man fell backwards, clutching his throat, then lay on the ground, twitching and gasping for air. The bat alighted on his head and began to fan its giant wings, scattering droplets of blood across his body. Then it arched its neck and vomited a stream of some dark liquid.

Crafty knew that this was the aberration known as a corpse bat. He'd seen a preserved one in the Relic Room, and read about them in the Grey Library. They didn't feed on flesh and blood, but ate the fungus that grew on the corpses of their victims. It had just sprayed the body of its victim with spores.

A second later it lay dead next to the slain courier. Crafty had put two crossbow bolts into its soft body.

He peered up into the darkness. The hideous flying aberrations were hard to make out. From the moment he glimpsed one swooping towards the battlements he had only seconds to take aim and fire. But now he wasn't the only one targeting them. He saw Titch bring down two of the creatures in rapid succession. The boy was a natural with that crossbow. However, Crafty reflected, each bowman aiming at these flying targets meant one less defending the battlements against the aberrations climbing the castle walls.

Maybe Captain Clayton would never have given the order to retreat. They might have fought there until dawn – or until there was no one left alive. But then something happened that made a tactical withdrawal the only possible decision.

Something truly terrifying was climbing the hill towards them now. It was roughly the same shape as the aberrations scaling the walls, with the same hairy bulk, long arms and fanged mouth. And it emitted the same sickly yellow-green light.

But it differed in one important respect. It was big. Very big.

The monster was perhaps four times the height of a man and at least twice as wide, with jaws big enough to bite off the head of a human. And it was heading straight for the main gate of the castle; Crafty could feel its heavy footsteps through the soles of his boots.

Of course, the strong metal portcullis protected the gate. The monster couldn't possibly get past that, could it? Crafty thought. And the gate was formidable, made of stout oak, edged with metal and reinforced with thick iron studs.

Below, the cat-like beasts had stopped their wild circling and fell quiet. They gathered behind the monster – along with the two One-Bites; even the White Lady was now much closer to the gate. Yes, they almost seemed to be waiting for something . . .

Now the huge aberration came to a halt before the portcullis, its nose almost touching the metal. What was it going to do? Crafty wondered.

Suddenly it gripped the iron bars with both hands. Then, as easily as bending pliant saplings, it pulled them apart, creating a wide gap. The scream of tortured metal had barely died away when Crafty heard a tremendous thud: it had sent one massive fist right through the gate, and the blow had shattered the top third, sending splinters of wood through into the castle.

'Retreat!' shouted the captain. 'Fall back into the courtyard!'

THE RETREAT

Captain Clayton strode over to Lick and started to shout into her ear, gesticulating wildly as he did so. Crafty couldn't hear what he was saying, but he saw Lick frown and shake her head in response.

'*Just do it!*' the captain roared as he left her. 'We'll hold the line as long as we can.'

Crafty, Lucky, Donna and Titch immediately ran to her side.

'He wants us to use my silver gate and evacuate the wounded,' she told them. 'I told him that he should come with us, but he insists on continuing the fight to let us get clear.'

No wonder Lick had tried to resist the order. It would be suicide for the captain and his men to fight on against such odds. They had little hope of survival.

Wasting no time, they followed his orders. As Crafty passed the victim of the bat's attack, he shuddered. The corpse was already covered with large brown protuberances – fungi sprouting from the dead flesh.

They ran down the steps towards the courtyard. At ground level, Crafty glanced back; he didn't like what he saw. The big head of the monstrous aberration was now visible through the shattered gate, its jaws wide as it roared out a challenge to those within. The head was peppered with arrows fired by the defenders in the courtyard, but it continued to smash the gate as if they were no more than irritating insect bites.

Now Crafty understood why the other aberrations were waiting patiently behind it. Once it had destroyed the gate they would surge into the castle to kill and devour every living thing.

He suddenly realized that someone was missing. 'Where's Titch?' he shouted.

They paused, and then Lick spotted him. Titch was close to the gate, laughing like a maniac as he fired up at the monster with deadly accuracy. Bolt after bolt pierced its huge eyes. It shook its head and roared with pain, but then continued to batter the gate.

Crafty went across and dragged him away; now Lick led them into the castle and along towards the Throne Room. Crafty hoped that the new large silver gate was operational – it would certainly make the evacuation easier – but when the door opened, he groaned. There was no sign of it. They would have to get people out through the much smaller silver gate in Lick's room.

'Alert everybody to the plan!' Lick shouted. 'I'll go and find the best locator.'

She headed for her office while Crafty, Lucky and Donna sprinted towards the sick rooms. Crafty knew what Lick would be looking for. She would be searching through her desk drawer, frantically checking the contents of the boxes. The gate wouldn't be able to take them directly into the Daylight World, so Lick needed to find a locator that would get them as close as possible.

They quickly found the medical orderly and told him about the order to evacuate. His face was slick with sweat and he looked close to panic.

'Another victim has died,' he told them. 'I did my best, but she succumbed to the effects of the poisonous breath. Hopefully the others should pull through.'

It seemed that the survivors were 'walking wounded': none of them would need to be carried, although they couldn't walk fast; some would need support to get to the silver gate in Lick's office. But in spite of the help being offered, it was slow work; Crafty could hear the sounds of battle getting nearer. By now many of the aberrations outside the gate must be racing into the castle; those climbing the walls would be descending from the battlements. Maybe the White Lady was also inside the castle, eager to get him into her clutches, Crafty thought.

Now he heard the shrieks and roars of their attackers and the shouts of the retreating couriers as they fell back towards the Throne Room. This was where they would make their last stand if the enemy penetrated the castle. The outer door was strong, but Crafty had seen what that monstrous aberration had done to the portcullis and the gate. The door might slow it down, but not for long.

Crafty could also see another problem ahead. They couldn't just send these sick people through the gate by themselves. When they emerged, they'd still be within the Shole, and they were in no condition to defend themselves. Somebody would have to go through with the first. But who? Those who had been guarding the sick were the obvious choice. They had weapons – a few even had crossbows, though they had little or no practice in using them.

When he reached Lick's office, he told her what he was thinking.

'A couple of us should go with them as well. I'll go if you like. I could take Titch with me. He's a great shot with the crossbow . . .'

But then the problem was solved: the acting sergeant came bursting into the room with two couriers, and Lick hastily explained the situation and what was needed. Without hesitating, Sergeant Jameson agreed to lead the way through the gate.

Lick sat in the chair holding a locator. Seconds later the swirling clouds cleared to reveal a dark wood of leafless trees. It was still a long time till sunrise. Anything could be prowling out there.

'This locator is the only one that gets us close to the south-eastern edge of the Shole,' she said. 'You'll still have quite a walk, I'm afraid.'

The sergeant went first, brandishing his axe. Two couriers followed, crossbows at the ready. Then Crafty and Lucky helped the first of the survivors through the silver gate. The queue behind them extended out into the corridor.

'How close are we to the Daylight World?' Crafty asked Lick.

'About a mile, on a direct route to Clitheroe Castle. It was the best I could do,' she replied.

'I'll go back and help the orderly get the last of his patients through,' Crafty told her, and hurried off.

The screams and howls of the aberrations were growing closer, and everyone worked quickly. Soon Crafty and the orderly, supporting the final two victims, reached Lick's office and saw a man preparing to clamber through the gate. It was Doon. He was brandishing a crossbow. 'Race you to Clitheroe!' he said with a confident wink.

Seconds later the captain and the couriers crashed into the Throne Room, locking the outer door behind them and sliding the big horizontal metal bars across. Crafty was shocked to see barely a dozen surviving men. So many of them must have died out there.

Just then Lick returned. 'The sick are safely through and the sergeant and his men are guarding them. We're about a mile from the edge of the Shole,' she explained.

Captain Clayton nodded. 'Once we're through, make your way to Clitheroe as quickly as possible. That door won't hold for long. Well done, everyone.'

As he led his men through the silver gate, Crafty saw a strange expression on Lick's face. He knew her well; he was sure she was concealing something.

'Go on, you four,' she said, nodding towards Crafty, Donna, Lucky and Titch with a smile that Crafty thought seemed forced. 'Do as the captain said.'

'What about you?' Crafty asked, but he'd already guessed the answer.

Someone had to stay behind to close the gate. Otherwise the aberrations that were now attacking the Throne Room door would simply follow them through into the wood. They'd soon catch their prey too. The sick would be making slow progress. For some of them, a mile would seem like a very long way.

Crafty couldn't allow Lick to sacrifice herself. He would offer to do it himself.

But Donna spoke first. She'd clearly guessed what Lick intended too. 'Let me stay behind and close the gate,' she pleaded. 'If someone has to sacrifice themselves, it should be me. I'm the most senior gate grub here and, after all,' she said, trying to make a joke of it, 'I'm dead already.'

'If it's anyone, then it should be me, not Donna!' Lucky cried, gripping her arm. 'I've been sick and useless – let me save you all as you saved me.' He clearly couldn't bear to lose his friend again. He would rather sacrifice himself.

'No, *I'll* stay,' Crafty insisted.

'You're all being ridiculous,' Lick said. 'I've no intention of sacrificing myself. There's another gate in the Chief Mancer's room. Once I've closed this down, I'll use that. I'll aim for a location a good distance away from the one Captain Clayton and the others used. They'll be safe and, even if I am followed, I won't be encumbered by the sick – I should be able to escape.'

'And how do you expect to get to that gate in the first place?' Crafty demanded. 'You'd need to go through the Throne Room door and along the corridor and reach it via the Waiting Room. And you know what's lurking out there . . .'

He could hear splintering, crunching noises from the direction of the Throne Room. Even as he spoke, the aberrations were breaking through the door. The corridor would soon be heaving with them – all desperate for blood.

'There's a secret passageway the Chief Mancer used,' Lick told him. 'It enabled him to reach any department without having to go through the main doors. I'll use that. So don't argue. Obey your orders and go through the gate. I'll see you later.'

Crafty wasn't satisfied with her answer. Was there really a way to the gate or was she just pretending so that they would feel all right leaving her behind? 'So there's a *secret passageway*, is there?' he asked, an edge of sarcasm in his voice. 'How come Ginger Bob told *you* about it?'

Lick frowned angrily. 'Because I needed to know!' she snapped. 'I required the same short cut. Working on ideas to fight the Shole, I needed easy access to specialist experts.'

That made sense. As she'd once explained, Lick was a Synthesist and was involved with assembling an explanation of the entire Shole. To do that she needed to be able to talk to people. Crafty realized that she was telling the truth.

'Sorry for doubting you,' he said, smiling apologetically. 'But you know as well as I do that there's strength in numbers. All five of us will use the secret passageway and the Chief Mancer's gate. So, close this one now, Lick. The faster we set off, the better.'

Lick seemed about to protest, but then Donna spoke. 'Crafty's right! Getting to Ginger Bob's room will be dangerous. Five of us will have a better chance than one.'

Just then there was the distant sound of the door crashing to the floor, and a bestial roar of triumph. It was time to go.

Lick shrugged, and then her face filled with determination. She closed the silver gate, and the stark trees were replaced by dark whirling clouds.

'All right,' she said. 'Have it your own way. Thanks for being concerned about me. I always intended to use that other gate, but there is a problem. We might have difficulty reaching it.'

35

THE TUNNEL OF FIRE

Without a word of explanation, Lick immediately jumped to her feet and picked up her crossbow. Crafty, Lucky, Donna and Titch grabbed theirs, then followed her out into the labyrinth of rooms behind the Throne Room.

As Crafty had expected, they were heading downwards. Reaching the foot of a flight of steps, he estimated that they were now on the same level as the mancers' rooms. But, to his surprise, Lick led them down even further.

They soon came to a rusty metal door. Lick took a key from her greatcoat pocket and unlocked it, then grabbed a torch from the wall and handed it to Crafty.

'You light the way! I'll lead. Donna, Titch and Lucky – you follow behind. It's narrow and we'll have to walk in single file. Here, Donna,' she said, handing her the key, 'you lock the door behind us. It will give us a bit more time. But don't lose that key. We'll need it later.'

Some of the aberrations would almost certainly pursue them, sniffing their trail. They had to keep running.

Lick pulled open the door and led the way into the passage. It was dark and claustrophobic, and Crafty didn't like it. He sensed the weight of the castle above, as if the ancient stones were pressing down on him. Shrugging off that unpleasant feeling, he raised the torch so that it gave out as much light as possible. They waited while Donna locked the door. He heard the sound of the key turning in the lock, and the dripping of water somewhere ahead.

'Right!' said Donna. 'Door secure.'

Lick began to move forward and they followed, their boots echoing on the dank stones. The passage soon widened out, but they continued in single file, warily keeping an eye out for each other. The passage then curved away to the left. As they rounded a corner Crafty's heart sank.

The tunnel was blocked by a tangle of white roots.

Lick turned and pulled two sets of pruning shears out of her pocket. 'This is the problem I mentioned, but I've come prepared,' she said. 'We don't need to clear the tunnel completely – just along one side, those roots at the right, so that we can squeeze through. Here – you're the gardening expert,' she said, handing a pair to Crafty.

They passed their crossbows to Lucky and Donna. Crafty handed the torch to Titch and set to work alongside Lick. The roots were relatively small, most of them no thicker than a finger. Lick first cut through two roots on their left, which gave them enough room to move forward. They were making good progress snipping through the roots at the right-hand side of the tunnel, but after a few moments Crafty started to feel even more uneasy. It seemed to him that some of the roots were moving – though maybe it was just the flickering of the torchlight that was giving this impression; or a breeze, he thought, before realizing that the cold air was still and their clouds of breath hung immobile before them.

Then, suddenly, he was sure: a root he was about to cut through twitched out of his grasp and, before he could warn Lick, the same thing happened to her. As she turned to face him, one of the severed roots suddenly coiled about her left wrist, causing her to cry out in surprise and pain.

Crafty lunged forward and immediately cut through the root with his pruners, freeing her wrist. But now all five of them were coming under attack. The roots ahead were still, but the ones they had severed now twisted and lashed out at them like lithe, angry snakes. One coiled about Titch's neck, and he coughed and spluttered as it tightened and he started to choke. Struggling to pull it away, he dropped first his bow and then the torch, which fell into the tangle of roots at his feet. There was a whoosh, a crackle and a flare of light as they caught fire.

As the flames leaped upwards, giving out a fierce heat, Crafty realized that they were in great danger of being burned alive. He had to free Titch so they could retreat back towards the door. He hoped that Donna had kept the key safe.

His thoughts were interrupted by a shrill scream that seemed to come from the very earth itself. It was like the tormented cry of a wounded animal. Suddenly the burning roots convulsed violently and withdrew upwards. Even those buried in the earth disappeared into the roof of the tunnel, like snakes slithering back into their holes – along with the one that had been wrapped around Titch's neck.

The torch was still burning feebly, but before Crafty could snatch it up it went out, plunging them into darkness. He couldn't see a thing. How could they hope to find their way out of the tunnel now? he wondered.

However, all at once he saw a flare of bright light, which soon settled down to a daylight glow. Lick had taken a small orb out of her pocket and cast it up into the air. It was a trick he'd seen her perform more than once, and he was grateful every time.

She gestured that they should continue, and without a word to each other about their close brush with death, they collected their bows and hurried off down the tunnel which, thanks to the fire, was now clear.

It was eerily silent, but for the sound of their boots on the floor and the occasional cough from Titch. The small glowing orb followed Lick, floating just above her head. The previous ones had just floated upwards and stayed there, Crafty recalled, but Lick was always tweaking and improving things. However, he noticed that the orb was already starting to fade.

They passed several doors – Crafty guessed that each led to a department – but it was only at the final one that Lick asked Donna for the key.

She unlocked the rusty metal door just as the orb winked out. They climbed some steps and went through a second door directly into the Chief Mancer's office. Crafty had never noticed the door before; it was hidden away behind a cupboard in a corner of the room.

They went round the desk, its surface littered with papers and books and biscuit crumbs, and made for the dark curtain in the other corner. With a swish, Lick pulled it back, sat in the grub chair and pulled a locator out of her pocket.

'This should bring us out further to the south, about four miles away from the others and a mile and a half from the eastern edge of the Shole. So, if we're followed, they should be in no danger. Ready?' she said, then stared at the silver gate and concentrated.

The clouds cleared and they clambered through the gate on to a farm track that meandered through a small copse. Crafty shivered. It seemed far colder than it had been in the castle and the ground was white with frost. He could hear the sound of running water somewhere to his left. It sounded like a sizeable river. As they marched on in silence, Crafty felt an acute sense of danger. A mile and a half, he reflected; that was a long way to walk through the Shole during the hours of darkness. Still, this part of the Shole should be relatively safe now, he told himself. After all, the voice had instructed the aberrations to attack the castle. The real danger would come if those gathered there decided to pursue them.

Somewhere behind them he could hear distant yelps, but he couldn't tell if they were getting any closer. The cat-like beasts worried him most. They seemed intelligent and might find the gate in the Chief Mancer's room; if they came through, they wouldn't be far behind. They were fast and fierce. If they caught them out in the open, he feared for their lives.

But despite Crafty's fears they reached the eastern edge of the Shole without mishap. Sighing with relief, they stepped out into the Daylight World. In the distance, directly ahead, the sky was already pink with the promise of dawn and it was much warmer. Crafty gazed northwards, where a river rushed along towards the dark wall of the Shole. It was the Ribble, its source somewhere far ahead. In that direction too lay Clitheroe Castle, the new home of the Castle Corpus. He was curious to see what it was like.

His thoughts were interrupted when Lucky suddenly cried out, 'Donna!' His voice was filled with anguish.

Crafty turned and saw that she had collapsed and Lucky was kneeling at her side. He had barely taken two steps forward when Titch stumbled and fell face down alongside her.

'She's not breathing!' Lucky cried.

Lick ran past him, knelt and turned Titch on to his back. She put her cheek close to his mouth. 'Titch isn't either,' she said, her face full of concern.

Crafty had seen the remains of human beings who'd died after being engulfed by the Shole. The flesh melted from their bones and formed a liquid pool under their bodies. All that remained was that slimy dampness and their skeletons.

Now he could see the skin on Donna's face beginning to bubble. Titch's face was mottled red and purple. Was this the beginning of the same process? He frowned in puzzlement. Yet this was happening in the Daylight World, not in the Shole!

'Help her! Help her!' yelled Lucky, looking up at the others.

But Crafty and Lick could only stare helplessly at the two dying grubs.

There was nothing to be done.

THE FIGHT GOES ON

All at once Crafty had a sudden glimmer of inspiration. There was one thing that might save them.

'Quick! Drag them back into the Shole!' he cried.

Lucky looked up at him as if he'd lost his mind, but Lick nodded, suddenly understanding too. 'It's worth a try,' she said, placing her bow on the ground and grabbing Donna's legs while Crafty took her shoulders. Together they carried her back through the dark curtain into the Shole, then returned to do the same for Titch.

'Crafty could be right,' Lick said as Lucky looked on anxiously. 'The Shole returned them to life. Maybe if they leave it, they will die again.'

Crafty knew that there were *excursions*, when some aberrations ventured out into the Daylight World, but these were rare; it might well be different for the dead whom the

Shole had brought back to life. They might never be able to leave it.

In any case he feared that it might already be too late to save Titch and Donna; perhaps the consequences of leaving the Shole were irreversible. However, within moments Donna was taking huge sobbing breaths, and soon she was back on her feet. Her face looked more normal, but she seemed very upset. Titch too was sitting up, rubbing his eyes and complaining of a headache.

Crafty and Lick explained what they thought had happened.

'If you're right, that means I'll have to stay in the Shole forever,' Donna said sadly.

'Maybe I should step into the Daylight World once more, just to see if it happens again,' suggested Titch hopefully. 'Next time I might be all right, eh? Maybe it was just the shock.'

'It's not worth the risk,' Lick told him. 'Next time the effect might not be reversible. We just don't know enough about this. We don't know what we're dealing with.'

'Lick's right,' said Lucky. 'Neither of you should take a chance like that. I couldn't bear to lose you again, Donna. Don't worry. I'll stay in the Shole with you . . .'

Donna shook her head and they began to argue, with Titch adding his own comments from time to time.

Crafty and Lick left them to it. Crafty looked around nervously. Although he had seen no guards, and Clitheroe

Castle was much further from the edge of the Shole than Lancaster Castle had been, those cat-like beasts might still pursue them into the Daylight World.

It was a long time before Donna and Lucky's heated discussion came to an end and they arrived at a decision. Donna forbade Lucky to risk his own life to stay with her. She told him that she wouldn't be alone – she had Titch for company.

Titch seemed to have calmed down somewhat and was far less twitchy. Maybe they would be able to help each other, thought Crafty. Donna certainly seemed to trust him.

'We'll look after each other,' she said firmly. 'And I hope we'll see you again.'

It was a very sad parting. Donna and Titch came right up to the edge of the Shole to wave farewell. Crafty felt sorry for them. Yes, they would support each other, but it would be a struggle. He hoped they could find somewhere to hunker down – and that they would all be reunited one day.

Meanwhile Lucky trudged after Crafty and Lick as they headed towards the castle, sobbing all the way.

At first sight, Clitheroe Castle was disappointing. It was right on the edge of the town, and smaller than Lancaster Castle. Would it be any easier to defend? Crafty wondered. But at least it was high, most of it set atop a steep rocky hill.

He pictured those hairy luminous aberrations racing out of the darkness to swarm up its walls; the terrifying monster that had battered down the huge gate. What chance would they have in a place like this?

Yet Clitheroe lay well to the east, and so far the Shole hadn't expanded much in that direction – just a few feet each year; there hadn't been any significant surges in forty years or more. Maybe it would leave them alone for a while.

The three of them were met by armed guards and escorted through the main gate, where they received some good news. Captain Clayton, the couriers and the rest of their party, including the sick, had all made it safely out of the Shole. They were delighted to hear it.

They also learned that the real Duke was still alive and making a slow recovery from his ordeal. Crafty was glad about that too. He'd always liked the Duke, and knew he was a brave man.

The bad news was that their new quarters would be very cramped. Several nearby farms had been commandeered to accommodate the Castle Corpus, but space was still limited.

For Crafty, that meant a return to sleeping in a hammock in a dormitory again. But after all that had happened he would have been grateful for a draughty barn and a heap of straw. He was exhausted, and was asleep even before the hammock had ceased its swinging motion.

And then he fell straight into another nightmare.

The witch began to cackle, her eyes filled with mirth. She took a step towards him and he shrank away.

Crafty was crouching on dirty straw in the dungeon at Lancaster; he was chained to the ring in the middle of the floor and Old Nell was standing very close, grinning down at him. He saw that her long sharp talons were encrusted with dried blood. If she attacked, he'd be at her mercy.

He knew he was dreaming and tried to wake up, but he was trapped there.

'This is just a dream!' Crafty told Old Nell. 'This isn't real.'

'How right you are, little grub! It be the easiest way to speak to you!'

Crafty had noticed that the witch's teeth were no longer those of a predatory aberration; she had just one set in each jaw and they didn't look particularly sharp.

'Your teeth are back to normal,' he observed.

'So, you've noticed, have ye? Well, Crafty, I was just having a bit o' fun with ye. When still alive, I healed folks but I liked scaring 'em too! What else can an old woman do to have a laugh?'

'That's not nice!' Crafty protested.

'But I be a lot nicer than you think. Ye might not know it yet but we're on the same side, little grub!'

'I find that hard to believe,' Crafty said, still attempting to will himself awake. 'How can that be true?'

Old Nell had taken a step towards him and was now so close that he could smell her. She stank of rot and decay. His eyes kept flicking from her face to her deadly talons.

'Two of a kind we be, Crafty. We're both Fey. Maybe we can help each other!'

Crafty opened his mouth to protest, but she gave another cackling laugh and kept talking.

'They hanged me, Crafty, and I didn't deserve it. You know that. All I did was help people by curing a few warts and boils . . .

Well, maybe that ain't the full truth. I did sell a few love potions, little grub, and a few curses . . . but it was mostly harmless! An old woman has to earn a crust somehow, don't she? But I didn't deserve to be hanged by the neck until I was as dead as a doornail, did I?'

Crafty didn't know what to say. The witch was very angry – her eyes seemed ready to pop out of her head. He didn't want to say anything that might provoke her.

'There are things out in the Shole that ain't like you and me. Pure evil they be. Aberrations that hope to inflict as much pain and loss as possible on humans – either that or remake 'em in their own image. Things like Viper. He loves to hurt and kill, he do. You were right all along. He was the evil one who slew the mancers in the castle. So I be on your side, Crafty. Things like that have to be stopped, don't they? So when shall we two meet again? In the flesh this time, not just in a dream! I know a secret place that'll suit us fine . . . We'll meet in the shadow of the Twisted Tree!'

She reached down and traced her forefinger down the length of Crafty's left cheek, the talon scraping against the skin. He felt as if his cheek was being sliced open.

He woke up sweating, the hammock swinging so wildly that he almost fell out. He touched his cheek, half expecting his fingers to come away wet with blood. But he could feel nothing.

For all that, he knew that it had been much more than just a bad dream.

THE TWISTED TREE

Soon after dawn Crafty went to have breakfast in the packed dining room. He was forced to sit on the floor until a place became available. The only person he recognized was Doon, who waved across cheerfully before turning back to his ham and eggs.

Crafty was hungry and soon polished off his own breakfast. He'd only just finished wiping his plate with a slice of bread when a guard arrived with a summons. The Duke wanted to see him immediately.

The Duke's residence here was very different from the Ducal Chambers at Lancaster. His new Throne Room was in an old orangery, built against an inner wall of the castle. When Crafty was escorted in, he saw that it was a large room with glass walls and ceilings. It was now late autumn, but the sun was shining strongly through the glass and the Duke's new abode was warm, bright and pleasant. It was full of plants in pots, some very exotic blooms that clearly did not originate in Lancashire. And at the centre was the most exotic bloom of all – the Duke himself.

His new container was much lower, so that his head was barely six feet off the floor, but connected to the sides and rear was a long box-like structure. As before, the purple cloth flowed down below his green tunic with its gold buttons, like a skirt to cover both the central container and the extensions.

The guard escorted Crafty into the room and left him there. Crafty looked up, and saw immediately that the Duke had not yet made a full recovery. His face was thinner, his complexion grey and his eyes tired. He seemed much older.

'Come closer, Crafty,' the Duke instructed. 'My voice isn't as strong as it was.'

Crafty approached the container.

'I wanted to thank you personally for your contribution to the defence of the castle and the subsequent withdrawal. I have heard excellent reports of your work. Thank you also for the personal help you afforded me, your Duke.'

Crafty didn't know what to say, so he gave a little bow. 'I just did my best, sir,' he muttered.

'This castle is a far safer location,' the Duke told him with a smile. 'Here we will have a welcome respite from the horrors we have faced. Of course, there will be certain disadvantages. That greater distance offers us safety, but it will make things more difficult. Couriers and guards will have further to travel . . .'

He paused, as though the effort of speaking was too much for him, then gave a little cough and wiped his mouth with a silk handkerchief before continuing.

The Duke gestured down at the silk-covered extensions that surrounded his pot. 'My roots continue to grow, but this time more slowly. Carpenters have made provision to contain them. After what happened at Lancaster, I don't want my roots to go too deep into the ground. They could come under attack again . . .'

Fear flickered over his face, and Crafty realized that he was remembering the agony he'd experienced when the aberrations attacked his roots.

'Do you still have the key I gave you?' asked the Duke.

'Yes, sir,' Crafty replied, taking it out of his pocket and holding it up. 'Do you want it back?'

'No, just the opposite. I wish you to continue your investigations, here in Clitheroe Castle. The key will work wherever we are based. Just showing your face unexpectedly will help keep the departments on their toes. You may even bring to light more of the Grey Hoods' conspiracies. It will be difficult, but I know that you will do your best. We learned a lot from observing that young man from the Relic Room. We were able to identify four more of his brethren and then deal with them all.'

'What punishment did they receive, sir?' Crafty asked.

The Duke's mouth tightened into a thin line and his expression became grim. 'All five were hanged . . .'

Crafty gasped. He'd anticipated a severe punishment but not execution. If he hadn't spotted the young man during the riot, he'd still be alive today.

'I can tell by the look on your face that you are unhappy with that, but I do not order such executions without serious deliberation. Those Grey Hoods had infiltrated the Castle Corpus and were actively seeking to undermine the work we do. We are in a war against the Shole – one that we cannot afford to lose. Extreme measures are called for. Now, we come to another reason why I wanted to speak to you . . .'

He paused and coughed into his handkerchief before dabbing his mouth again.

'Captain Clayton has recommended that you be trained as a courier. He believes that you are truly suited to the role. I agree, but unfortunately we cannot spare you from your duties as a gate grub at the moment. The research we do on the Shole is more vital than ever. But when we do manage to find your replacement, you will be transferred.'

Feeling far from happy, Crafty made his way to the new Waiting Room. He had been disturbed by the news of the hangings. The Duke thought they were necessary, and who was Crafty to disagree? But he couldn't forget that he was partly responsible for the deaths of five men.

Nor did he want to become a courier. Despite the danger, he wanted to carry on working as a gate grub with his friends. However, the Duke had clearly made up his mind on the matter, and Crafty hadn't felt able to refuse him. Maybe he would summon up the courage when the transfer came through – if it ever did. Fey who could be trained as grubs were hard to find. It might be a long time before they found a replacement.

The new Waiting Room was small, with just a single door, but it had a wide mullioned window with a view over the walls. The fields were green but the trees dark and leafless against the blue sky. Winter was coming.

There was a small round table and four seats. Two were occupied by Lick and Lucky.

'What, no draughts?' asked Crafty as he glanced at the bare table.

'I'll see what I can do,' Lick said with a smile. 'More likely to be chess though. In the meantime I might be able to lend you a few useful books to pass the time. They managed to bring some of the stock from the Grey Library, though much of it still needs to be catalogued. It's chaos so the librarian won't miss them. You've scratched your cheek,' she said, pointing at Crafty's face.

Lick had dismissed his visions of Old Nell as nightmares, but she could see the scratch on his cheek where Old Nell had scraped it with her talon. Yes – it really *had* been more than a bad dream.

'It's nothing, Lick. Are we likely to be busy today?' Crafty asked.

She nodded. 'Yes, there'll be lots of the routine stuff that happens after the Shole has engulfed a new area. Remember last time when we took samples from the canal? This time there's a much bigger area to study. The border is now north of Lancaster. We're particularly interested in getting samples from the river.'

'But not the castle, I hope,' said Lucky.

'I think we'll give that a wide berth for a while,' Lick replied. 'Preston, where the Shole first began, is usually considered to be its most dangerous part, but I think the castle might prove just as deadly. A host of monstrosities could develop from that root system under the foundations. During the last few days we've learned a lot of new things about the Shole, none of them good.'

'So what's the main conclusion you've reached?' Crafty asked.

'That what Bertha told you was correct: the Shole is alive – it really is like a great beast, steadily growing in power. And it may be able to replicate anything that's been changed into an aberration, holding it in its memory and recreating it in a different form. It made a copy of the Duke, and later one of Viper – both grew out of those roots. It can control aberrations as if they are just extensions of its mind –'

'But some can resist, can't they?' Lucky interrupted. 'Donna helped us. She's still our friend, and so is Titch!'

'And don't forget Bertha,' Crafty added.

Then he thought of something else. 'You once said that, with each new surge, a new aberration came into existence. Last time it seems like it was Viper. This surge was far bigger, so what can we expect?'

'Your guess is as good as mine, Crafty. But we might have already encountered it: that root system under the castle is a terrifying new threat. And don't forget that the original Viper is still out there. The danger is increasing all the time.'

Before Crafty could speak again, the door opened and the tall, thin form of the Chief Mancer appeared. There were the usual food stains on the front of his black gown, and he still looked rather supercilious, but Crafty was glad to see him.

'Sorry to cut short your briefing once again,' he said, 'but there is important work to be done. Proudfoot, you will accompany me; Benson, you will assist Miss Crompton-Smythe.'

Business as usual, Crafty thought.

As they followed the Chief Mancer out of the room, Crafty mulled over all the difficulties that lay ahead. How would Donna and Titch survive in the Shole? He would have to find some way to help them. And what about his mother – where was she now? He missed her so much – though sadly he now hoped that his father and mother never again came face to face. He remembered his father stabbing his knife into the empty cupboard. What if his mother had been hiding there? He missed his father too. It seemed a long time since they'd last talked together. How would he feel about Crafty becoming a courier? Would he be proud? Since arriving at Clitheroe they had yet to meet up. Crafty resolved to find him as soon as today's duties were over.

Then he thought sadly of his brothers, Brock and Ben. Even if the Shole did bring them back to life, it seemed that, like Titch and Donna, they would never be able to leave it. And what had happened to all the other dead grubs removed from the experimental graveyard? What use had the bargeman for them? That was another mystery.

In spite of all their work, the Shole seemed to be becoming more and more dangerous. He remembered the brave words of the Duke a few months before the castle had been engulfed. He'd wanted to become known as the Iron rather than the Wooden Duke – someone who protected his people and defended the castle at all costs.

He now seemed a much weaker version of his former self, though he was a wise and compassionate leader, and perhaps their new location would rally the Castle Corpus to intensify the fight against the Shole, Crafty thought. He took a deep breath and tried to think positively.

It was hard. The Duke thought that they would be safer in Clitheroe Castle, but Crafty remembered Old Nell showing him the field with the dark patch expanding outwards and then forming new Sholes. Could something like that really happen? What if another Shole began to form near Clitheroe Castle? Maybe nowhere was safe any more.

He followed Lick into her new room. As he sat down in the chair, she handed him a locator and gave him a smile.

Suddenly, driven by curiosity, Crafty asked her, 'Is there a place in the Shole called the Twisted Tree?'

Lick looked surprised. 'Where did you hear about *that*?' she asked, a little abruptly.

Crafty told her the truth. 'Last night I had another nightmare about Old Nell. She said that she was on my side and wanted to help. She claimed that she'd been using dreams to communicate with me. In the dream she scratched my cheek with her talon – the mark is still there. Now she wants to meet me in person – at the Twisted Tree.'

'The Twisted Tree is a legend, Crafty. The couriers secretly believe in it; some of them even claim to have visited the place. Although the Shole began in Preston, they believe its centre is that tree. I've tried to get them to help me find it so it can be investigated properly, but they just clam up. It means something very special to them.'

'You do know that, if they can find a replacement, I'm going to be a courier? It's Captain Clayton's idea and the Duke has approved it. I don't want to go, but it seems I don't have much choice!'

Lick nodded. 'I know, Crafty – the captain told me about it. I'll miss working with you – it won't be the same. Still, it could take months to find a replacement for you.'

'Wouldn't we still work together sometimes? Don't you use the gate to contact couriers?'

She nodded. 'Yes, but you'd be away in the Shole for much of the time.'

'Maybe it'll still be possible, Lick. I'd be a member of the Castle Courier Guild, wouldn't I? Then I can find out all about the Twisted Tree.'

'You'd break the rules of their guild by telling me?' she asked, looking shocked.

'Of course I would! I'd do *anything* to defeat the Shole. You boffins need all the information you can get. What do a few guild rules matter compared to that?'

Lick whistled through her teeth. 'Let me think about it. In the meantime, let's go and take a look at the river,' she said.

Crafty nodded, held the locator tight and began to concentrate.

A battle might have been lost, but the war against the Shole would go on.

Glossary

Aberrations

The generic name given to creatures that dwell within the Shole. The majority evolved from creatures (including humans) who were engulfed and, instead of dying, changed their shape and adapted to life in that new environment.

Black barge

Within the Shole, a mysterious black barge, drawn by a horse-like creature, follows the canal to Preston and back. Leading the 'horse' is a thin hooded figure who is over seven feet tall. The barge always leaves Lancaster at midnight on Tuesday and returns three nights later. Its purpose is unknown but it is being investigated by the castle couriers.

Black gates

A type of gate that is believed to be under development by the boffins who work within Lancaster Castle. If successful, it would enable mancers and gate grubs to access the world of the damned dead as easily as they do the Shole.

Boffins

Highly skilled theorists, researchers and technicians who develop new methods to combat the effects of the Shole.

Bog

This is the first example of what is known as a geographical aberration. It seems to be controlled by Bertha, the Bog Queen, who can make its usually calm surface stormy, and can even expand the area of the bog at will.

Bowland Fells

A range of hills south of Lancaster. Although enveloped by the Shole, most of the green summits rise above it into the Daylight World.

Canal

This runs from Preston to Kendal, passing through Lancaster. It is used by horse-drawn barges carrying all manner of wares. A large portion to the south has now been engulfed and only the northern section between north Lancaster and Kendal is still viable.

Canines

These are aberrations that resemble dogs. There are many sub-categories and the majority of these are carnivores and hunt in packs. A few, such as a One-Bite, are lone predators.

Castle Corpus

The collective name for the people who work from Lancaster Castle to learn how to counter the threat from the Shole.

Chair jobs

A task that is carried out from the chair facing the gate. The grub is often strapped in to minimize the danger of being dragged into the Shole by one of the aberrations.

Combined field operation

Where two or more gate grubs pass through their respective gates and work together in the Shole.

Corpse bat

This flying aberration rips the throat out of its victim and uses its wings to scatter blood across the whole body. It then regurgitates pellets from its upper stomach and sprays them on to the bloodied corpse. Within minutes the spores root themselves in the flesh and grow into big circular fungi, each about the size of a human head. Thus, the bat does not feed upon corpses but upon the fungi that it cultivates.

Courier craft

The skills used by couriers to protect themselves when travelling through the Shole. Some are magical, others technological. For example, a triangle of three candles can be used to ward off aberrations, while the use of silver alloy is applied science.

Couriers

These are recruited from the Fey, and thus largely immune to the effects of the Shole. They carry messages and sometimes medicines to the Daylight Islands encircled by the Shole. They also make regular patrols, noting areas of change and danger, and are skilled in map-making. They are also skilled in the use of courier craft.

Daylight Islands

Pockets of the Daylight World cut off and surrounded by the Shole after a sudden surge. Why they are untouched by the Shole remains a mystery.

Daylight World

The ordinary world, as yet untouched by the Shole.

Duke of Lancaster

The ruler of the Palatine of Lancashire, answerable only to the King. He has the power of life and death over the county's inhabitants.

Excursion

This term is used to describe the situation when an aberration ventures out of the Shole and enters the Daylight World in search of victims. The *White Lady of Whittingham* and the *Grim Ploughman* are both examples of this. The Grim Ploughman had seven excursions before returning to the Shole. He has never been seen since. Such aberrations are also referred to as *excursionists*.

Fey

The Fey are humans with potential magical ability which may or may not manifest itself as they grow up. Some have a single ability while others have several. Couriers and gate grubs are traditionally recruited from the Fey. Mancers (from the managerial staff of the Castle Corpus) are not recruited from the Fey, who are sometimes thought to be reckless and unreliable. They are considered to be a necessary evil – except for the few with extremely high academic ability, who become boffins.

Field operations

These are jobs involving a gate grub passing through a silver gate to carry out some task in the Shole.

Fixed locations

Only gate grubs can find new locations within the Shole, but subsequently they can be revisited by mancers using the ratchet-dial on the side of the gate. They are then termed 'fixed locations'.

Flappers (stone)

A stone flapper is embedded in stone and thus, denied sustenance, withers away and dies within weeks. Most are blind, but experiments have proved that a few have exceptional vision.

Flappers (tree)

Tree flappers are aberrations embedded in the branch of a tree and partly fused with the wood. They moan and flap their limbs. They can survive for many years in that condition as the sap of the tree provides nutrients. Mostly, humans change into aberrations quite slowly, but both types of flapper are exceptions to this. They change within minutes.

Forensics Room

Those who work here apply magical theory and practical technology to the study of deaths and changes in the Shole. Any samples are routinely handed over to the Relic Room within seven days unless the Chief Mancer authorizes an extension.

Gate grubs

Fey humans who are able to venture into the Shole without fear of either dying or changing. Using a silver gate, they also have the ability, using sympathetic magic, to find aberrations, locations and objects within it. Most gate grubs do not survive much longer than a few months.

Geographical aberrations
These types of aberration consist of local changes in the landscape of the Shole rather than to a human or an aberration. The first of this type to manifest itself in the Shole is known as the bog.

Grey Hoods
This is a cult that worships the Shole. Its members believe that one day it will engulf the whole world and they will then live forever. They actively work to undermine the objectives of the Castle Corpus.

Grey Library
This contains the cumulative knowledge gathered about the Shole over a period of almost seventy years. The name refers firstly to the Shole, which is grey and murky; and secondly to the books in the library, all of which have grey jackets. Thirdly, metaphorically speaking, it refers to the understanding that the facts about the Shole are neither black nor white. All is uncertain and in a state of change – the known facts are grey.

Grim Ploughman, The
This aberration walked out of the Shole and visited farms on the outskirts of a village called Grimsargh. It was physically

intimidating, being tall and gaunt with very large hands. At first it appeared benign and would offer its services as a ploughman. In return, all it wanted was a plate of mutton and a hunk of bread. However, it turned on the final man who hired it, taking in payment the lives of the whole family. It ate them before returning to the Shole, never to be seen again.

Guillotine

A sharp blade suspended above the area between the chair of a gate grub and the silver gate itself. It slides down between two vertical poles. A gate mancer controls it, by means of a foot pedal, to kill any aberration attempting to enter the Daylight World through the gate. Unfortunately, gate grubs are sometimes killed or maimed by the blade. For them, it is the second most likely cause of death. (The first is failure to return from the Shole after a field operation, when the precise cause of death is usually unknown.)

Human hybrids

These are people partially changed into animal, vegetable or mineral forms. Those changed into predatory animals are the most fierce and dangerous. The triple rows of teeth are what most have in common. The bargeman is one example.

Lancaster

The chief city of Lancashire, lying on the river Lune. At its centre is Lancaster Castle, which is the focus of attempts to contain the threat from the Shole.

Lancaster Castle

This castle is very old and was once the centre of the county's judiciary and military. Now it is the centre for research into the Shole and home to the mancers and other experts who hope one day to reverse or destroy it. It also has its own guard, a quasi-military force which is responsible for the security of the castle and for policing the city. They also patrol the boundaries of the Shole to prevent its aberrations entering the Daylight World.

Locators

These are cylindrical objects that have been cut in half. One part is usually buried just outside the Shole. When it advances and engulfs the locator, a gate grub can take the other half and, using his or her Fey abilities, move the gate to where its twin is buried. This is useful because a new section of the Shole is extremely unstable and silver gates do not work well there.

Lure

This is an illusion with which a mancer entices an aberration towards a gate so that a gate grub may snatch it.

Mancers

Specialized mages who have magical and technological power within just one field of expertise. Their magical abilities are developed over time using discipline and meditation, whereas Fey magic is innate and chaotic, and potentially much more powerful. *Gate mancer*s are one of many such categories; *necromancers* are another. The Chief Mancer manages and has authority over all types of mancer.

Menagerie

This is where live specimens from the Shole are kept for study and experimentation.

Mimics

This category of aberration pretends to be something else, copying its shape, while it waits for its prey. There are many sub-categories, ranging from insects that mimic twigs to carnivores that look like stone statues. Most take on the shape of trees; they can move very fast and feed on flesh.

One-Bite

This aberration takes the form of a large fierce dog with the typical three rows of teeth found in predators within the Shole. It first manifested itself in the heart of Preston at a time when the Shole was relatively small. Emerging from the Shole, it attacked its human prey at great speed and would bite a single chunk of flesh from its victim. It never went back for more. However, that one bite often proved to be fatal. The first of these aberrations was snatched from the Shole and put on display in the Relic Room. One of them is caged in the Menagerie but others are still at large.

Ouroborus

This is a great serpent sometimes called the *Earth Dragon*, and the fact that its head is joined to its tail is a symbol of rebirth. It was important to ancient tribes like the Segantii. It was often represented upon their weapons and amulets.

Porter magic

This is used to transmit objects over a distance. It is the means by which many of the Daylight Islands are fed. But the Shole waxes and wanes in strength, and sometimes porter magic does not work.

Preston

A market town south of Lancaster, where the phenomenon known as the Shole first began. At first it merely covered a terraced house in a small street called Water Lane, which is next to a busy thoroughfare called Fylde Road.

Relic Room

This is where artefacts taken from the Shole are stored by its curators. They jealously guard its contents, sometimes undertaking further study of the items without sharing their findings with the Forensics Room.

Samples

Items from the flora or fauna of the Shole, removed to be studied in the castle. Samples may be large and active, or small, or even dead. All, or a piece of them, is taken for further study.

Segantii
An ancient tribe inhabiting Lancashire before the invasion of the Romans, of which Bertha was once Queen. Some believe that they had a port on the west bank of the river Wyre.

Shade
This is an alternative term for the Shole which is in popular use. Another variant is the *Shadow*. Mancers always use the term *Shole*.

Shadow stains
The remains of a human caught within the Shole. Most victims drop dead within moments of being engulfed and within hours are reduced to a skeleton, only their bones remaining. Very occasionally the dead become shadow stains: wet patches which are roughly human in shape, thrown against a wall, a tree or the ground. Sometimes they move and shriek with pain. There is no evidence that any awareness remains, but the possibility should not be discounted. One of the earliest gate grubs claimed to be able to converse with shadow stains but was slain before that could be verified.

Sheol
This is one of the ancient names for Hell. Some believe that the word Shole was derived from it.

Shole

This first manifested near the centre of Preston, in a house in Water Lane, close to a busy thoroughfare called Fylde Road. It gradually expanded to cover most of the town centre. After seventy years of sporadic growth it has extended thirty miles north and now threatens the heart of Lancaster. The Shole changes or kills most creatures within it, including humans (except the Fey). The changed are termed *aberrations* and they are at their most dangerous after dark.

Silver gates

These are mediums resembling framed windows through which a gate grub may access the Shole.

Snatches

When performing a snatch, a gate grub (secured in his or her seat by restraining straps) seeks to drag an aberration out of the Shole into the Daylight World for the purposes of research.

Sympathetic magic

This can be a form of malevolent magic. A doll representing an enemy can be pierced with pins to cause pain or even death to that enemy. Such magic can also be used benignly. A person can be located when a Fey holds an object that once belonged to them or even a piece of skin, bone or hair. It is the principle upon which silver gates function.

Glossary

Twisted Tree, The
This is one of the Castle Courier Guild's secrets; they will not discuss it with outsiders, therefore its location is unknown. It is supposedly a place within the Shole which they believe is its new centre of power.

White Lady of Whittingham
Several 'white ladies' have manifested themselves either within or just outside the border of the Shole. The White Lady of Whittingham was the first. She befriended a group of children. One had a withered leg, which she healed. Other folk from nearby villages were also healed of a variety of health problems. She met a group of children every week, but the last meeting ended badly. Neither the lady nor the children were ever seen again. It is believed they were abducted and taken into the Shole.

JOSEPH DELANEY used to be an English teacher, before becoming the bestselling author of the Spook's series, which has been published in twenty-four countries and sold millions of copies. The first book, *The Spook's Apprentice*, was made into a major motion picture starring Jeff Bridges and Julianne Moore.

IF YOU'D LIKE TO LEARN MORE ABOUT JOSEPH AND HIS BOOKS, VISIT:

www.josephdelaneyauthor.com

www.penguin.co.uk

THE SPOOK'S SERIES

WARNING:
NOT TO BE READ AFTER DARK

DO YOU DARE ENTER
THE WORLD OF ...

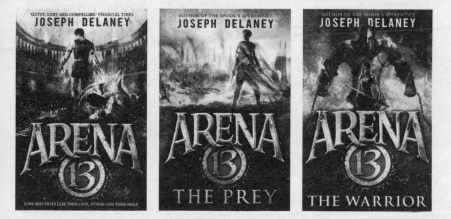

WHEN LEIF'S FAMILY IS DESTROYED BY AN EVIL CREATURE,
BATTLE IS THE ONLY WAY TO GET REVENGE ...